The Lies Between Us

The Lies Between Us

JEN BRAY

SANDYCOVE
an imprint of
PENGUIN BOOKS

SANDYCOVE

UK | USA | Canada | Ireland | Australia
India | New Zealand | South Africa

Sandycove is part of the Penguin Random House group of companies
whose addresses can be found at global.penguinrandomhouse.com

Penguin Random House UK,
One Embassy Gardens, 8 Viaduct Gardens, London SW11 7BW

penguin.co.uk

First published 2026
001

Copyright © Jen Bray, 2026

The moral right of the author has been asserted

Penguin Random House values and supports copyright.
Copyright fuels creativity, encourages diverse voices, promotes freedom
of expression and supports a vibrant culture. Thank you for purchasing
an authorized edition of this book and for respecting intellectual property
laws by not reproducing, scanning or distributing any part of it by any
means without permission. You are supporting authors and enabling
Penguin Random House to continue to publish books for everyone.
No part of this book may be used or reproduced in any manner for the
purpose of training artificial intelligence technologies or systems. In accordance
with Article 4(3) of the DSM Directive 2019/790, Penguin Random House
expressly reserves this work from the text and data mining exception

Set in 13.5/16pt Garamond MT
Typeset by Falcon Oast Graphic Art Ltd
Printed and bound in Great Britain by Clays Ltd, Elcograf S.p.A.

The authorized representative in the EEA is Penguin Random House Ireland,
Morrison Chambers, 32 Nassau Street, Dublin D02 YH68

A CIP catalogue record for this book is available from the British Library

ISBN: 978–1–844–88691–3

Penguin Random House is committed to a sustainable
future for our business, our readers and our planet. This book is
made from Forest Stewardship Council® certified paper.

For Alan and Michael

PART ONE

I

A fierce rapping tears me from sleep. Knuckles on wood.

There's a brief silence, a moment when I am suspended between dreams and reality. I sit up, dazed, trying to make sense of shapes in the dark. The streetlight throws a half-hearted amber glow through the window, and I remember where I am. Mum's holiday cottage. I crashed out when I got back from the beach. Susannah is cooking dinner downstairs.

Then: high heels on ceramic tiles as Susannah makes her way through the house. A whoosh of air moves up the stairs and presses against the door. I move awkwardly into a sitting position on my bed and wonder if it could be true.

Is Tara here? After all this time?

A voice floats underneath my door, the tone sinister. It's not Tara, because it's a man talking. I can't unscramble his words.

'Get the hell out of my doorway,' Susannah says.

I hoist myself off the bed and go over to the small sash window. The sea and sky and clouds have fused into a swirling blackish blue. The weather has turned; there's a violence to it. I see the tip of angry waves licking up over the high wall that separates the beach from the road, which inclines up into a hill behind the cottage. Over the slapping sound of the sea, I can barely pick up what is going on below. I squint down and see a man in shadow. This time, I hear him loud and clear.

'You leave tonight, or else I swear to God—'

The rest of his sentence is cut off by the sharp whistle of a gust through the windowpane. As the door slams shut the force reverberates throughout the cottage. I watch him slip through the gate to the shared parking area, his figure distorted through the glass, his features obscured in the gloom. Before turning onto the road, he pops up his collar, glances around him, takes a left. I watch him disappear into the hotel.

I make my way down the staircase that bisects the house and leads to the navy front door. On one side of me is a sitting and dining area. On the other, behind the wall that separates the stairs from the rest of the open-plan ground floor, is the kitchen. It's cleverly designed, keeping the cottagey feeling – the front door is a stable door, for God's sake – while making it airy and modern. Reaching the bottom of the stairs, I see Susannah has laid the dining table with a ruby-red runner, vintage china, crystal glasses and a long thin dinner candle at either end. Nothing is out of place. Susannah is the kind of person who cleans the inside of her wheelie bins: she's a perfectionist.

When she said she was inviting Tara, I was shocked – they've been estranged for years, since what happened in New York. But she's set four places. Who else is she expecting?

'Who the hell was that?' I ask, craning my neck around the wall to look into the kitchen. She has her back to me. She is wearing a long silky mauve dress tied with the thinnest shoestring straps, revealing her bare arms and shoulders. Something feels wrong. Her hands are splayed out on the kitchen counter. Her shoulders are tensed up towards her ears. I feel a tightening sensation in my own upper back. And yet, when she turns to face me, Susannah looks like a woman just back from a week in a high-end spa. Her green eyes sparkle under her expensive make-up; her long brown hair is sleek and shiny. I haven't seen her look this good in ages.

'Who was who?' she says, but before I can answer she has moved on. 'Lucy, what are you wearing?'

I look down at my outfit – blue velour tracksuit bottoms and a man's jumper I picked up in Penneys.

'Who cares? Sass, who was that at the door? Who were you fighting with?'

I plonk myself down at the table, where I can still see into the kitchen. I wonder if it is my fate on this trip to just continuously be asking questions, because at this stage, I have so many.

'Oh,' she says, bustling around the kitchen now, 'one of the neighbours two doors up said I parked my car in his space. Honestly, men; after a certain age they just become interminably grumpy. They can't help it.'

Her pitch is too high, and when she scratches at her wrist aggressively with her nails, I feel the sting on *my* wrist – which is annoying, but on the scale of annoyances I have to put up with because of my condition, it's minor.

All my life I have lived with mirror-touch synaesthesia. I feel what others feel on or against their body. And I feel their emotional states too. If, say, someone is in a state of anxiety, their foot tapping off the floor rapidly, breath held high in their chest, I soon experience that same restlessness.

Being so in tune with others also means I'm adept at spotting a liar, and Susannah is lying. But I know my sister, perhaps better than I know anyone else in the world. She's private and guarded and defensive. So, there's no point asking her yet what's going on. Once she's had a few glasses of wine and relaxes, she'll open up. Even though I'm worried, and even though I don't like what I heard at the front door, I park that particular interrogation for the moment.

Instead, I try another question that has been eating away at me all day. I have attempted to raise it a few times since this morning, to no avail.

'Sass, what is *Sea of Mirrors*?'

Sass, I hope, takes the edge out of the question.

But my timing is off again. She has just opened the oven door and made the mistake of peering into it, so she's getting a full blast of steam. She jumps back, wailing. 'My make-up!'

I sigh and ask again, louder this time. 'What the hell is *Sea of Mirrors?*'

After breakfast I found the manuscript for her new novel – at least that's what I assumed it was. I only scanned a few pages, but it was enough to freak me out. A main character called Lucy, which seemed odd, but I supposed it was a stopgap name till she was editing. But when the fictional Lucy turned out to be a garda and I found a scene set in Dunmore East, my head started spinning. I heard her coming downstairs, and I had to shove the manuscript back into its folder, but I've barely thought of anything else all day. I was so exhausted I needed a nap before this weird family dinner she has planned.

I've finally got her attention, but she doesn't even look guilty. 'Truth is stranger than fiction,' is all she says, cleaning a non-existent smudge off a wine glass.

My eyes follow her around the room as she goes to the fridge, removing a bottle of Sauvignon Blanc, and then over to the freezer for an ice jacket to put around it. She is so consistently *extra*. It's something I've always loved about her – how much effort she makes. I admire it especially because I'm not like that. She's got her look coined, right down to her perfect shade of Chanel lipstick. I wear men's clothes.

When she brings over the wine, I open it and pour my glass nearly to the top. We must be a family of alcoholics because we all do this.

'Did you write a book about me? Because I don't consent,' I say, feeling increasingly hangry.

Susannah checks her wrist. I get up from the table, cross the room and pick up her phone from the table beside the front door. She has never had a watch in her life and relies on her phone to tell the time. Yet she is always looking at her wrist for this mythical watch.

Without thinking, I press the power button to light up the screen. I'm nosy, always have been.

There are two WhatsApp messages from David.

'What the actual fuck?'

That's the first.

'Are you going to publish it?!'

Before I can digest the words, Susannah snaps her phone out of my hand.

'No one likes a nosy Nellie,' she says, although her tone is cool and unbothered.

She's going to pretend that I didn't see the messages, and I guess I'm supposed to pretend that I didn't see them too. *Snap!* I think, recalling our mortifying conversation about texts from my boyfriend this afternoon – now I've read her husband's pissed-off messages just like she's read my boyfriend's pissed-off messages. We're even.

Giving up on the questioning, I help her take the lasagne and garlic bread out of the oven. I ask her if she's OK. I'm not prepared for the look she gives me. It is yielding, empathetic, understanding – like she knows what has been going on with me and knows that the real question is if I am OK.

'Luce, do you believe that everything happens for a reason?'

I think a moment.

'No,' I say, thinking of my split-second decision all that time ago in New York. There's no way that any god would let what happened to me be a thing that happens for a reason. And if there was a reason, it was a shit one and I have no interest in ever hearing it.

'Some things just happen because of chance, or circumstance,' I say, burying my sadness.

'I used to think that, too. But I'm starting to change my mind.' She pauses. 'Why do you think we are the way we are?'

'What do you mean?'

'Anxious over-thinkers. People pleasers. Afraid of confrontation. Addictive personalities.'

'Are we?'

'Yes. You, me, Tara. We're hostages to our past, that's why. And you can't expect a different future if you don't face up to the past,' she says.

For some reason, that stings. And perhaps all three of us sisters have at least one of those traits, but not all of them together, surely.

Her phone beeps and she holds it up close while reading the message. A pained look crosses her face, as though someone has grabbed a hold of her heart in their hand and is giving it a good squeeze. She types something quickly before turning her attention back towards me.

'Put those back in the oven to keep them warm,' she says, pointing absently towards the food. She crosses to the hooks on the wall beside the front door, grabs her coat, ties a thick black scarf around her neck and looks at the phone again. Then she peers around the room, as though sizing it up, assessing something that I cannot see. She seems suddenly fearful.

None of this is making any sense.

'Lucy, don't ask questions, just listen to me. Listen! Lock all the doors and windows. Make sure everything is properly locked, including the front door behind me. Don't let anyone in. Promise me.' As she speaks, she's coming towards me, finger pointed, barely stopping short of jabbing my chest.

'Jesus, Susannah, what the hell is going on? Where are you going? What if Tara shows up?'

'Forget about her, Lucy. Just do as I say, OK? Stay in. Answer the door to no one except me.'

I'm taller than her; I could stop her leaving if I wanted. But she's out the front door before I can ask any more questions.

'Bolt the door. And stay inside!' she shouts from the other

side. I do as I am told. I watch her pass the sitting-room window and hear the sound of her phone ringing. Then I hear her boots crunch on gravel, until the sound fades away. Anxiety thrums through my veins, spiking my heartbeat and making my mouth dry.

Ever since we got to Dunmore East my normally poised and together sister has been acting completely out of character. Usually, when Susannah tries to whisk me off on a mini-break, it's because she feels guilty about New York. Standing dumbstruck by the front door, I start to suspect that this trip is about much more than guilt.

2

New York, April 2011

David steps out onto the rooftop terrace, his breath puffing out in a plume of icy air. Tara beckons him over.

'It's going to snow in the next few hours, definitely, and hard,' she says, her scarf wrapped around her, mummy-like. One hand pokes out, holding her cigarette. She's leaning against a red-brick wall. She sees David do a double-take. She guesses the louche look is not quite her, but she stays put and holds her nerve. Let him come over to her. She smiles encouragingly.

What she is thinking as he strides over, rubbing his hands together, is that David looks like a dream. And that this feels impossibly romantic – the two of them here on a rooftop, Manhattan skyscrapers going up, up, up, millions of lights sparkling just for them.

Downstairs, Susannah's dinner had been interminable. Poor Lucy looked bored out of her mind sitting at the end of the table, over-stimulated by all the noise and chatter. She was only sixteen after all, so a literary dinner was hardly her scene. Still, Lucy wasn't Tara's problem right now.

Although she feels ecstatic when David wraps her up into a hug, Tara tries not to look it. She hopes it's not a brotherly hug. She *needs* it not to be a brotherly hug.

'Had enough?' he says, pulling away just far enough to end the hug but still close enough to keep his hands on her shoulders. She hopes David can't see how drunk she is. Her cheeks feel warm and her eyelids heavy. She gives him what she hopes is a languid look.

He's peering right into her face.

See, she thinks, *he is flirting with me. It's not in my head. There must be something here. Why else does he find my eyes across the table when everyone else is talking? It's not just tonight. Or could it be that he catches me staring at him, and is too polite to look away?*

And yet on this trip – and it is the only reason she came, to be near him – she feels that he has been paying her closer attention than ever.

He may be her sister's husband, but from the moment she first met him on that Christmas Day in 1998 – Susannah proud as punch as she introduced her boyfriend to the family – Tara knew she had to have him. She feels a wave of bitterness even thinking about that Christmas. Susannah was just twenty-one and her first book had been a sensation at the Frankfurt Book Fair a few months earlier. Already her life was full of promise. Tara was in the second year of her hotel management degree. And then Susannah turned up with the guy she'd been seeing for nearly a year. Tara could see that Susannah had decided that David was the one. That didn't stop Tara falling for him.

With five glasses of Malbec on board, Tara decides *this is it* – there will never be a more perfect moment, with David looking so handsome and her feeling so brave and the world around them exuding so much beauty and promise. It would be a crime not to kiss him.

David had just asked if she'd 'had enough'.

'Not of you,' she says, standing on her tiptoes and cupping his chin in her hand. Their lips meet. A thousand flowers bloom inside her.

David's not exactly devouring her but he's not pushing her off. He seems to be savouring the moment, testing his limits, thinking.

She knows their first kiss will be a scene that she replays a thousand times. The bristle of his stubble, his Adam's apple in her hand, his chest pressed against hers.

It's magic, until it's over. He pulls away.

'Ehhhh,' he says, bushy brows furrowed.

'Wow,' Tara says.

He takes a purposeful step back. The space between them feels as wide as the Atlantic. Tara scrambles for a seductive thing to say, something to reel him back in, but her brain has not caught up with her body. Nothing comes.

The metal door to the rooftop swings open and Susannah stands there in her little red dress, like a Hollywood siren. 'There ye are,' she says, sashaying over, apparently not noticing the tension, the heat. She opens a small, sparkly clutch bag and pulls a cigarette out of a pack. She lights it with a flourish and throws her hair over her shoulder.

'Jesus, Tara, you look pissed.'

Tara thinks there's a knowing glimmer in her sister's eye. It's a look she often gets from Susannah, as if her sister is saying: *I know who you really are. What you really are.*

Tara doesn't think she's being paranoid. It's all there in Susannah's novel, where one of the daughters in the family is a whiny child, who becomes a meek teenager and an aimless adult. Tara knows it's a dig at her. That novel is enraging on so many levels – a part of her is still astonished that Susannah wrote something so personal – but she doesn't have the tools to challenge Susannah about her writing. Since reading an early proof that was lying around their mum's house, Tara has decided to ignore it. Not a word has passed between them about the book. And yet it's the reason they are all in New York, to witness Susannah's triumphant comeback to the literary scene. Tara fervently hopes that her sister fails at the awards ceremony tomorrow.

The door opens again and Summer, Susannah's agent, sticks her head through. 'Hey – we're doing the toast now, come on!'

Susannah throws the cigarette on the ground, crushing it

with the pointed tip of a designer-heeled shoe. She grabs her husband's arm and says something like, 'Let's go, love,' before throwing her sister a warning look.

Too late, Tara thinks. The spark has been lit. It may reignite tomorrow, next year, or in a decade, but Tara believes that she will get what she wants.

And then Tara is standing there alone, with only her thoughts, shivering. Susannah's clutch bag catches her eye, sitting on a low ledge. She picks it up and opens it. Lipstick, a nearly full pack of cigarettes, a keycard. As she walks over to the door, she tosses it in the bin.

3

Two hours have passed since Susannah left, and I have felt every second. The old wall clock ticks loudly, so I can't forget the worrying passage of time.

I've tried her phone a few times, but it's off. Wherever she went, she went on foot and stayed on foot, because her car is still parked in the large circular shared driveway. Each time I try to relax, drinking a glass of wine, distracting myself with the small TV in the corner, I'm propelled back onto my feet. Because now that I think about it properly, there have been some glaring red flags that something is amiss with Susannah. And I've been so slow to spot them. It almost makes me doubt that I was, once upon a time, a police officer.

First – Susannah's strange plot to get us into Mum's holiday home. We had arrived in Dunmore East just after 4:30 p.m. and pulled up outside the cottage. At this point, I might have expected her to simply produce the keys to the cottage. Not so. Instead, I listened as she made a call, asked if she had reached Turner's Letting Agency and then said, 'Mary Wall here,' told them she had arrived and asked for the PIN to get the keys from the box by the front door. The person on the other end confirmed some details before giving her the PIN. Despite how odd this seemed – why would she need to book Mum's cottage under a fake name, couldn't she simply have asked her for the keys? – I didn't question her. She always has a plan of some kind, and I figured it would materialize in its own good time. So, instead, I frowned and went back to scrolling through Instagram. That's the first black mark against me.

Second – Susannah instructed me to tell no one that we were taking this trip to Dunmore East. I didn't mind – I had no one to tell.

She picked me up yesterday afternoon. Sunday, 3 April. I was glad to be out of my so-called studio apartment. It's in a crumbling old house and is so cramped that the sink is in the bedroom, right beside my head. A man from upstairs keeps leaving creepy notes under my door. I keep hoping I'll catch him.

The drive from Dublin took two hours and Susannah blared songs about angry women the whole way, and I found I quite liked them – I have so much repressed rage, I'm only dying for someone to volunteer themselves as my victim.

On the way down she was categorical: not a soul. No exceptions. In my defence, Susannah sometimes does this. She takes on too much and spreads herself so thin that every few months she snaps and goes off the grid, ignoring everyone – me, Mum, David, her cat Buttons. We have learned to just leave her be and eventually she reappears. I thought maybe this time was different, that she was having the kind of meltdown that called for company.

Third – and this is probably the most curious thing – the novel.

After breakfast Susannah was jittery. I presumed it was a hangover from the wine we knocked back in the pub last night. Earlier, she had suggested a swim as the tide was moving out and much of the beach was now accessible. I can never understand people who throw themselves headfirst into freezing-cold water. I simply do not buy that there is a thrill – unless nearly catching your death is thrilling. But in the interests of peace, I shrugged and said, 'Yeah, why not.'

Susannah said she was going to shower and put on her swimming suit. I crunched into my second slice of burnt toast, thinking I'd never needed a holiday more. While I was sitting there at the white wooden kitchen table, idly wondering what I was going to do with the rest of my life, my eyes landed on Susannah's laptop sitting on top of a thick folder on the kitchen bureau. It wasn't like her to leave her stuff lying around. Nosy as ever, I had to investigate.

It was the folder that piqued my curiosity. It was stuffed. It reminded me of work – before my life spectacularly imploded, of course. All those folders, all that paperwork.

I padded over, feeling sand on the ceramic tiles under my bare feet. I slid out the folder, opened the flap and pulled out a thick wedge of bound paper. The top page had just four words: *Title: Sea of Mirrors*.

Ah, a new novel.

No offence to her books, but I tend to stay away from the kind of stuff Susannah writes. It's not because I'm a literary snob – I've always loved fantasy. But she writes domestic thrillers and I get enough of that kind of thing in work. Or at least I used to when I was a garda.

I held the file tight at the binding in my left hand and flicked through it with my right. I stopped when I saw the name 'Lucy'.

Odd, I thought. I don't know much about books, but I would expect most authors to steer away from using their siblings' names for their characters. And yet, here she was, a fictional Lucy.

I hoped Susannah's 'Lucy' put all of us Lucys in a good light. I'd hate for someone to decide not to name their child Lucy because they'd read a novel featuring an absolutely psychotic Lucy.

Lucy knew she had to pull from all her reserves: remember every tool she had been taught and every trick she had learned in her training as a garda.

I felt a strange fluttering feeling in my chest before I even had time to register the words. This character, Lucy, was also a member of An Garda Síochána. With increasing unease, I read on.

She asked the wind and the water for an answer, hoping that the very spirit of Dunmore East would help her find the solution, for a way out of this mess.

My next thought: *Am I in a dream?* Because it all felt very meta.

A crash upstairs jolted me. I shoved the manuscript back into the folder, replaced it under the laptop and ran upstairs. Susannah was in her bedroom. A mirror lay in shards at her feet. It seemed she had somehow knocked it off the wall.

'Seven years' bad luck,' I said.

She's not superstitious like Mum, and she rolls her eyes when I count magpies. She threw her eyes to heaven and said, 'Some certainty, at last.'

After that I could not stop thinking about Susannah's novel. I prayed that she wasn't writing a fictional account of how my career had ended. Depending on who you ask, I either quit or was fired from the job I loved. It all amounts to the same thing. I didn't just fail, I failed on a spectacular level. I wasn't sure I would ever shake off the sense of shame over what happened.

I decided to wait until Susannah had the hair of the dog on board before asking what on earth *Sea of Mirrors* was about and, more to the point, why I appeared to be in it. I waited till this afternoon, when we were sitting outside the Strand Hotel, looking out over the sea. It felt warmer than it had the right to be for a late afternoon at the start of April, but there were plenty of clouds shielding us from the sun's full glare. The water was calm, with just the faintest ripple as the tide rolled ever in.

Despite the cloud cover, Susannah sat opposite me lathering her face with dollops of SPF. It was almost aggressive the way she applied it, and she caught my look.

'You're still in your twenties, Lucy. Take the advice I never did and start wearing SPF even if it's cloudy. Maybe you can avoid the crepe-head. Save yourself a Botox bill.'

She pointed at some insignificant lines on her forehead. It's not that Susannah is obsessed with getting older, just with the idea of perfection and the fear of what she looks like in other people's eyes. She puts on a good show of pretending not to care but she's riddled with insecurity. She thinks I can't see it because I'm her younger sister, but she's easy to read.

'My days of worrying about beauty are behind me,' I said.

I wanted to come across as jokey but, annoyingly, I sounded sorry for myself, and I guess maybe I was.

'Don't say that about yourself, Luce,' she said, with a sad frown. 'You're beautiful.'

Automatically my hand went to my chest, to where the spidery scars were hidden under a thick jumper. The ones reaching up my neck to just above my jaw line are harder to camouflage, but I make a decent fist of it with make-up. In my more charitable moments, I think my scars look like the branches of a tree running up my body onto my face, like I am at one with Mother Nature.

This was a conversation I didn't want to have, especially with Susannah. It pains her to remember what happened in New York – no one wants to imagine someone they love being a victim, especially their teenage sister. I picked up the bottle of rosé and poured a generous measure.

'Drink up, Sass.'

'Are you trying to get me drunk? Again?'

Between the dirty big glass of wine and using her pet-name, I wasn't being as subtle as I hoped. When I started calling her 'Sassanah', because she had a smart answer for everything, there was an edge to it. 'Sass' has no edge. Exactly the opposite.

I waited until she had taken a decent gulp and opened my mouth to ask the burning question.

'I wanted to ask you about—'

'We need to talk, Lucy,' she said, cutting across me.

She spoke as if I was the one with questions to answer.

'O-kay,' I said, taken aback.

She was normally so sure-footed that I barely recognized uncertainty on her face, but she seemed to be steeling herself. I gave her a moment or two. The only sound between us was the gentle crashing of waves, each one chasing the next as the tide inched closer, the fresh folds of water seeping in over the dry sand. The atmosphere felt briefly sinister, as though I was being cornered by a force of nature I could not escape.

'There are two reasons why I have brought you here, and I'm not sure which one I should start with,' she said, lowering her voice as a group of women in Dryrobes ambled past our table.

'Well, this sounds ominous,' I said with a half-laugh.

She reached into her pocket, took out her phone and started scrolling, her fingers flicking up and down the screen. When she found what she was searching for, she placed the mobile, screen down, on the wooden table.

'We need to talk about Tim.'

I groaned and threw my hands up in the air.

Not this again, I thought. Susannah has always made clear her dislike of my boyfriend and I have always made clear that I don't need a second mother.

'Susannah, can you just, for once, drop it?'

I had a rant forming in my head about how this was supposed to be a holiday, a break from normal life, a time when you leave your baggage at the door, but I wasn't given a chance to get the words out.

'Tim has been texting me,' she said. She squirmed slightly.

I was totally at a loss, because to the best of my knowledge the dislike between them was mutual.

'Why would Tim be texting *you*?'

She picked her phone up off the table.

'Remember when we went out three weeks ago?'

Three weeks earlier was when Susannah dropped over unannounced, though she knows I hate it when people do that. Standing there in my poky doorway, in her Max Mara wool coat, she peered in, a pained look on her face. She insisted on taking me out to a fancy new wine bar. Over drinks, she said she was becoming concerned about me because I wasn't responding to her Snapchats, WhatsApps, Instagrams or phone calls. In her words, I'd 'gone dark'.

Briefly I was back in that moment, with Susannah scrutinizing me. She had a similar quizzical expression now, as we sat outside the hotel. Behind her, a wave broke and foamy water sprayed up. Seagulls circled low over the water. The sun had disappeared behind clouds and it was chilly. I shivered and snapped back to attention.

'The wine bar? What about it?'

She opened her mouth but then clamped her lips together. Instead of speaking, she handed me the phone. I saw a string of texts in blue and white bubbles. The first message was from Tim.

'Hi Susannah, Tim here! How are you?'

'Fine. What's up?'

'Could I check something? Confidentially. Just between us.'

'I know what confidentially means. What is it?'

'Was Lucy v drunk last night? She didn't ring me to say goodnight.'

I felt my blood cool, and a pit of dread opened low in my stomach, but I tried to keep it off my face. I read on.

'No. And so what if she was?'

'Ah yeah,' Tim replied. Then another from him straight after. 'Was she talking to anyone but you?'

'Like who?'

'You know – tall pretty girl, drinks involved. You sure no blokes were trying to take advantage?'

I was conscious of Susannah peering at me closely as I read, so I smothered a sigh.

'Are you asking if she was talking to other men? Or insinuating that I'd let creeps near my little sister?'

'Look, never mind.'

And that was it. I pushed the phone back across the table and finished the rest of my glass of wine in one go.

Though I was impressed by how she handled Tim, I was annoyed that she had this insight into my life. Also, this outing was supposed to be when I got to question her, not the other way around.

'He can be a bit possessive,' I said finally.

'A bit?'

'I don't want to get into it. He can be jealous. And clearly, he can be a bit thick too, judging by those messages. Anyway, you'll be delighted to hear that we've split up.'

It was half true. I just hadn't quite got around to telling him yet.

Susannah pulled her heavy coat over her shoulders while keeping her gaze trained on me, her eyebrows knitted together. I thanked God for the beautiful seascape around us that I could focus on instead. I fixed my eyes on the horizon. The closer the sea came to us, the choppier it became, but way out in the distance the ocean was so calm and blue it looked like silk.

'Lucy,' she said gently, 'I'm not trying to be nosy, but is everything OK? You never mentioned that you'd broken up. Is this why you're so quiet lately?'

Was everything OK?

I wasn't ready for the question. My throat constricted and I could feel emotion well up inside me. I guess that was the answer.

I reached over to take Susannah's pale bony hand in mine. She relaxed at the touch and I felt my own nervous system quieten down too.

'Everything is fine,' I lied. 'Men will be men. Now, my turn to ask the questions. You said there were two reasons you brought me here. What's the second?'

Susannah's eyes were still fixed on mine, but she looked glazed, the way someone looks when they are pretending to listen but their mind is somewhere else entirely.

'I'll save that for dinner, Luce. Which leads us to the next . . . thing. Now, please don't make a massive deal of this, but I've invited Tara to dinner.'

My head reeled. I didn't know whether to laugh or shout, 'What the hell?' I opted for the latter.

'Lucy, don't—'

How could I not? Susannah hadn't spoken to Tara for years, not since New York. That trip was eleven years ago, in 2011. I always sensed that a lot more happened than has ever been revealed. And, of course, I was right there in the middle of it all.

But now – *this*! Susannah had suddenly reached out the hand of friendship. My mind was blown.

'Has she responded? Does she know I'm here?' I asked.

'Er, no, she doesn't know you're here, I was hoping it would be a nice surprise for her. And she hasn't responded yet, but I'm optimistic. I told her I was making a special dinner tonight.'

There was a curtness to her tone. Just then I felt a vibration against my leg. I slid my phone out of my pocket: Tim. Given the half-truth I had just told Susannah, I couldn't talk to him then. I silenced the phone.

'So, go on,' I said, tipping the last of the bottle into her glass. 'After all these years why are you trying to call a truce?'

Her eyes were darting all around the other tables, as if she was about to divulge a huge secret. She twisted her long caramel curls into a rope and tucked it into her coat. Though the sun remained hidden, she pulled her massive Cartier sunglasses down over her eyes. Her look screamed *luxe* – the sunglasses alone probably cost more than my monthly rent.

'It is thirty-nine years to the month since Tara and I were last here. We came on holiday in April 1983. I was six. Tara was four.'

This really surprised me. I'd never been here before but I assumed Susannah and Tara must have used Mum's cottage.

'And do you know something even weirder?'

I said nothing. Already I was hooked. She does this captive audience thing – in her defence, it's because she usually has a captive audience. It's her thing – storytelling. She's good at it in writing, and she's good at it in person.

'Years later Mum came here for a break, also in April. She and Dad had a fight, and she came here to get some space. She only reminded me about it a few weeks ago. I was revising for the Leaving, so was trying to ignore the pair of them. It's almost like a mirror, isn't it? All of us coming here on the same month all these years apart.'

At the mention of the word 'mirror', I remembered what I was supposed to be asking her all along. About her book, and my apparent presence in it. But before I could say anything she was off again, lighting a cigarette – another annoying habit of hers – at the same time.

'Maybe I'm getting sentimental, but I thought it would be nice to see Tara here again . . . for us sisters to be together.' She blew smoke out between her lips and held the cigarette aloft, looking poised and in control. 'I think it's time to start again with a clean slate. We're not getting any younger.'

'What on earth has got into you?' I said, waving smoke away from my face. Susannah has so many vices – between the Pinot Grigio and the fags and being so tightly coiled; I wondered if I should tell her it wasn't the lack of SPF that had put lines on her face.

'There's something about this place, though, isn't there? I would have invited Mum, but it would probably have only reminded her of Dad,' she said.

She shoved the sunglasses back on top of her head. Her green eyes bored into mine. Her intensity was becoming more unsettling. All she had said – about getting sentimental, starting again – was just so unlike her.

'So, little sis, here's to a reset,' she said.

Susannah clinked her glass against mine – hard – but I couldn't speak because I was trying to gather my thoughts. Susannah can hold a grudge, so her olive branch to Tara was out of character. Strange, too, for her to mention Dad. Though they grit their teeth and get on with it the odd Christmas he comes around to say hello, they barely tolerate each other – the barbs come out when the Baileys are on board, and there are always Baileys on board. Then there was this 'reset'.

Suddenly I remembered the novel again. With all the curveballs out of the way, it was time to find out what Susannah thought she was at. I looked at her straight, ready to ask my questions, but she was frozen, glass of wine suspended in mid-air. Her mouth was a little open. She appeared shocked, or horrified, or both. I had never seen a look like that – fear – on her face before. I followed her gaze and turned my head to look over my shoulder towards the glass porch leading into the hotel. I couldn't see anything out of the ordinary.

When I turned back to her, she was necking her wine and clambering up off the bench. 'Let's go – now,' she said.

I glared at her. She has always known that I hate being rushed. Feeling other people get panicked and flustered around me just makes me panicked and flustered.

'I'm grand here for the moment, what's got your knickers in a twist?' I asked.

She fumbled in her bag and put a black debit card on the table between us.

'Use this to pay, you know the PIN. Don't mind me. I've just had an idea. I have to get it down in my journal before I forget,' she said, making a writing gesture in the air. 'I'll see you for dinner,' and she ran out onto the winding road, up the slope, about 30 metres to our cottage. I saw her open her car door, bend over and remain in that awkward position for about a minute. She stood then, like she had remembered something.

And then she looked directly at me, as though she was going to come back. I frowned and put my hands up in a questioning pose, as if asking, *What?* But she didn't respond.

She fumbled in her pocket, produced the key that she had taken from the safe, turned to open the front door and shut it forcefully, so loudly I could hear it slamming.

By now I had completely lost my bearings. The old me would have twigged that something was very out of place. But instead of being present and spotting the warning signs, I got lost in my thoughts.

I thought of Lucy the cop in Susannah's novel and how I still hadn't a clue about her. That made me think about how much I missed my job and how Susannah thought it was salvageable but didn't know the full truth of what happened. Every time I thought of it, my stomach lurched.

I thought about how much I wished I had the courage to break up with Tim and about Susannah's pitying look as she watched me reading his texts. I knew what she was thinking: *You can do better, but you just don't believe it.* Was it any wonder if she made me a character in her book, when mine is a tragic story that makes strangers feel awkward?

I touched my neck above my jumper, tracing my scars, some jagged and deep, some superficial and thin. Of course, that brought me full circle, to what happened in New York when I was sixteen. Everything comes back to that.

4

New York, April 2011

A rare spring nor'easter drops a foot of snow on New York City and temporarily hushes the sirens and horns.

It is the biggest day of Susannah's life.

It hasn't gotten off to a good start. She got up to use the bathroom at seven and there was no light. A note from the general manager, slid under the door, confirmed that the power was gone throughout the hotel. An hour later it's still gone, as is the promise of an extravagant breakfast of eggs with hollandaise sauce and champagne.

From under the Egyptian cotton sheets of their four-poster bed, Susannah whispers into her husband's back: 'David? *David!* Wake up! I'm starving.'

'Mmmphh.'

'How are you still asleep?' she says, hauling herself up onto her side to get a look at his face. She shakes his shoulder, until he turns to glare at her.

'What? They'll ring when the power is back. I'm wrecked here, woman.'

With that, he turns on his side again, bashing his pillow into shape with irritation.

'You're hanging is what you mean. Too much boozing with my sister last night,' she says. 'Seriously, I have to eat.'

One of the things she and David had bonded over was a love of food. They met at a writers' retreat in the Midlands in spring 1998. She was twenty-one, there on the advice of her English professor, and on the cusp of finishing the book that would change her life. He was four years older, a short-story writer and editor of a literary magazine, the *Novel Idea*. Both being younger than the other guests by at least two decades, they clicked immediately. One night they snuck out to a pub in Mullingar. They agreed that the meaning of life was great wine and better food. In his speech at their wedding, he said watching her horse into a bowl of chicken wings was the moment he knew he would marry her.

'A fancy place like this is bound to have sorted something,' David says. 'See what's in the mini-bar – that'll keep you going. There's no need to get into a state.'

'Do you think it's still going ahead? The ceremony? Because if it doesn't, I swear—'

Releasing a sigh, David sits up and turns to look at her.

'You are the most insecure person I know,' he says.

'What? How is that insecure?'

'Don't be so sensitive. I'm just saying.'

Seeing her expression, he lies back down and pulls her into the space just between his shoulder and neck.

'Sorry, sorry, sorry. Such a little flower. If anyone saw this side of you, they would die of shock. C'mon, the ceremony will go ahead. The electricity will be back in no time. Right?'

'But what if the judges can't make it because of the snow? Or the other nominees can't get here? Or the hotel staff can't make it in because it gets worse?'

David runs one hand over his stubble. Susannah knows she's being impossible and he's probably wondering how he's going to put up with a whole day of this. But she can't help herself. Today is a big deal. Huge.

'Listen to me now, I will say this only once more. The. Awards. Are. Happening.'

He punctuates every word with a playful jab into her side, causing her to squeal and burrow further under the sheets. With her voice muffled, she says, 'But the storm.'

'But the storm, my eye. Everyone you're talking about has already arrived. You saw them all last night. Didn't you say you saw Stephen King getting into one of the lifts? Let's hope he's not still stuck in there,' David says, prompting more laughter.

Susannah slides out her side of the bed and makes her way into the bathroom, automatically reaching to flip the light switch before remembering – no power. She opens the blinds in the bathroom, which looks out onto Sixth Avenue. Apart from a couple of yellow cabs, and a police car crawling slowly over the grey-white snow, it's weirdly empty.

She shuts the bathroom door and then sits on the small stool beside the bath and closes her eyes, allowing herself to picture the scene that she has replayed over and over again; a well-worn movie, but one that never fails to make her stomach flip and heart race. She would never say it out loud to anyone, never admit the extent of her vanity, but she is picturing her name being called out after the list of nominees is projected onto the screen at the front of the ballroom.

Book number four, her lucky number. While *The Broken Bay* is selling well, winning will send it to the top of the bestseller charts. But it's not just about sales. It's about vindication. After the runaway success of her first two books, *Under the Echo*'s failure had blindsided Susannah and rattled her confidence. And she had seen a mean side to the publishing scene, authors she barely knew sympathizing about the reviews, hardly bothering to conceal their delight. Clearly, a lot of people had been longing to see the girl-wonder cut down to size. Her girl-wonder days are past, but if she wins today it will be one in the eye for everyone who wrote her off as an overhyped flash in the pan.

It all swirls around in her head. She wants it to stop – she can't let bitterness put a dampener on this wonderful day. Then she hears the words that have haunted her since she was seventeen.

She'll amount to nothing. That's what they say in the school. Face it, she's a loser!

She had heard her father's voice through the kitchen door, reporting back from a parent–teacher meeting. His words cut right to the bone. They would change the course of her life.

David raps on the bathroom door, reefing her back into the present.

'Tara's at the door.'

'Ugh. What on earth does she want? Tell her to take a hike.'

'Susannah, I'm not dealing with the sniping between you two today. I'll let her in, and you can tell her yourself.'

For the umpteenth time Susannah wonders why she invited Tara. She has never met anyone with Tara's ability to whinge and create a drama out of nothing. She could have foretold that Tara would try to make everything about herself. But still, Tara is her sister, and she would never hear the end of it if she left her at home.

Susannah pulls on her blue satin robe and yanks the bathroom door open. She intends to leave Tara under no illusion about what she thinks of her lush behaviour the night before.

Tara is talking at David, who is standing lamely in his boxers scratching his head. Tara then turns to her, tugging her wispy brown hair behind her ears. It's an anxious tic she's picked up from their mother.

'Lucy is missing.'

'What do you mean Lucy is missing?'

'She's not answering her mobile, or the phone in her room. She said she was going to bed at like nine o'clock and she was acting weird after dinner—'

'Tara, why do you always have to be so dramatic? She was probably just sick of your drunken antics last night.'

'If you'd let me finish, for once? I was worried and got reception to let me into the room. Her mobile is on the bedside locker. So is her bag.'

Despite herself, Susannah hears her mother's words, during one of their many conversations when she was trying to convince Evelyn to let Lucy come to New York.

'It's not safe for her over there,' Evelyn had said. 'She's only sixteen. And New York is loud and chaotic – I'm not sure she'd be able for it.'

She puts that to the back of her mind. This is Tara all over – catastrophizing and trying to make a fun occasion miserable.

Tara is still talking. 'I'm going to ask reception to have a look through any CCTV footage when all the generators are up and running, although they probably cut out too. In our hotels, generators only power the essentials, fridges and the like. But if Lucy went out, in that weather – I mean it would be madness—'

Generators, Susannah thinks, *thank God!*

'Tara, get a grip! You know Lucy – she's nosy. She's just gone for a wander. She won't have gone far. Can you leave us to get dressed.'

'You are unbelievable! You wouldn't listen to Mum and now you won't listen to me. I know something's up. I'm calling the police.'

With that, David comes to life. 'Tara, hang on! This place is like a labyrinth, straight out of one of those fantasy novels that Lucy reads. Susannah's right – she's bound to have gone exploring. You know what she's like. I don't fancy explaining that to a New York cop.'

Though she looks dubious, Tara seems becalmed. 'Do you think so, David?'

'I do. Imagine Lucy's reaction if we panic when she shows some independence. She's in a fancy hotel in the middle of Manhattan. She's fine.'

'I suppose you're right. I'll have another look.'

Without looking Susannah's way again, Tara turns on her heel and leaves the room. Susannah makes the namaste gesture to David. He smiles, rolls his eyes and goes into the bathroom. Drama over.

Susannah thinks of the text she sent Lucy an hour ago, and the response. Tara would hit the roof if she found out, and for what? *All will be fine*, she thinks. She puts it out of her mind and focuses on the momentous day ahead.

5

When I wake, it's to the sound of the sea sighing. I have one blissful moment of peace before it is shattered.

Susannah!

I jolt forward and shout her name. But there's no answer.

I stayed up for hours. I paced the room and stared out the window, analysing every shadow and watching each passing car with mounting dread. I lost count of the number of times I tried to ring her. I thought about going out onto the beach to look for her, but I remembered her telling me to stay put. Even so, I stuck my head out the door, but a gale blew bitter surf onto my lips. Her car remained parked outside.

I sat on the couch and poured another glass of wine, and then another, hoping it would tamp down the fear. A question rose up, insistent and embarrassing: *What would a garda do?* If I was still in that job and this was happening to a friend or colleague, what would I say to them? What advice would I give?

I was at a total loss. It was almost as though I was a new person entirely, so far removed from the path I once trod, the life I had mapped out for myself.

'Susannah?'

Nothing.

My mouth is parched, and my tongue sticks to the top of my mouth. It's already mid-morning and I blink the sun out of my eyes. It is pounding in through the window with a surreal and overbearing intensity. I pitch myself fully upright, the muscles in my neck and back aching intensely. After sitting up waiting for her to come back through the front door, I fell asleep on the small couch in a contorted position, my legs hanging off one end. This house is too small for me. I now know that if I ever buy a house, it won't be a cottage.

I make my way upstairs. Reaching the landing I stand at the bathroom door. It's bright in the morning light – pristine white tiles shining, a pretty blue mosaic of a lighthouse. It could not look less sinister. Part of my brain still can't accept that there's anything amiss.

So, I call Susannah's name again.

No answer, again.

I splash water on my face and I allow my senses to flood back in fully, one by one. I listen, but nothing stirs beyond the sea.

Surely there is some logical explanation.

I press a hand into the wall and try to focus. In the pocket of my tracksuit bottoms, I feel my phone vibrate and I'm flooded with relief. This will be her ringing with an explanation, and I am going to kill her for making me so worried.

When I look at the screen, I see a missed call and three unread messages from Tim.

Of course, a normal person would have called their boyfriend by now for advice. But if I was having doubts about Tim before – and I was having serious doubts – his texts to Susannah confirmed them all. It was one thing when stuff was between us. It's a different story now that he's dragged my sister into it.

Tim is my first boyfriend. I met him when I was in the garda training college. I'd been in Maynooth before then, studying criminology. I loved the course, delving into the nuances of criminal behaviour and how different societies handled it. But I found it hard to make friends. People seemed so self-contained, so sure of themselves. I lived at home with Mum in Whitehall, getting two buses to Maynooth every day and two back. I never stayed out to socialize.

Being in Templemore was the first time I'd lived away from home. The whole vibe was different from a big university campus. We all wanted each other to succeed. For the first time, I felt a sense of belonging. I made my first real friends there, and though they brought me out of my shell – which wasn't an easy task after what had happened to me, and with my synaesthesia too – I was still shy and working on my confidence. And that's when Tim became part of my life.

All of us recruits would troop off to a pub in the town on a Thursday and get tanked, and it was nearly always Tim serving us. There were a few things I liked about him immediately. He was as tall as me, with big broad shoulders. And he was charming, always flopping his black hair out of his eyes to give me a lopsided grin. He seemed to like me and brought me out of my shell even more.

I can see I was perfect girlfriend material for someone like Tim. He could camouflage his insecurities by exploiting mine. His family owned the pub and a few other businesses around the town. Along with his sister, he was the heir apparent. So, while he might have been loaded, Tim was beholden and felt trapped. Looking back, I was so pliable – so insecure about my attractiveness, so preoccupied with hiding my condition. I was grateful for his attention, and willing to change the contours of my world for him.

I moved back to Dublin when I got my first posting in 2018. That's when things started to get complicated. He always wanted to know everything I was doing and everywhere I was going. He expected me to get down to him at every opportunity, especially after I lost my job and couldn't bear to hang out with my garda friends from college. I screened their calls and didn't get back to them. Those friends were hard-won, and eventually, understandably, they gave up on me. Then the pandemic happened. I'd already cut myself off and this was the perfect opportunity to make my life even smaller. It was comforting in a way that only introverts will understand.

How easy it was to use the excuse of having a cough or sniffle not to visit Mum, to ditch my Saturday walks with Susannah. My 10k walk became a 5k walk and then, no walk. And of course, the pubs were closed so Tim was in a bad headspace too. I spent far too much time FaceTiming him. Just him, no one else.

I've known for a long time that I don't love him. I just depend on him for a feeling of connection outside my family. I've been afraid that if I tell Tim and his controlling behaviour to get out of my life it will sever my last link – beyond my sisters and Mum – to normality and humanity. But despite knowing that I need to break things off, in the last few months I've managed to become more enmeshed with him than ever. He's been paying my rent.

The arrangement came about because I told him about an incident in the café where I've worked since last autumn, a job I took against Tim's advice. The incident was no big deal really – a story about a man standing up for me after an obnoxious woman lost the rag when I mixed up normal and oat milk. Tim suggested that I needed to go part-time. He said I was obviously struggling with sensory overload and he'd help with my rent. When I said the incident had nothing to do with my condition and I could handle the job, he accused me of 'invalidating' his opinions and said I didn't care about him. It wasn't the first time he'd turned on me like that, and it scared me, so I let him talk me into his plan. Somewhere between then and now, working part-time became working no time, and helping with the rent became paying the rent.

Up to now I have tried not to think about how odd this is. It took coming to Dunmore East and squirming through that conversation with Susannah to clarify how messed up the situation is. If I achieve one thing today, I decide, it'll be finally telling Tim where to go. I am going to cut the cord. The thought thrills me. And I'll pay him back somehow. However, sorting things with Tim will have to wait.

I walk back into my bedroom and peer out of the small window. I see a picnic table painted a deep marine blue. Past the winding road, just metres away down a steep slipway, is the sea, pinned by steep cliffs on either side. The ebbing tide leaves behind it a smooth glass expanse of wet sand, which reflects the blue sky and clouds above. The water glitters in the sunlight. I am momentarily stunned by the sheer beauty.

I narrow my eyes and the glittering water looks like a thousand diamonds in a sea of mirrors. *Sea of Mirrors*. I think of Susannah again and go into her room. The bed is made up, unslept in.

I try her phone again, in hope rather than expectation. Still off.

Shit, I whisper.

In light of her sudden disappearance, Susannah's request that I tell nobody about our trip here is looking very strange. *Sorry, Susannah*, I think. *Needs must.*

I ring David. The line is dead. Straight to voicemail.

The last person I want to ring is Mum – she tends to overreact and be impetuous – so I do the unthinkable. I ring Tara.

This time the phone rings but there's no answer. In desperation, I phone Myles. If they're both at home, I can tell him how urgently I need to talk to her. Maddeningly, he doesn't answer either. What exactly has everyone so busy on a Tuesday morning in April?

Then the phone rings, and thank God, it's Tara.

'What is it, Lucy?'

Her voice is weary and quiet. It's the 'I have kids' voice.

'Jesus, nice to hear from you as well,' I say.

Tara sighs. 'Sorry, it's just not a good time,' she says. She's whispering.

'OK. The thing is, right, and please don't get annoyed, but I'm worried about Susannah. She's in Dunmore East, as you know, and she seems to have done a runner. Have you heard from her?'

'Susannah and I don't speak, Lucy.'

'Yes, but did she not text you yesterday about coming to dinner? I'm starting to get really worried here, Tara. I'll have a wander around the area but I have this . . . this horrible feeling, right in the pit of my stomach.'

'Wait, you're in Dunmore East too? With her?'

Her voice is no longer weary; there's a sharpness there.

'Yes, why?'

'What on earth are you doing there? And where have you been recently? You've been very quiet. Were you abroad or something?'

'Can we do the small talk another time, Tara? Can you get down here if she doesn't show? I dunno what's going on.'

'There is no chance of that happening. I've got my hands full with the kids,' Tara says, sighing again. I can almost feel her exasperation inside my own body and then my chest deflating as though I have been let down by someone. Extreme empathy – that's how one consultant once described my kind of synaesthesia.

'Christ! OK, look, just let me know if you hear from Susannah. Something weird happened last night, some guy came to the door and was shouting. Then she got a text or something and told me to stay in the house and lock the doors, and that's the last I saw of her. I'm trying not to panic but it's just weird. I'll keep you in the loop. It's probably best not to say anything to Mum. I don't want to freak her out if there's nothing to worry about.' As I say this, I'm trying not to freak out myself.

On the other end of the line, Tara is hesitating. Unlike Susannah, this is very much like her.

'Maybe you should call Mum. Susannah would be more likely to get in touch with her than me, if something was up.'

'Let me think about it,' I say.

Seconds after I hang up, the screen lights up again. It's Myles.

'Lucy, hi. Sorry I missed you. You wouldn't believe the messing here today.'

He puts a heavy emphasis on the word messing. In the background I can hear screeching – the soundtrack of teenage angst, a girl shouting at her brother. Myles talks over it.

'I thought it would be easier when they got older, Lucy, but do you know what, it just gets bleedin' worse. Take my advice – never have kids, OK?'

I respond with a dutiful half-hearted laugh. He loves doing the exasperated dad shtick. It got old a long time ago and I'm certainly not in the mood for it now.

'Don't worry, Myles. I'm sorted. I got a hold of Tara there.'

'Oh? That's nice of her to answer the phone. Maybe you could ask her to answer my bloody calls occasionally.'

'Is she not there with you?'

'No, she's not here. Sorry, I have a call coming in from the geologist. I have to take it, OK? Bye, bye, bye.'

How odd. Where is Tara, and why is she lying?

I don't have time to ponder this fresh question as my phone starts pinging with a surge of breaking news alerts and push notifications. They all say the same thing: 'Gardaí launch a murder investigation after a woman's body is found in Dunmore East.'

6

New York, April 2011

By nine the hotel has rustled up coffee and pastries. Susannah figures that will do for now. It's that or head out to find a diner, but she wants to get her bearings. The power has yet to return, therefore the lifts aren't working. Battery-powered lanterns sit on ornate ebony tables. The hallways of the hotel are fitted with royal-blue carpets, in an intricate pattern that's hard to make out in the dim light.

'Spooky,' David says.

'Hmmm,' Susannah responds.

'You worried about Lucy?'

'Nah,' she says, though not being entirely truthful. She is anxious for Lucy to turn up. Still, she's sure there's a simple explanation – probably that she's become completely absorbed in something and lost track of time, which would be Lucy all over.

They round a corner and push open double doors leading to a staircase. Judging by the cold tiles, Susannah is guessing that guests rarely, if ever, use this way down.

David walks ahead, using the torch on his phone to give them more light.

'Tara was very anxious about her. I suppose, given the way Lucy is—' he says.

Susannah cuts him off. 'Aaargh, diversionary tactics. Tara's probably mortified about being three sheets to the wind last night. I haven't seen her that drunk in ages. What was she saying when you were up on the roof? You never told me.'

'Oh, nothing much – just chit-chat about the dinner,' David says.

'Anyway, Lucy is sick of being mollycoddled. She told me herself. It just makes it harder. We wrap her in cotton wool and it's not good for her. She'll have gone for a wander, and she's got distracted and doesn't realize what time it is. She's probably found a diner and is tucking into a stack of pancakes, syrup and bacon.'

As they turn the corner down yet another flight of stairs, out of nowhere David sighs and says, 'Wouldn't it be great to do a Lucy on it – just go for a wander, forget about the bloody ceremony!'

'Where did that come from? Don't say that, even as a joke! You know this could change everything.'

They were far from stuck for cash, but as writers with no pension or sick leave, a win today would probably give them lasting security.

'Yeah, you're right. Sorry.'

They walk the rest of the way in silence. Ten flights down Susannah stops and says: 'This is it, first floor.'

She pushes the door open into another dimly lit hallway and puts her nose right up to a brass plaque on the wall.

'This way,' she says, signalling ahead.

A faint light spills out the doorway of a conference room. Inside, there are no windows, just big round tables covered in white tablecloths. Even with the benefit of poor emergency lighting to obscure its features, the room has zero charm.

A scattering of people sit around. While she's still adjusting to the scene she hears her name, on the double. Following the voices she sees Summer as well as Fran Morris, her US publisher, waving her over. Summer has an open laptop and three notebooks splayed out in front of her. Fran is stuffing a croissant into her mouth, a steaming cup of black coffee in her other hand.

'OK, let's get down to it, we don't have long,' Summer says, running her sleek blonde ponytail through her hand. Summer is all business in her oversize two-piece suit and white blouse.

Susannah throws her eyes to heaven. 'Here we go,' she says.

Even in the candlelight, she sees a muscle twitch under Summer's eye. Christ! She and Summer have an odd relationship. Summer is tough. Unlike most agents, who are some combination of therapist and cheerleader, Summer is more like a demanding coach. Her briskness used to suit Susannah, but recently things feel strained. She's not sure what's going on. It's complicated because they met through David. Summer was his agent first. When she and David got together, he told her Summer Hayes was young and extremely pushy – she gave him grief about only writing short stories – and he thought if anyone could get Susannah an amazing deal it was Summer. And that's exactly what she did.

In the years since they met, Summer has become one of the biggest agents in New York and is managing a huge roster of writers. Susannah knows she could easily drop her. The David connection often helps in smoothing things over – Summer has a soft spot for him.

Susannah slumps into a chair beside David and pulls out her phone. She's not in the mood for Summer or Fran getting on her case – on today of all days. She lets David go into manager mode. He already liaises with the publicity people, but he's always a step ahead. He goes through the list of proposed interviews again. Fran reminds him how they plan to maximize *The Broken Bay*'s reach in the US if it wins. Susannah has heard it all before. She zones out.

After a while she hears Summer's voice.

'Susannah!'

She looks up, startled. She didn't even notice Fran leaving the table.

'I have two questions, Susannah.'

'Go on.'

'Number one, have you a game plan for this afternoon?'

Susannah pauses, pushes herself up in the chair and puts a hand on her hip.

'Yes. If I win, I accept the award. If I don't, I clap for whoever got it. Simple.'

Summer sighs, but Susannah doesn't know what she was expecting her to say.

'And what's question number two?'

'If you win this thing we are going to need to move fast to capitalize on the attention. If *The Shallow End* could be published next spring, it would be perfect timing. I've already had the conversation with Fran, and Amelia in the UK. Fran doesn't want to put pressure on you today, so *I'm* going to ask: how are you getting on with the revisions?'

Susannah glances at David, who jumps in.

'I hear what you're saying, Summer. And we already had a look at your notes. There were a few things that didn't add up so it's taking longer than intended to finalize the new draft.'

'What do you mean about stuff not adding up?' Summer says.

'There's a reason why the murder has to happen in the last part of the book, and not the start, because when I originally thought about Kayla's character—'

'That's enough,' Susannah says, snapping her phone shut. She clocks Summer's baffled expression.

When I originally thought . . . Jesus!

She turns on the charm. 'Sorry, Summer. I know you're only thinking of my best interests. Of course I do. I'll come back on your mark-up in a few days. But cut me a bit of slack.'

'You're right. Sorry. We'll pick it up next week.'

Susannah stands up, making it clear that the meeting is over. Summer packs her notebooks away hurriedly, shuts down the laptop and walks off. She pauses at the door to call back, 'Don't forget the pre-ceremony gathering this morning. And try to eat something substantial – it's going to be a long day!'

Susannah can feel her blood still boiling as she marches out of the room ahead of David. She is pissed off. In the gloom of the never-ending stairwell, she climbs onto the first step and then spins around, putting her face level with David's.

'You did that deliberately,' she says. She is practically hissing.

'Did what?'

'*Did what?* Spare me. You know what you did. It's not the day to steal my thunder. You might have helped with my books, and I appreciate that, but they are not *yours*.'

She can feel her bottom lip trembling.

What a day for this to come out into the open, and like this. They've never discussed just how much David contributes to her writing, especially over the six years since *Under the Echo* was published. Because working together created so much tension he had, by mutual agreement, stayed hands-off with *Under the Echo* and concentrated on admin and some freelance editing. But after it got such a mauling from the critics they had, again by unspoken agreement, reverted to their old MO with *The Broken Bay* and now with her latest — Susannah writing, David reading and giving her detailed notes, often coming up with suggestions. But that's all they were — notes and suggestions. She still wrote the books.

'Don't ever do that to me again. Don't treat me like a thief. Write your own fucking book.'

David stays perfectly still. Even in the poor light she can see his colour has risen, his lips have tightened, and his eyes have narrowed. The air between them crackles and she can feel that he is seething. Him not having written his own novel is a sore point for David. *He* was the promising young talent when they met. He's always said he doesn't mind being the supporting act, and she has always chosen to believe him. And now he's decided to casually imply to her agent that he's the writer behind her books.

David opens his mouth to say something, but she doesn't want to hear. 'No,' she says, palm in front of his face. His head jerks backwards, as if she's slapped him. She turns and stomps up the stairs. If she doesn't get away, she *will* slap him.

7

Murder?

I devour the news reports, taking in the details as quickly as I can.

A dead woman . . .
Found by walkers early this morning . . .
A well-known location, Badger's Cove . . .
Gardaí on the scene . . .
Murder investigation . . .

Susannah, I think. *Susannah.* I throw on a pair of jeans, suede boots and a top of Susannah's that I find on the banister. I grab the first coat I find on a hook in the hallway and race out the door, nearly knocking myself out on the low frame as I do so. I have no idea where I am going.

The patio opens out onto shared parking area, surrounded by six other thatched cottages. Beyond the parking bays is a gate onto a steep road which slopes down towards the beach. There are only two cars, including Susannah's. I check the driver's door and it's open. But I don't know what to do. It's like I have stepped onto the set of a movie that I have no part in. I hear kids screeching down on the beach, their excited yelps so out of place in the nightmare that's unfolding. I feel my heart constricting inside my chest.

I take out my phone and type Badger's Cove into the maps app. The cove is only ten minutes by foot. I go through the gate out onto the road and turn away from the beach, climbing up instead. At the top, as I pause for breath, I see a sign in the side of a stone wall – 'Harney's Hill'. Underneath it is a quote about love that I can't quite read, the concrete worn down by weather and time. I feel my heart thump high in my chest.

It can't. It just can't be my sister. As if to reinforce this point, I shake my head side to side, saying, *nope, nope, nope.*

As I reach the top of the hill, out of breath, my phone rings. It's David.

'Lucy, what the hell is going on? Tara texted last night saying Susannah's in Dunmore East? Are you with her? Why isn't she answering her phone? Jesus Christ, I'm up the walls here after hearing the news. Why won't she answer me?'

His questions tumble out on top of each other before I can jump in.

'I tried to ring you this morning. She went out last night and didn't come back.'

I know I'm leaving out a lot, but in my panic I feel my throat closing around the extra words I want to say.

'What do you mean she didn't come back? And why are you even in Dunmore East? That's it, I'm coming down there.'

His alarm is making me feel even worse. My breath comes in quicker bursts.

I need to check the map again, so I take the phone from my ear. David's frantic voice sounds tinny now, just a stream of questions, more than I can keep up with. According to the map I need to take a left and then I can get to the cove through the Dunmore East park.

'David, I don't know what's going on. I'm going to find out. Give me twenty minutes and I'll ring you back, OK?'

He protests but I cut him off. His anxiety isn't helping mine.

I race up the road, a low wall to my left, the park sprawling out beyond it, all small rolling green hills and gnarled trees that reach high up into the sky. On my right, as I race along the path, is a church with one old clock high up in its turret, backlit with a fading amber glow. Screeching crows encircle the spire. I can see crowds gathered up ahead at the entrance, which is a small kissing gate. I see four squad cars, at least a dozen uniformed gardaí and a coastguard helicopter thunders overhead. People are standing in clusters here and there. A woman has her hand over her mouth, while a man nods his head solemnly.

It can't be Susannah, it can't. If I just keep telling myself this, maybe it will be true.

I barge through the kissing gate all the way down a path to the entrance to Badger's Cove. It's taped off with a police cordon. Two young gardaí are guarding the entrance, one with a clipboard in his hand, the other keeping watch. They look a little out of their depth, I think, knowing exactly how that feels.

They eye me suspiciously. I am dishevelled; my eyes are smudged with yesterday's mascara, and I am panting. I am near tears, too. The female garda is sturdy, blonde and has an unlikely shock of pink blush high on her cheeks. She looks around my age. As she scrutinizes me, I see the lines deepen around her eyes.

I need to keep myself in check. Even being around gardaí in a situation like this is hugely triggering. It would be so easy to let my defences down and succumb to my emotions.

'This is a crime scene, please,' the female garda says.

'My sister is missing. She disappeared last night. I'm a former garda. Can I go down there and speak with the inspector on duty?'

The words are out before I even have time to think what I'm saying. And while my words are measured, my tone of voice is not. It's becoming almost impossible not to think the worst, and my pitch betrays it. I want to tell them that someone came knocking at the door last night and threatened her. I want to say that she was acting out of sorts and ordered me to go into lockdown. But it feels like I'm inside one of those dreams where you try to scream and nothing comes out.

'One of us will let him know when he comes back up. Can you step back, please,' she says.

I crane my neck past the two officers to see a path that gives way to steep steps that descend to a clearing of rocks by the sea. The clearing is blocked from view by a large white tent. I know it was put there to protect the body from the elements and from curious eyes.

The body is the evidence.

How many times have I heard this phrase in training?

The body is the evidence.

Susannah's body.

I feel eyes on me and realize that people are watching me from different vantage points. My palms are clammy, the anxiety surging through me from head to toe. It's a horrible feeling, an overwhelm, like I'm being lifted out of my shoes by worry. I see a short, bald man halfway down the path behind the officers. He has his hands in his suit pockets, and he is watching me intently. I know this is the detective inspector in charge, I know it just by looking at him.

'Is it Susannah? Let me see my sister, I want to see my sister.' I don't mean to shout but it comes out far louder than I intended.

'You can't stop me,' I say, trying to charge between the two gardaí to get to the path.

The pink-faced officer grabs me firmly by the shoulders and tells me to control myself, or else. The inspector approaches and asks what's going on.

'This woman says she is the victim's sister.'

'What's your sister's name?'

'Susannah. Susannah Brown – you might have heard of her, she's a writer. Her married name is Susannah Murtagh. She's from Dublin.'

I feel my pulse tapping rapidly against my wrist.

Quietly, almost hesitantly, he says, 'We have identified the victim and her family has been informed. Her name is not Susannah Brown. She has no sisters. Now, please step back.'

In that moment, all I can hear is the sound of the sea bashing against the rocks somewhere just beyond me. I want to fall to my knees with the relief.

I hear the inspector tell the clipboard-wielding garda to bring me home and arrange for someone to take a statement. He steers me by the elbow, like I'm a bold child. Everyone stares.

My wave of relief is followed by rising dread. A woman has just been murdered. And Susannah is nowhere to be seen.

8

New York, April 2011

Ancient chandeliers glow overhead, and the room is filled with the sound of corks popping and glasses clinking, despite it being just past breakfast. Having briefly shocked Manhattan into stillness, the worst of the weather has passed. The power hasn't returned but just in time to save the day, the rest of the hotel's diesel generators have come to life. The authors' pre-awards gathering is proceeding, with no food in sight.

'I hate this shite,' Tara mutters into her flute of sparkling wine, earning a sneaky smile from David. It gives her that familiar giddy feeling. She can't blame it on the warm morning wine; she feels what she feels. As they stand there, she breathes in his unmistakable scent – the darkest musk, wood and spice. If 'more' had a smell, this is what it would be.

They watch Susannah as she glides around the room, air kissing the authors she vaguely knows and shaking hands with the ones she doesn't.

'I used to like it,' David says.

'You did not,' Tara says, nudging his shoulder with hers.

'I did! I swear. There was this feeling of being surrounded by your own kind, people who understood what a lonely job writing can be, creative people who were genuinely interested in what you were doing, being with your tribe, all that jazz. Yadda yadda.'

'Huh, if you say so. I haven't a creative bone in my body.'

'Neither have I, apparently.'

'Ah, stop. You'll write again,' Tara says.

'Been a while.'

'We're all rusty in one way or another,' she says, her flirty tone embarrassing her once she's spoken the sentence out loud.

David smiles at her, but she can see the flash of a warning in his eyes and then he turns away to gaze over to Susannah. She knows better than to push it. Besides, she isn't feeling great about what happened last night. At some stage today, she hopes to talk with him about it.

Tara mulls over what he just said about losing his creativity. She wonders if, when he met Susannah at that writers' retreat, and she told him about the book she had been working on since she was seventeen, he had any idea what lay ahead. And if the sensational success of that book had dimmed his light the way it had dimmed Tara's. If maybe that's why he doesn't bother writing anymore.

Just then he turns towards her, giving her a quizzical look.

'What are you thinking about?' he asks.

Nothing I can tell you, she thinks. *Not yet.*

'Lucy. I'm worried about Lucy. I know you think she's perfectly normal, but—'

'Oh, I never said that. There's nothing normal about Lucy. She's one of the most unusual people I've ever met.'

'That's what worries me. That she's . . . unique. And she's sixteen and a six-foot blonde who looks like Claudia Schiffer. She's bound to attract attention – the wrong sort of attention. What if she's gone out?'

'Wow, you really are worried, aren't you? But so what if she's gone out? It's mid-morning in the middle of Manhattan. There was no proper food here until they got the generators going. Susannah thinks she's out having a big greasy American breakfast and she's lost track of time.'

'Susannah is only thinking of Susannah. She's the one who begged Mum to let Lucy come. She promised to keep an eye out for her.'

David says nothing, but she knows he agrees. He goes back to sipping his drink and watching Susannah make her way around the room. He's not looking at his wife with pride or curiosity. It's more of a barely disguised grimace. She drinks in his features. His dark hair now is a little too long. His five o'clock shadow, that's a permanent feature. His Adam's apple juts out in an unbearably masculine way. If there's trouble in paradise, Tara is here for it – David is too good for her sister.

Suddenly he glances back at her, and perhaps seeing how she catches her breath, he asks, 'How are the kids?'

Bubble. Firmly. Burst.

'Mia stomps around acting like the boss of Mark. He's too tiny to do anything except squeal at her and try to eat marbles. I'm convinced she leaves them out deliberately. She wants her mother to have a heart attack, obviously.'

'And Myles?'

'Myles!' She sighs before she can stop herself. 'I'm not a hundred per cent sure Myles understood how hard this parenting lark would be.'

'What do you mean?'

'Oh, you'll see one day.'

'I'm not quite sure I will.'

'What do you mean? I thought that was all part of the master plan?'

'Susannah is still very focused on her career,' David says grimly, before turning suddenly cheery and saying, 'Her ladyship is giving me dagger eyes. Wonder who that is that she's talking to. Hard to know if she wants me to come over or stay where I am.'

Being a foot shorter, Tara cannot see who is talking to whom across the room. She checks her watch again and places her long-empty glass on a table.

'I'm going to check Lucy's room again and if she's not

there I'll head out and have a look for her. You're welcome to join me.'

'OK. I'll meet you in the lobby in ten minutes. Maybe we can grab some food while we're out. I'll just let Susannah know where we're going.'

In Susannah's experience, events like this are a blend of rewarding and revolting. It just depends on who you get stuck talking to or sitting beside or smoking with. Granger Jones, a perennial *New York Times* bestselling author who writes prize-winning novels about marriage and friendship, may be a literary legend but she's an absolute head-melt.

'I see they optioned your last two books, but nothing came of it. Don't worry, honey, these things take years to come to anything. But think about it this way, what a lovely extra bonus, and it's good for PR.' Granger tosses her long red hair to one side while licking the gloss off her lips. Susannah thinks she could not be more the textbook literary diva.

Over Granger's shoulder she sees David trying to catch her eye. Thank God. They haven't exchanged a word since their row on the stairs. He didn't come back to the room, and she wasn't even sure he would turn up to this gathering. But before she can beckon him over, she realizes he is not the only one scrutinizing her. At the back of the room propping up the bar is a man she cannot quite place. He has blue eyes that blaze unnecessarily bright. A flicker of recognition ignites in the recesses of her mind. It is in the way he holds himself as he stares her down, sneering, as if he can see right through her. The hairs stand up on her arms and a shiver runs down her spine. She knows exactly who he is. Every fibre of her being tells her to run out of this room and never look back. She drags her attention back to Granger's mouth. God knows what Granger is saying but Susannah tries to sound like she is listening.

'What? Oh. Honestly, it doesn't bother me. I wouldn't be one of those authors up at the director's chair demanding creative input anyway.'

Granger gives her a puzzled look. 'Well, you say that now, but when *Love Beyond Love Beyond Me* was in production—'

Granger drones on and Susannah's mind races. If there is one thing she was determined about today, it's that it would go without a hitch. Even if everything and everyone is in league against her, she can still course correct. Nothing – not the snowstorm, not Lucy doing one of her disappearing acts nor Tara making a fool of herself nor David taking credit for her writing – nothing is going to mess this up. And she is going to tackle this ghost from the past head-on.

As graciously as possible Susannah takes her leave from Granger, puts her head down and pushes her way through the crowd. As she approaches the bar, the man with the bright blue eyes reaches behind him, picks up a glass of sparkling wine and hands it to her.

'To your great success,' he says. He has short and scruffy black hair that tears off in all directions. He is well built, the buttons on his white shirt straining under the pressure of the muscles on his chest and arms. He's in his early thirties, around the same age as her.

She takes the drink cautiously and gives him her best coy smile, pulling her long hair around over one shoulder until it grazes her waist.

'Do we know each other?' she says sweetly.

He laughs, a low guttural *hah* that's closer to a snort of derision.

'I suppose it's been so long, you might have forgotten me. If you weren't such a star now, I might have forgotten you too.'

'I'm sorry?'

'Jack Fogarty.'

This cannot be happening. It just cannot.

She hopes her face bears a look that suggests the name rings a faint bell, so faint she can barely recall it. Benign confusion is the look she's going for, as if she hasn't a clue what is going on. This is what she needs to do for survival, to have a chance of getting out of this interaction unscathed.

'Jack, Jack . . . ummm.'

'Ah now, don't play coy. It doesn't suit you, Susannah. I know you, and you know me. Let's not play this game.'

'Honestly, I'm confused—'

He cuts her off with a raised hand as he reaches behind himself again, this time producing a copy of her book.

'You're not confused, Susannah. It was the strangest thing when I saw the publicity about this thing. You know, I hadn't thought of you in such a very long time. My memories were always so hazy, so confused.'

Inside Susannah, a lift is plummeting to the core of the earth. *Fix this*, she tells herself, *fix this now*.

'Let me tell you, things were never the same after the Browns left Waterford.'

'I'm going to cut you off there. My husband—'

'No. You're going to listen to me or else I will stand up on that magnificent-looking stage and give the guests a few home truths. You don't want to test me, Susannah.'

Susannah plasters a smile across her face and takes him by the elbow, steering him towards the quietest corner of the room. She cannot have David hearing or seeing this.

'OK, what the hell do you want?'

'Whoa! So, no more of the Little-Miss-I'm-So-Confused act. Someone is worried,' he says.

'I'm serious, Jack.'

'Do you have no shame? After what happened, you write *this*?'

He slaps his hand down on the cover of the book.

'It is nothing to do with you,' Susannah says.

'Oh, but it is; it's the version of me and my family that you dreamt up in your sick little mind. All to get attention and praise.'

'I'm going to ask you one last time, and after that point, I am no longer listening. What do you want from me?'

Jack pauses, as if to give the matter some thought, and then seems to come to a resolution.

'All my life I tried to get to the bottom of what really happened. I mean, why did your family run away from Dunmore East that time? So many confusing memories. And, lo and behold, what turns up in the *Sunday Independent* last month but an interview with one of Ireland's great cultural ambassadors, Susannah Brown. You wouldn't know there's a recession looking around the room here, would you? Chandeliers and champagne for breakfast. It's not like this in Waterford, I'll tell you that. Not one bit.'

There's a gleam in his eyes now. Susannah knows her time is running out.

'Imagine how shocked I was when I read the revelations in these pages.'

'It's fiction, Jack.'

His eyes, so bright just seconds before, turn impossibly dark.

'It's not fiction. I was there,' he says.

When Susannah wrote the book, she wasn't thinking about people reading it. Or about a fictional past catching up with her actual present. And although she pushed and pushed for it, she never believed the book would be such a success, especially after falling on her face with her last book. It is only in this moment, under Jack Fogarty's unyielding stare, that she realizes what a truly awful idea it was to write this book.

'So, here's the deal, Susannah. I could have emailed you, or called you, but from my extensive research, your husband reads all your correspondence. Hired him as your glorified personal assistant, did you? No surprise there – I recall you were the bossy sort. Anyway, I came here to tell you something in person.'

She knows she should just let him finish but she can feel her anger rising. She takes a deep, steadying breath. Keeping calm is imperative; she knows this, but it's proving hard.

'For a man talking about recession, you found a way to fund this ridiculous mission,' she says, clutching at the first straw she can.

'Aha. And therein lies the crux of the issue. I am not affording it. You are. You just couldn't let sleeping dogs lie and now you have to pay the price, Susannah. Do you know what happened after your family left?'

His voice is louder now, with a hard edge. Over his shoulder she can see David is around fifteen feet away, coming towards them, a frown on his face.

'My mother won't even talk to me,' he spits out, 'and my father had to sell all his land. And now, thanks to the gombeen government that allows you tax breaks for your shitty books, his house is going to be repossessed. I want your personal email, and I'll tell you exactly how much it will cost you to hold on to your perfect little life.'

As David appears at Susannah's side Jack's expression morphs from dark to jovial. His face is transformed.

'Ah, this must be the famous David! Great to meet you, man,' Jack says, thrusting out his hand.

'Ehm, hi? Susannah, are you going to introduce me?' David says.

She matches Jack's smile of delight with one of her own.

'You won't believe it, but Jack and I knew each other when I was younger; our families hung out.'

'Oh? Wow. Small world. What brought you to New York, Jack?'

'I'm a garda. Was supposed to be here for a boxing match between our club and an NYPD club, but it's been cancelled because of the weather. Couldn't believe it when I heard this was on, I just had to call in. Such a coincidence.'

'Wow, boxing! I did this white-collar boxing thing once—'

'Sorry to interrupt, David, but I have an interview that I'm late for,' Susannah says.

'Of course, that's why I came over. We have to go but feel free to hang around, Jack,' David says.

Susannah is about to remind Jack that the ceremony is invite only, but before she can, he says he must be off.

'But don't forget to give me your personal email, Susannah; we must catch up and reminisce on those childhood holidays.'

David digs one hand into the pocket of his trousers and hands Jack a card.

'Just add 1977 before the "at" – that's her private address.'

'That's great. Thanks, David. Great to meet you. Good luck later, Susannah. I'll let you both get on with it so,' Jack says and walks away.

David has started talking about what's next on the to-do list. Susannah nods in agreement, but she has tuned out. Who is Jack Fogarty to come sneaking in here, blaming her for all his family's problems? And what does he know, really, beyond what he thinks he has put together from a work of fiction?

She can't concentrate on a word coming out of David's mouth. She thinks about all the years of hard work and sacrifice, locking herself away night after night in front of the computer, missing evenings out with friends, holidays with David, saying 'No' over and over to get this book written and push her life forwards, upwards. Can she let this man destroy one of the biggest days of her life with his vitriol and his poison?

'One second,' she says to David, rushing out of the room into the hotel lobby. She catches up with Jack and taps him on the shoulder.

'I'll send you what you want but consider that it. Whatever debt you think my family owes, that's it paid. And don't you ever, ever, turn up like this again or I swear to God, I will make you regret it. Because despite what you think you know, you know nothing.'

'Threatening a member of the force, is it? Well, while we are throwing it around, something for you to remember too. If you ever show your face in Dunmore East, or even the county of Waterford for that matter, I will kill you myself.'

9

I pace around the cottage in small circles, trying to put the pieces together.

Where on earth is Susannah?

What the hell happened in that cove?

I feel a throbbing between my temples, a mix of the wine I drank last night and the stress of the morning. I turn on the radio to hear the noon headlines, hoping to glean something new. The story is at the top of the bulletin, just a rehash of what's out there already. 'A murder investigation has been launched after the discovery of a woman's body in Dunmore East.' After, it's back to a current affairs show. The presenter comments on how shocking the story is. 'Obviously, we have very few details about what's happened in Dunmore East, but this will be the sixth violent female death in Ireland this year.' She recites the names of the other women who have already been killed in 2022.

It is overwhelmingly grim. All these women brutalized. A picture comes into my mind, clear as day – a woman, splayed out on the ground, a gash across her face.

A picture from my past.

I hold my breath and count to four. Then I breathe out for a count of four. I repeat this and imagine myself fully grounded to the earth. I try my best to tamp down the anxiety. But it's too late – the memories rush in, my emotions overpower me and I can't stop an agonized sob coming out.

This is what lost me my job – not being able to control my emotions. For Susannah's sake I need to focus on what I am good at, on using my strengths. But I'm trapped by who I am, with the past and present battling for my attention.

Who I am is someone who struggles to avoid being overwhelmed, mainly by other people. Of course, it took a long time to find that out. Mum took me to loads of doctors and refused to accept any of the labels they wanted to give me. She was relentless. Finally finding out what the accurate label was for my behaviour, synaesthesia, was a help. It gave us something to work with.

By the time I got to Templemore, I had come to embrace my unusual traits. I started training college with a huge sense of trepidation, given my appearance and my condition. If anyone asked about my scars, I would just say 'I was glassed' and that was usually enough to stop any further questions. I told no one about my condition. I became known for my amazing memory and an almost uncanny ability to read what other people were feeling. It was no problem for me to remember that under section 40 subsection 2 of the Road Traffic Act 1961, it is an offence for a driver not to show their licence. No one could come close to me when it came to that kind of stuff. And while other students griped and moaned about having to keep every hair in place, or making sure there wasn't so much as a scuff mark on their shoe, or practising the parade in the mornings, I loved nothing more than the sense of order. I learned how to keep my emotions off my face and bottle up the agony I felt watching others train and practise. It was my ultimate act of control, and I felt euphoric that I was achieving it, that I was the master of this condition and not the other way around. But in the end, the synaesthesia was in control, not me.

After training I was a probationer garda in uniform in Finglas. The way things worked I was on the front desk by day and would go on patrol with a senior officer at night. The day shifts were mad. I often regaled Mum with the stories – I thought funny stories would reassure her that I was fine. One woman wanted to make a criminal complaint about her neighbours feeding the seagulls, which were now shitting all over the local gardens. I can still hear her shrieking, 'It's a crime!'

On the night shifts, it at least felt like I was doing actual police work. But real police work would be my undoing. It was a routine domestic violence call-out that sent my life spiralling. I was out with Detective Garda Arthur O'Sullivan and we were fresh from an attempted robbery at an off-licence when the call came in. A woman had phoned the station saying she was worried about her neighbours. The husband was beating his wife. She said she could hear it through the wall, and so could her young children, and she was terrified that the woman would not make it through the night.

The front door was open when we got to the house. There was blood all over the floor tiles in the hallway, and the wall to the sitting-room door had wide horizontal streaks of it, like it had been smeared on with a paintbrush. Someone had tried to reach the front door and been dragged back. The sitting room was even more grim. Against the back wall a woman was slumped, covered head to toe in blood. A massive gash ran from her forehead around the curve of her cheek to the corner of her mouth.

O'Sullivan had taken a step back, perhaps to get a better look at the scene, perhaps in shock. Either way, I was not aware of anything except the sound of a woman screaming. It was a bone-chilling, high-pitched noise that could be heard by every house on the street. *We need to find her*, I thought. *Make sure she's OK, try to calm her down.*

It was only when O'Sullivan started shaking me by the shoulders that I realized I was the person screaming. And I wasn't stopping. I couldn't stop. Emotions that had been bottled up for eight years had been unleashed.

The woman was dying. I could hear it in the rasps of her final breaths. And then, horrifyingly, I felt it within myself. I felt *my* breath slow, *my* heartbeat become erratic, *my* vision become cloudy. As the woman died, I died too.

I woke up two hours later in hospital to find my boss, Inspector Richard Murphy, at the end of my bed, his leathery features pinched. He looked at me kindly, the way a father might, but I knew. It was there in his eyes.

When they found out the extent of my synaesthesia, how entangled I became in other people's sensations and emotions, I knew it was the end of the only thing I ever believed I was destined to do, that I was truly good at. What happened on the call-out convinced my colleagues – but, even worse, it convinced me – that despite all my talents I was not up to the job. How I held it together for so long, after everything I had been through, only to let one incident derail me, still devastates me.

That was three years ago, years in which circumstance, shame and a pandemic made me hard to reach. When Susannah hijacked me two days ago for this trip to the seaside, I thought it would blow off some cobwebs. But somehow, *somehow*, I've ended up at the location of a murder and she is missing. I'm triggered, shocked, confused and petrified all at the same time.

I make an effort to slow my breathing again, and a strange feeling starts to settle over me. Something like resolve. A present-day version of me is squaring up to a past Lucy – the real version versus the ghost. The real me says: *Get a grip, Lucy. Get a hold of yourself.*

So, I do. I turn my mind to all the unusual things said and done in the last twenty-four hours. And the red flags come back to me: Susannah instructing me not to tell anyone about our trip and pretending to be someone else to get into Mum's cottage. From that I can deduce that she did not tell Mum we were coming here. I need to find out why, but without alerting Mum that something's up. After what happened in New York, she tends to fear the worst. Still, if there is bad news it won't be long until she has to be told.

The next thing isn't so much a red flag as a loud klaxon. That man turning up at the door has something to do with this. He must have. Otherwise why would Susannah have instructed me to turn the cottage into a fortress when she rushed out last night?

Before I can consider anything else, there's a call from Tara. The words that come out of my mouth sound like they belong to somebody else: 'The body is not hers. But she's still not back. I don't know what's going on. Don't call Mum until we figure out whether there is something major to worry about or not.'

I'm almost embarrassed by my matter-of-fact voice, like I'm playacting at being a garda. It's mortifying and I feel myself redden in the way you do when you know that the other person knows you're embarrassed, and it makes you more embarrassed in turn.

'David and I are on the way,' she says, with uncharacteristic assurance.

Relief.

And then her words sink in.

David and I . . .

What is Tara doing with David? I remember now that David mentioned Tara had been texting him last night. But I have always been under the impression that the cold war between my sisters has been raging for over ten years. I refused to take sides, and Susannah and Tara felt so bad about what happened in New York that they let that go. But there's no way Susannah would have given David a free pass. If he's in touch with Tara, it's behind his wife's back.

10

New York, April 2011

Dumping herself onto the cracked blue leather seats in the diner booth, Tara takes off her glasses and wipes them aggressively. Snowflakes are sprinkled over her hair. They've searched for Lucy for blocks and blocks around the hotel, and then along the perimeter of Central Park, and no joy.

Across from her, David grips the menu with both hands.

'I am starving. Starving,' he says, eyeing up the options. 'I can't wait till the lunch – I have to eat something now.'

Tara puts her glasses back on and peers around the restaurant as if her younger sister might emerge from the bathroom or come out from behind the till. She fishes her phone out of her pocket. More texts.

'I'm going to have to ring Mum. Ever since she woke up she's been texting asking how Lucy is getting on. She's getting suspicious,' Tara says.

'Crap. I bet Lucy's back in the hotel by now – she knows Susannah will kill her if she's late for the ceremony. Let's make a deal. The thing kicks off in an hour. We'll grab something quick here and if she hasn't returned when we get back, we'll alert the hotel manager and take it from there. What do you think?'

Tara puts down the phone. She sits gazing at her knuckles, which have turned blue from the cold. The window next to them is dripping with condensation, the stuffy heat of the diner a stark contrast to the icy white world outside. Noisy snow ploughs are scraping the streets and traffic is starting to build again, normal city sounds returning as the worst of the weather has passed.

David reaches across the table and covers her hand.

'Don't worry – Lucy's fine. If I had a dollar for every time she went off on a mystery tour, I'd be minted.'

'Yes, and that's why Mum was worried about her coming here. It's not Dublin!'

'Susannah is right, Tara – Evelyn wants to wrap her in cotton wool. But Lucy knows her limits.'

'I hope so,' she says, emotion welling up in the back of her throat, sparks flying in her chest. All too soon, he takes his hands away and resumes examining the menu, as if things are normal. But for her, every touch like this is magnified. Every look from him is loaded with meaning.

A young waitress appears with a pot of coffee.

'Fresh brew? Ready to order?'

'Oh God, yes,' David says, ordering a portion of fries.

The waitress pours steaming black coffee into two mugs and looks at Tara expectantly. Though she has no appetite she orders the same.

The waitress flicks her long auburn hair over her shoulder as she turns, taking a flip phone out of her pocket as she does so. She's the epitome of unbothered cool, with a loftiness that Tara envies.

'That was so reckless of me last night,' Tara says. 'We could have been caught.'

David takes his gaze away from her face and instead focuses on the faces passing on the street outside. It is clear he does not want to talk about it. He remains silent. She tries again.

'Do you want to talk about it?'

When he turns his brown eyes back to her, a blazing stare, straight into the depths of her very soul, she knows that she would do it all over again. However long that kiss lasted –

she would like to say twenty seconds, but it was probably less – it was one of the highlights of her adult life.

'I suppose we better. You first,' he says.

As she opens her mouth the waitress returns with serviettes and cutlery, and they wait until she is gone again. Tara takes a deep breath and puts her hands under the table. She pinches the inside of her thigh three times in the vain hope it will stop the blood rushing to her face.

'I know how wrong it is for me to say this, David. I know it's terrible. And I feel terrible. But . . . I have always had feelings for you. And I think you know. And if you didn't, well you do now. I've sort of always thought that you felt the same. Christ, maybe that's delusional. But there have been times, you know – moments we've shared. You know what I mean. Or do you? Maybe it's all in my head. Christ!' She splutters into silence.

David stirs a sugar into his coffee, seeming to gather his thoughts.

'Yeah. Um. Look, I do know. I did know. Obviously, after last night, it's out in the open. I think the truth of the matter – and you can never say this to your sister. I mean this seriously, Tara – give me your word that this conversation will stay here between us and go no further.'

Her heart is thumping. She will promise him the furthest constellation in the galaxy just to hear what he will say next. So, she swears that the conversation will stay here in this diner, just between them. Finally, she is having the conversation with David that she's dreamt of for years, and she just wants him to keep talking.

'Look, if I had met you and Susannah at the same time, it might have been you that I went for. I can't believe I'm even saying this. But yeah. I do feel different when I'm with you. Calmer. Susannah is like a hurricane tearing through the world. She's a hothead. She's . . . a wanter, if that could be a word; Susannah's a lot. Being with her is a lot. But – and I can't emphasize this enough – it doesn't matter that any of those thoughts have crossed my mind. Because I am with Susannah and, for all her flaws, I love her. I really do. I'm not a cheater. And I certainly would never betray her with her own sister. Think about it, Tara. You wouldn't want to be with someone who could do something like that.'

Tara bites her lip. It might make her the worst sister in the world, but she hates the words that have come out of his mouth. How is it possible that Susannah always gets her way, even when it's not right?

Tara never gave her parents trouble. She was a quiet, shy child who grew into a quiet, shy teenager. While Susannah was skipping classes, getting suspended for smoking weed, going missing from home and turning up completely out of it, puking at the front door, you name it, Tara was getting straight As and making her parents proud. She did everything right, did everything to keep the peace in the house. And then, what happens? Susannah turns into a beauty and then a literary sensation. She gets the looks, the talent, the attention, the fame, the money, the house, the man. She even has cleaners and gets in a fancy private chef to cater her parties.

Cleaners! She doesn't even have kids. *If there is anyone in this family who needs a cleaner and a cook,* Tara thinks, *it's me.*

And what's all this about 'calm'? Calm is just another way of saying, *You're a bit boring, Tara, but how lovely to get a break from all the passion.*

She burns with mortification. She thought David enjoyed talking to her because they were on the same wavelength. Other people talk over her. Or they tune out when she's making a point. She used to think it was because she is soft-spoken, and it would be different if she were a man with a low booming voice. Lately, it feels that it's just because she has nothing to offer. She thought it was different with David.

If Susannah is 'a lot' then it looks like she's 'not a lot'. And it seems that fate has decreed that Susannah can have the hot marriage, and she can have the hand she's been dealt, the hand she deserves, apparently – stodgy marriage, stodgy job, stodgy life. Her thoughts continue in this bitter vein but what comes out of her mouth is conciliatory and sweet-natured, because the last thing she wants is for David to see her dark side.

'I know. I know you love her. So, are you going to tell her what happened last night?'

'No. Because nothing happened,' he says. He sounds definite.

'That's not quite true,' she says.

'Well, I think it is.'

'I kissed you. And you—'

'Pushed you away,' he says.

'Not immediately.'

'Tara. Nothing happened. We kissed for a few seconds. I barely registered what was happening and when I did, I stopped it. We were both drunk, you got confused. But look, no one got hurt. I'm glad we've been honest about . . . things. Now we know where we stand. Susannah would disown you if I told her. And she would disown me if she heard this conversation, and for what? Pointless harm, really.'

With that, Tara's mobile rings. David glances down. 'There's Myles ringing – divine intervention!'

Tara picks up her phone and pushes her way through the diner door onto the street. Bloody Myles. Still, he could not have called at a better moment because her embarrassment and exasperation with the conversation had been reaching an uncomfortable peak.

Myles wants to talk about the house they're supposed to be buying. She's not in the least bit interested in the house right now, but she lets Myles drone on, while taking a few silent deep breaths and gathering herself.

'So, you'll get that deposit over?' she hears him say.
'Yeah. Leave it with me. I have to go. Bye.'

The day before leaving for New York, after seeing that heavy snow was forecast, Tara had gone out to buy thermals. Arriving back to their apartment, even before she reached the front door, she could hear Mark screaming. It was the sound babies make when they are in serious pain or extreme hunger. In the kitchen, she found him strapped into his highchair with Mia standing in front of him on her tiptoes, holding a spoonful of potato mash towards his mouth and wearing a look of panic.

'He won't stop crying,' she said, her bottom lip trembling.

'You're a great sister, Mia,' she said, as she lifted Mark up out of the chair. She kicked a basket of dirty laundry out of her way to get to the poky sitting room. Myles was sitting hunched forward on the couch, elbows leaning on his knees and a PlayStation controller in his hands.

'Myles,' she said in a fierce whisper.

No answer. He was wearing earphones.

Before she knew what she was doing, she walked over and kicked him hard in the leg. He let out a squeal and pulled out his earphones.

'What the hell did you do that for?'

By now Mark was having full-on convulsions.

'This. *This!*' she said, holding the screaming red-faced baby towards him. 'This tiny person here is your son, and he's been bawling his head off in his highchair for God knows how long. What the actual fuck, Myles?'

'He was grand sure, just a second ago – what's up with him?'

She gasped. Trying to gaslight her was the final straw. The utter brazenness of it. She pinched her nose between her fingers, trying to contain the terrifying wave of rage surging through her body.

Now Mia was tugging at her elbow, crying too.

Tara hated fighting in front of the kids, which was why she let so much go. She had been so adamant that her home would be different from the one she grew up in.

Peering into Mark's nappy she saw that not only did he need to be changed, he had needed to be changed for ages. Myles's inability to put on a wash was one thing but failing to take care of a helpless infant – his own son – was another.

She turned away from Myles and brought the children into the bedroom so she could change Mark's nappy and try to soothe the pair of them. Her frustration spilled out as tears. *I've married a man-child*, she thought. *I don't love him anymore. He doesn't help me. He just suits himself.*

She thought then of David, the man who always snuck into her mind unbidden. How many times had she fantasized about a life with him? Wasn't that *really* why she was willing to make the long journey to New York, to be close to him?

Could I really leave Myles? she wondered. *I swore I would never, ever, do what my parents did to me and my sisters. I would never let my children grow up in a broken home.*

She had to make it work, surely. But as she laid Mark down on the changing mat on the bed, rubbing his tiny toes in the exact way that always calmed him down, she knew the other truth. One day, something would tip her over the edge. One day she would flip.

Tara arrives back at the table just in time for the two portions of fries. They dig into the food in silence.

Eventually, David clears his throat.

'Everything OK?'

'Myles is annoyed that I haven't sent across the deposit.'

'Oh, is this for the fancy new house in Tipperary?'

'Yeah,' she says, pushing the fries around the plate. 'It's a sad situation. The house was repossessed after the crash. Some of the rooms still have kids' toys in them.'

'Is that why you're dragging your feet?'

'I feel bad for the family, yeah. But I have other doubts. I wanted to wait before putting down the deposit and signing the contract. To come here first.'

The house is in the middle of nowhere in Tipperary, but much larger than their apartment in Dublin. Moving to Tipperary seems so final. She knows she will miss living close to her mum. And she will have to move jobs. And it feels so far away from everything. So far away from David.

'Are you going to? Send the deposit, that is,' he asks, snapping her out of her thoughts.

She looks at him. 'Should I?'

She can see he understands exactly what she is asking.

'Yes. Yes, you should.'

She nods and says: 'I will so. But I have a bad feeling about this.'

They finish their food quickly and leave the diner. David hails a yellow cab. As it pulls up, Tara says: 'It's my birthday tomorrow, you know. Thirty-two.'

She just wants one last hit of affection. Pathetic.

'Ah, no way, Tara! Is it? Happy birthday!' He pulls her into a bear hug and whispers into her hair, 'You're a really good person, do you know that?'

She doesn't answer. She doesn't want to be a really good person, and in any event, she's pretty sure she's not. After all, she was willing to betray her own sister without a second thought. And again, she senses it – a feeling of unfinished business, a longing that has to be satisfied – and she knows if she gets the chance, she'll take it.

Five thousand kilometres away, in the house Tara and Myles will eventually own, a thin crack creeps down the length of the back wall.

11

I am hanging up the call with Tara when I see a man approaching the front door through the small porthole window. Almost breathless, I wrench the door open. His hand is raised as if he was just about to knock. There's a silver badge around his neck. A garda.

'Lucy Brown? I'm Detective—'

'Is it Susannah? Have you found her?'

My pulse shifts from fast to rapid as the images flood into my mind. Susannah attacked and left for dead. Susannah splayed out on the beach.

Bizarrely, the garda smiles.

'May I come in?'

I stand back to let him in. His black steel-capped boots bring mud and sand across the floor. He looks all around, tapping his fingers off the buckle of his belt. Without asking, he sits on the couch, hitching his trousers up at the knees as he does so. There is something distantly familiar about him.

He motions for me to sit on the couch opposite. I don't know why, but I feel like slapping him. It's the smile. Who smiles in a situation like this? For a second, I imagine myself in his place. I would have brought empathy into the room. I would have shaken my hand. I would have asked to sit down and not sat down first. I wouldn't be smiling and gawking around the cottage.

'I'm Detective Garda Jack Fogarty. I'm investigating the murder of Olivia Philips.'

'Who?'

'Olivia Philips. The woman who was found dead in Badger's

Cove this morning. I'm informed that you arrived at the scene believing the deceased to be your sister? Why was that?'

The detective has unfolded a small black notebook and looks me full in the face. Then his eyes slide down to my chest, which is partially visible over Susannah's scoop-necked top. It's not the kind of top I would pick for myself: too revealing. He flinches. I'm used to this, but still, it stings. I have a life of two halves: Before New York, and After New York. Two different women. One who was beautiful, one who is not.

I clear my throat and take a deep steadying breath in an effort to shake off these thoughts. I remind myself that we have the same training, that there's no need to be intimidated.

'My sister is Susannah Brown, married name Susannah Murtagh. I came here with her for a break. We arrived two days ago, on Sunday third of April. Yesterday evening she prepared dinner here in the kitchen. A man called to the door, and they exchanged what sounded like tense words. After getting a text message, she suddenly took off without telling me where she was going. That was coming up on 9:15 p.m. She hasn't returned. She's not answering calls or texts. I saw the news alerts about the body and thought it was her. That's it.'

He looks surprised by my officious tone. I feel like there is a power struggle playing out between us. No sooner do I have the thought than I realize how ridiculous it is. Who am I? A humiliated ex-cop. The power struggle is all in my head. What I really need is for him to have the answers.

'I'm sorry, what did you say?' I ask. I was so busy thinking about imaginary power battles that I tuned out.

'I said: did you see who this man was? And do you work in the force?'

'No, it was nearly dark, and I was upstairs. And yes, I was a garda.'

'What do you mean *was*? You quit?'

Blood rushes to my face, and I hate my body for it. I scramble for a smart answer but nothing comes.

'Something like that.'

His tan face is concentrated into a deep frown, his blue eyes boring into me. I feel him flinch again and I flinch too. This is the worst thing about what happened. There are days when I feel I have made peace with my scars. But other days, when I see people look at me and I feel what they're feeling – shock and revulsion – that peace is shattered. I can never quite shake the feeling of being disgusting.

'Right,' the detective says, 'moving on. Do you know if your sister knew the deceased? She was a pianist from London. I believe your sister is a writer. Maybe they move in the same circles.'

'A pianist? I doubt it. She never mentioned her to me. And, like I said, we only just arrived.'

'OK. Would Susannah have suffered with any mental health problems?'

'Are you trying to ask if I think she's topped herself?'

'We prefer to talk about someone "taking their own life" rather than what you just said there.'

'Are you seriously arguing with me about phraseology? Your bedside manner could do with work.'

Now I just sound petulant.

It is unmistakable – a flicker of anger that makes him jut out his chin.

'In answer to your question: no. She is the strongest person I know. And there is no way on earth she threw herself off a cliff, if that's what you're getting at.'

He remains still for a moment, and then to my surprise he closes his notebook. Despite arriving barely five minutes ago, and all the indicators pointing towards a serious issue, Detective Fogarty is done. He stands up and ambles to the front door, going for an attitude of serene detachment. But

I see his nostrils flare briefly, the quick clench of a fist, his chest puffing out ever so slightly. Beneath the surface, all is not calm.

'Is that it?' I say, my tone conveying just how indignant I am.

He opens the door, and the sunlight pours in.

'If your sister doesn't show up by tonight, drop into the station.'

'Wait, you're not even going to ping her phone? To find out where she is?'

'Ms Brown, we are in the middle of a murder investigation. We don't have time to go chasing errant authors around the village. But, as a matter of interest, where were you last night between the hours of 9 p.m. and midnight?'

I do a double take. This is farcical.

'Me?'

'Yes, you.'

'Here.'

'In this house? Alone?'

'Yes. This house. That couch. Right there. Alone, once my sister left after 9 p.m., as I keep telling you.'

He pauses.

'Ms Brown,' he says, using my name as a goodbye.

And then he is gone, and in the silence I am left with the embarrassing truth of what just happened, which is that I acted like a child. I treated him like the enemy. I spent the vital time in which I had the attention of a garda comparing my skills to his. I thought of me first, my sister second.

I walk to the sitting-room window, wondering if I should call him back, and wondering what I would even say if I did. I see him idle at the gate. As he looks left and right, a memory stirs. He pops his collar and strolls nonchalantly into the hotel. And the ghost from last night is revealed in the clear light of day.

12

New York, April 2011

Tara and David have barely stepped into the hotel lobby when Susannah rushes towards them, anger blazing across her face.

'Where the hell have you two been? The ceremony is starting now, the award will be given out in twenty minutes. Everyone is sitting at their tables and I'm in there with Summer and Fran like a spare tit,' she says.

David puts his hands up and says: 'Whoa, you need to calm down.'

'Don't. Tell. Me. To. Calm. Down,' she hisses, turning her attention to Tara.

'Why exactly did I bring you here anyway? You're supposed to be supporting me, not running around Manhattan with my husband.'

'Oh, shut up, Susannah, you're acting like a spoiled brat. Lucy is missing and all you care about is a stupid award. While you were in here preening yourself, we were out looking for Lucy.'

'I'm sick of everyone treating Lucy like a two-year-old,' Susannah says through gritted teeth.

'You mean you're sick of everyone paying so much attention to Lucy.'

David steps in between them.

'Girls,' he says through clenched teeth. 'People are staring. Can we wrap this up, please.'

Susannah steps back and just for a moment considers punching her sister square in the face, but decides against it.

'It's fine,' she says quietly, 'Mum is on the case.'

'What? What do you mean Mum is on the case?'

'I rang her. She's going to ring around. Now can we please go in? And can you take those massive coats off? You're going to look weird bundled up like two Michelin men – but on second thoughts I'm past caring.'

'Ring around where? What is it that Mum can do all the way from Dublin, exactly?'

Susannah throws her eyes to heaven, as if she is exhausted trying to explain simple things to a dummy.

'Diners, shops, hospitals, I dunno.'

'Hospitals?' David says, and Susannah can hear alarm in his voice. She shouldn't have mentioned that Evelyn said she was going to ring hospitals. Susannah couldn't talk her out of it, and if it keeps her busy while they're tied up at lunch, what harm? When Lucy eventually rocks up, she's going to kill her. The last time she went on an unplanned skite for the day, she'd ended up in the Chester Beatty Library looking at the manuscripts and Qur'ans. The girl is a one-off. She'll have ended up on some random excursion like that. The amount of grief a simple text has caused.

Tara's face turns an even whiter shade of pale.

'She could have slipped and hurt herself on the pavement,' Susannah says.

Across the lobby, Summer calls her back into the function room. David and Tara, peeling their coats off, trail after her into the room where the air is hot and sticky and laced with tension and booze. They are led through crowds to a table right in the middle of the room. Just as they sit, the lights dim and a willowy grey-haired man in a three-piece suit taps the microphone on the stage. He pushes half-moon glasses up his elegant nose. The audience starts to cheer and applaud.

The man begins by telling jokes. Susannah sees David and Tara exchange sideways glances. She doesn't have time to figure out what's going on there. She pretends to be fascinated by the words coming from the man's mouth on the stage, but she hasn't heard a word he's said.

Susannah can concentrate on one thing only: winning the award and the money and prestige that comes with it. The validation. The proof that she matters again, that she isn't a has-been. Winning will push her career into the stratosphere. She'll prove the doubters wrong and be on top again.

Tara knows how big this is for her sister but sitting here in her shadow, observing her vanity, her naked ambition, Tara just wants to scream. Especially when she thinks of what's in that novel.

Tara wonders why Susannah even invited her. Most of the time she seems to hate her. She thinks it's because Susannah knows she sees through her, that she sees the real Susannah. The vain, selfish, stroppy Susannah.

A woman wearing a silky green dress is on stage announcing the next category and nominees. It's the one before Susannah's. In her pocket, Tara feels her phone vibrating. She looks at the screen and excuses herself, prompting a glare from Susannah. But she has to take this call.

In the cool, calm air of the lobby, Tara answers.

'Mum, what's up?'

On the other end of the line, her mother is sobbing.

'Mum, I can't make you out – what's happening?'

Evelyn tries to catch her breath before speaking.

'I found her.'

The world around Tara goes completely still.

'She's in hospital. I think she's been attacked. I rang the hospital nearest to your hotel.'

Evelyn falls apart again, sobbing loudly into the phone.

'Oh my God!' Tara says, steadying herself on brass railings that lead up a grand staircase. 'How serious is it?'

But her mother can't speak.

'You told me you'd look after her,' Evelyn says eventually. 'You promised me. I warned you. You need to get to the hospital now, Tara, I don't give a damn about that bloody novel getting an award. The hospital's called Mount Sinai. Go and find her now, right this second.' Evelyn grows more distraught with every word.

It feels like the world is spinning out of control. Despite her dazed state, somehow Tara's legs carry her back into the function room, all the way to Susannah's table in the middle of the room.

She sits down beside David. She needs to share the news, but wants to avoid making a scene. She feels slightly paralysed. David will help.

'What's happened?' he asks.

'Ssshh,' Susannah says.

'It's Lucy,' Tara whispers across David to Susannah. 'Lucy's been attacked. She's in Mount Sinai Hospital. We have to go now.'

David's mouth drops open. Susannah gazes at Tara as though she is making it up.

'We have to go. Now!' Tara repeats, getting to her feet.

Susannah reaches over and pulls Tara back down by her arm.

'I'm literally the next category. We can leave right after. It's only a few minutes.'

Tara leans across David. 'For God's sake,' she hisses through clenched teeth. 'For all we know, she could die at any second and we will have been sitting here clapping a stupid book. Cop on to yourself.'

Tara can feel people from around their table staring over.

'Tara, stop. Stop it. David! Tell her.'

But David reaches over his shoulder to scoop his coat off the back of his seat. He nods at Tara, indicating that he is ready to go. He turns to his wife.

'Stay, if you must. We'll go,' he says.

David follows Tara out of the room, not stopping to look back. Susannah remains seated.

13

Am I right about Jack Fogarty? Or is this a coincidence?

Anyone who has gone through a crisis will know that time does not flow along its usual course. Some seconds last minutes, and some minutes last seconds. So, I can't say how long I remain standing at the window, staring out at the spot I saw Jack Fogarty, trying to remember everything about the man who was at the door last night. But really, it's not my memory that's the issue; it's my crippling lack of confidence.

My gut says I'm right. But the pervasive voice of doubt in my head is trying to tell me that I'm seeing things. For Susannah, I need to find that sense of certainty again.

I know that the garda who was here just now is the man who appeared at the door last night and threatened Susannah, shortly before she disappeared. Same shape, same voice, same mannerisms. This man could know where she is.

The phone rings again. David. As I take the call, I hope he has calmed down since we last spoke. I've already worried my way through the cuff of Susannah's fancy top – I can't handle any more anxiety.

'Lucy, are you OK?' He sounds genuinely worried.

I try to say 'Fine', but my voice sounds shaky, and it comes out three different tones, betraying the truth.

'I'll be there soon.'

I can tell that he's calling from the car.

'I thought you were coming with Tara?'

'It's in hand.'

What's that supposed to mean? But now is not the moment

to ask David what's going on with Tara. I'm better at spotting lies when I see someone's face.

However, some questions can't wait.

'What's the story with those texts you sent Susannah last night?'

'What texts?'

I'm too impatient to play dumb.

'You know I have a photographic memory, David.'

I can see the texts, and I remember them word for word.

'*What the actual fuck?*'

'*Are you going to publish it?!*'

'If it's OK with you, Lucy, I'd rather sort my problems out with my wife, and not her sister.'

It's not just what David says, but how. Cold and harsh. I've known him my whole life, practically – I can't remember a time before David – and normally he treats me like his little sister. I've never seen this side of him before.

'Look, we'll be there soon. We can search together,' he says, back to normal. 'We will find her. You know what she can be like, following up some idea, wherever it may bring her.'

It's clear I'm not going to get answers about the texts. I feel the hairs on my arms prickle though, an alarming feeling spreading through me.

'There's something else, David,' I say.

'What is it?'

'A man came to the door last night. I was upstairs. I'd gone for a nap and the sound of raised voices woke me up. I think I heard Susannah telling him to leave – but I'm also sure I heard him threaten her, and tell her to leave too. When I asked her what was going on she said it was just a neighbour annoyed that she took his car parking space. But I could tell she was lying – the guy had spooked her. About ten minutes later, just as the food was coming out of the oven, she got a text, became all flustered and said she had to go out. She told me to lock the doors and windows and she disappeared. And . . .'

'And what? Lucy?'

'I think the guy at the door was a garda. The same one who just came to take a statement from me.'

'Christ! What the—'

'She was scared of him, David.'

'Hold tight, Lucy. I'll be there as soon as possible. An hour and a half, max.'

Now that I've explained what's happened, and admitted that I'm scared, the strangest thing happens. The feeling of terror loosens its grip and I hear Susannah's voice in my head.

Don't wait for David.
Don't wait for anyone.
Don't trust anyone.
Move fast.

14

New York, April 2011

As the shiny award is pressed into her hands, Susannah looks out over a sea of faces, some reflecting happiness in her achievement, some a perfect picture of envy. She can't quite take it in. She has won. She has actually won.

When the clapping subsides, and she's navigated a wave of hugs and handshakes to return to her table, Susannah feels deflated. Summer and Fran yelled their delight and embraced her when *The Broken Bay* was announced as the winner. In the absence of her husband and sisters, she appreciated their excitement, while knowing it was for themselves as much as her. They gave her warm smiles and pats when she took her seat, but now they are both busy on their phones. As she sits there, award on her lap, strangely abandoned, she is dry-eyed. It should be the happiest moment in her life. David should be here to see it. Her sisters should be here. But no one is here, a strangely familiar feeling.

Susannah checks her own phone. It is hopping with congratulations and good wishes from friends and acquaintances who have seen the news online. But nothing from her family.

Despite feeling sorry for herself, Susannah has sudden blinding clarity. She *deserves* to be abandoned. Her behaviour today is impossible to explain or excuse, other than by egomania. Her tunnel-vision about this ceremony, her refusal to consider that something could have happened to Lucy, has been unforgivable. And now Lucy is in trouble.

Lucy is in trouble.

The thought sinks in and panic seizes her.

'Summer, have you heard from David or Tara?'

'Hmmm?'

Summer is completely absorbed in her phone.

'Summer!'

'Sorry, sorry, sorry, what?'

'I said, have you heard from David or Tara?'

Summer flicks at her screen. 'No, nothing.'

Susannah types a message to the two of them.

'Where are you? Is Lucy OK? PS: I won.'

It takes just twenty seconds for Tara to reply.

'Lucy was glassed. She needs major surgery. She could have died.'

She watches the three dots as Tara writes another message.

'I don't give a shit about your award. You've shown your true colours.'

And another.

'I will never forget this. And I will never forgive you.'

15

I've come down onto the beach, partly to search for Susannah, futile as I know this is, and partly to calm myself down. There are perks to being a six-foot-tall woman, but in the cottage I feel oversized and out of place, hemmed in by walls that feel too close together, pushed down by the low ceilings. Each time I come downstairs I bump my head off a beam because I forget to bend forwards. What had seemed quaint when we arrived is borderline unbearable today.

I'd always been curious about the cottage. We call it Mum's pension, but she shares ownership with her brother, my uncle Adam. They've had it all my life, if not longer. Adam lives in Australia and doesn't seem to have any interest in it. During the summer, Mum rents it out and in the off-season she gives the keys to her friends in, as she calls it, the 'artistic community' for painting and writing and the like. How she and Adam came to own it has always been a mystery – not only is there no family connection with Dunmore East but despite how much she loves the sea, Mum seems to hate the place. From what Susannah said on the way down, neither she nor Tara have been here since childhood. When I was younger, I wondered about the cottage a few times, suggested coming down for a weekend, and she always shut down any conversation. It's just an income, she has always said. Just an income.

To my left, a little boy stamps his feet in the wet sand and bends down to pick up a pearlescent shell. His orange hat, covered with hundreds of miniature dinosaurs, slips off his head and lands at the edge of the water. His mum comes running to rescue the hat and grab her little boy. As she swoops him up, they both find it hilarious. Their laughter is raucous, and for a moment I glimpse a joy and lightness of being that transports me back to when it was just me and Mum, before I realized I was different.

On my first day of school, I screamed down the entire classroom because the alphabet block with the letter 'a' was the colour red. How could they not understand that it grated against my eyeballs? The letter 'a' was meant to be yellow. That was the start of it. The doctors and neurologists and sensory experts flip-flopped between different labels that they would attach to me.

First, they said I was autistic, so Mum tried to make sure I had the proper kind of teaching and attention in the classroom. When the new schoolyard opened months later, and we could play outside at lunchtime, that brought on more screaming. I seemed to feel someone else being touched or pushed or hurt as if it were happening to me. When my friend Kelly pushed my other friend Caoimhe to the ground, I felt every scrape on both my knees as if it were me. Mum had noticed these traits and perhaps that's why Susannah and Tara were always so gentle with me.

When you're only five years old, you think everyone else is exactly like you: feels like you, sees like you, thinks like you. I had no way of explaining something I didn't understand wasn't normal.

Teachers didn't know what to make of me. There was talk about 'attention-seeking'. Mum knew it was something more but getting anyone to believe she wasn't a highly strung mother, overly protective of her precious late baby, was an uphill fight.

It didn't help that she was doing it on her own. I was about eight when I overheard Mum tell one of her yoga friends that I had been a difficult baby who had needed a lot of soothing, an overwrought child. She was reassuring the young mother, explaining how hard it had been for her when I was little but that she got through it. I figured it explained why Dad left right after my first birthday.

Despite all the doubters, Mum persisted with having me tested. Things finally started to fall into place when they did more sophisticated tests of cognition and memory. I saw letters and numbers as colours, and I saw the colours as if they were imprinted on the inside of my eyeballs. I could see the overarching colour of the word when all the colours of the individual letters combined, and I could remember that final colour perfectly.

I received my first diagnosis – grapheme synaesthesia, the association of letters and numbers with colours – at ten. That's still how I see words – the spectrum of colours in my world is immense. It took longer, though, for the experts to believe that I could feel within my own body the sensations experienced by another person when they were touched.

When I was a teenager, friends would test my reflexes by punching each other or holding their breath. They thought it was the coolest thing ever. But it was hell. What they didn't think was cool – and why it took a long time to find a group of girls who weren't weirded out by me – is that I seemed to have uncanny intuition. More than once I got into trouble because I could read my friends' feelings and was too young and naïve to hide it. For example, I thought it was quite clear that there was tension between Cara and our better-looking friend Aideen. She was just quieter and more reserved around Aideen than our other friends. I asked both of them if there had been a falling-out. What had been an unspoken nothing, a simple jealousy between teenagers, became a topic of gossip in our paranoid group of girls. My speaking about it only made things worse between them. Everyone thought I was a shit-stirrer.

All of this – the colours, the sensations, the ability to intuit and feel other people's emotions – was why Mum didn't want me going to New York. Of course, if she hadn't been so stubbornly independent, never wanting to impose the details of my diagnosis on Susannah and Tara, maybe they would have understood her objections. While Susannah was at college in DCU when I was little, she already had her own life by then so wasn't home much. And she bought a house and moved out to Malahide when she got all those deals for her first book. Tara went off to do hotel management in Galway when she was eighteen. So, they didn't really understand what it was like for Mum. Both of them, but Susannah in particular, told her she was being over-protective. But Mum was sure that a cacophonous place like Manhattan would be overkill for my senses. And she was right.

At least what happened had some use – it led to my second diagnosis. They called what I have mirror-touch synaesthesia. Counselling that Susannah paid for after my breakdown in the guards brought me as close to understanding my condition as I ever have. The easiest way I have found to describe it is telling people that they have certain neural systems in their brain that are activated when they watch one person touch another person. For most people, there is a threshold that keeps those sensations out of their own body. For me, the threshold is so low, it's practically non-existent.

All my life I have see-sawed on whether being synaesthetic is a blessing or a curse. Being able to intuit how someone is feeling by being so in tune with their expressions, by literally *feeling* their movements, might seem like a gift, but most of the time it's a burden. In recent years I tend to avoid mentioning my condition, even if it would explain apparently over-the-top reactions. It's just too exhausting.

The decisive argument for saying my synaesthesia is a curse is what happened in New York. Though one small part of it I don't regret. The NYPD officer who found me, Peter Millar, blew me away. Even barely conscious, I fancied him a little, yes, and I was enthralled by how he spoke to me, how methodical he was, his quiet authority, how skilled he was in an emergency, his sense of purpose, his sense of ownership over a situation. That innate power. It made me want to become a garda. And despite losing my career, I have good memories of the training. When other trainees were receiving demerits, I was being applauded by the sergeant, embarrassing as that was. Templemore was the only time I felt in control and good at something.

Suddenly I notice that my breathing is shallow. The memories – my condition, my lost career, my dead-end relationship – Tim's last WhatsApp message read, 'You don't cut contact with me, Lucy! It works the other way around.' – it's all overwhelming.

And as always when I get into these spirals, I keep coming back to New York. None of this would have happened if Susannah hadn't been so insistent that I should go on that godforsaken trip. I would never have been attacked. I might still be beautiful. I might still be confident. I might have chosen a job that didn't expose me to other people's trauma. I might not have had a catastrophic meltdown. And I definitely would not have suffered the humiliation that followed, a story that's the stuff of legend amongst young gardaí, and not in a good way.

I hear the lungs of the sea pull the water in and release it out again. I try to match my breath to it. I try to banish these thoughts.

Susannah is missing. How could I let that slip from my mind, even for a second?

And David will be here with Tara shortly. Another thing I'll have to figure out – how the two of them are coming here together – though it's not a priority.

And sooner or later, I will have to ring Mum. And I'll have to tell her I have no idea where Susannah is. That I don't even know where to start looking.

Not knowing where she is . . . it's torture. The anxiety is unbearable and concentrating feels impossible. No wonder my mind is hopping all over the place. Even beating myself up for forgetting about her is self-centred. For the second time this morning, I'm thinking about myself, not her. Maybe I'm more like her than I think.

Over the years I've often wondered what exactly was going on in Susannah's head when I went missing in New York. I know Mum raised the alarm early and Mum was also the one who located me. So, neither my sisters nor David covered themselves in glory. They have all been vague about how 'confusing' things were that morning, with the snowstorm and the power cut in the hotel. As soon as I was free of the heavy meds, Tara made a point of letting me know that she and David had rushed out of the awards lunch as soon as she got the call from Mum but had waited nearly two hours for Susannah to show up.

I've never been brave enough to ask Susannah why. She knew what had taken me out of the hotel that morning. Knowing that, why didn't she do something about finding me? And why was she so late getting to the hospital? Of course, I know the answer – she was obsessing about her award. But a part of me would like to look her in the eye and hear her admit it. I swing wildly between blaming her for abandoning me and feeling bad for her. That's because we share an unspoken secret about New York, a secret that I know has prompted Susannah's over-the-top generosity since – buying me expensive stuff that I don't want, funding therapists, bringing me on trips. If she knew Tim was paying my rent for the shithole I'm living in, she'd want to set me up in an apartment.

Until New York Susannah was a doting big sister, but in a normal careless way. Ever since then her attention has been laser-focused. She is always on the lookout for things she can do for me. It's almost oppressive, knowing that you're the source of so much guilt in another person. And somehow, I always felt there would be some karmic reckoning for her, because we must all face our misdeeds eventually. We must all face our demons, and the consequences of our actions. But this – her simply disappearing in a panic – this is off the scale of anything I could have imagined. This is all wrong.

16

New York, April 2011

Tara and David have been given part of the picture after talking with the emergency room nurses who first looked after Lucy. There are still parts of the puzzle missing, but now as Lucy is in theatre, about to undergo surgery on her chest, neck and part of her face, they have an outline of what went down. They sit side by side in a waiting room trying to digest what they have just learned. Neither can grasp the full horror.

Much of what they know is thanks to an NYPD officer, Peter Millar, a desperately pale man with slicked-back red hair who happened across the scene of Lucy's attack while headed home from a night shift. He had been crawling along in his car and spotted a distressed elderly woman in a fur coat waving and screaming at the entry to an alleyway. He hopped out of his car and the woman – gasping for breath – explained that a girl had rescued her from an attempted attack but then been attacked herself. As she talked, she dragged him down the alleyway to where a young girl lay slumped on the ground, covered in blood.

Officer Millar had called in for help and stayed with Lucy, doing his best to staunch the blood with a scarf, trying to get her talking, to keep her awake.

Lucy muttered that she was 'only going out for my sister'. Going out where, she didn't say. While she was out walking along the street, she saw something.

What did you see? Peter had asked.

A shadow, she said.

At this, the other woman spoke. She said as she had been passing the alleyway about fifteen minutes earlier, someone had jumped out and tried to wrestle her bag away from her. She had put up a fight, but he dragged her down the alley, pushed her up against a wall and started choking her. The woman, shaking with the memory, marks from her attacker's fingers still visible on her throat, told Officer Millar that her attacker suddenly seemed to lose interest in the bag. Instead, as he peered into her face, he seemed to be getting pleasure from her fear and she felt one of his hands reaching into her underwear. But before she knew what had happened, he was off her, seemingly attacked by this young girl.

Officer Millar turned back to Lucy. In a voice that was barely audible, she said when she saw the shadow squeeze the woman's throat, she could feel her own windpipe close. And when she saw him thrust a hand down the woman's trousers, she felt a hand grab her there too. She said she couldn't bear it and she had run towards him and knocked him to the ground.

Officer Millar looked at Tara and David in bafflement. They just stared back blankly, so he continued.

What came next happened in a flash, Lucy told Officer Millar. The shadow was on top of her. She saw jagged glass coming towards her. She felt a tearing sensation across her chest, and then went cold.

The other woman said that she had seen a broken bottle in the attacker's hand but by the time she got to her feet to run for help, he had slashed the girl several times.

Officer Millar told Tara and David that in an effort to keep Lucy conscious, he had tried to get her talking. He had asked her name, where she was from, where she was staying. But there was so much blood and soon she was starting to hover on the edge of consciousness, so apart from 'Lucy' he could no longer make out her replies. When Lucy could no longer talk, he just kept talking to her, making sure she was at least staying awake. He had accompanied her in the ambulance to the emergency room. He felt he could not leave her until someone came looking for her. He stayed with her all morning, as the hours ticked by. Finally, to his relief, the call came in from Lucy's mother.

'How was she when she got in? Did she know how badly injured she was?' Tara asked, dissolving into tears. David pulled her into him and let her sob into his shoulder.

'The opposite, if anything. She didn't seem to understand just how serious it was,' Officer Millar said.

'What do you mean?' David asked.

'They gave her some meds, and she was kind of laughing. So, I don't think she realized then how badly cut she was. But she does now.'

'Did one of the doctors tell her?' David said.

'No. She was being pushed in a wheelchair by a porter...'

Tara stared at the officer. He was clearly struggling to get the words out.

'Yes?' she said. 'And?'

'Well, she saw her reflection in the bottom part of the door as she was wheeled into surgery. I was just behind her. The door is kind of mirrored on the bottom. And she saw everything. She screamed, and I think she passed out.'

'Oh, my God. My God,' Tara said.

'Yeah. It was awful.'

'Where is the bastard who did this to her?' David said.

If Officer Millar had previously been awkward, he was visibly squirming now.

'We have officers out looking for him.'

'You mean he got away?'

Officer Millar explained that the attacker was probably an addict who had targeted the first victim because of her fur coat. More than likely, he knew the streets like the back of his hand, so was able to make a quick escape when the woman had run up the alley screaming for help.

'By the time I understood what had happened, he was gone. But the lady was able to give us a description to go on. I can assure you we're searching for him.'

David put his hands over his face as Tara stared at the police officer, stricken. Speaking to no one in particular she said, 'Why was she even out? Why was she out, on her own, in the snow?'

17

So many times I have been asked by people why I was out on the streets of Manhattan, on my own, in the snow. The answer was in the texts between Susannah and me that morning.

'Hey hon, hope you slept OK. I can't find my bag from last night and I've run out of cigarettes. Can you be a legend and pick some up in the shop we were in last night? They won't ask you for ID.'

'Sure! Wasn't going to go out but it'll be nice to see the place in the snow. I'll head out now.'

Not once in the years since has Susannah referred to this exchange, even hearing people probe me about that morning. I suppose it's bizarre that we've never spoken about it. I imagine she, like me, recognizes that it was a sliding doors moment, where my life severed into 'before' and 'after'. Had I refused to do her this favour, or waited till later, who knows how my life would have unfolded.

Going into meltdown as I looked at that bloodied dying woman in Finglas was like an aftershock many years later, the trauma of the attack catching up with me. In therapy I decided that I couldn't load the blame onto Susannah – after all, she didn't force me to go out that morning. Given my condition, it's possible that even if I had never been attacked, I would still have felt the woman dying within my own body. But if I'd never been attacked, I probably wouldn't have been a guard. And so it goes, around in circles.

I force myself back into the moment, back into my body. By now, I have searched the entire beach and the Strand Hotel, which is kind of the heart of Dunmore East from what I can see. I walked up Harney's Hill, past the park, into the small village. Every time I saw a woman with long brown hair, my heart leapt, but of course it wasn't Susannah.

Back at the cottage, I push the front door open, feeling the now familiar sense of claustrophobia settle over me. It's 1:30 p.m., and the radio I've left on is playing a truncated half-hourly news bulletin. There's no update on the murdered woman.

How many hours has Susannah been gone? I want to shake myself. From my training I know very well how vital the hours can be in a missing persons case.

My phone buzzes. A text from David: 'We will be there in 20 minutes.'

We.

How easily he and Tara slip into a 'we'.

A hazy memory comes to mind. It was the night before my fateful decision to step out into the blizzard. We were at a stuffy dinner for Susannah. Tara was very drunk. She was as quiet and meek as ever, but I was watching her closely and I could sense her longing as she watched David make a speech about Susannah.

Now I do shake myself. I need to focus on one thing only right now: finding Susannah.

In the bathroom, I wash my face and wet my greasy hair with water to try to make it look like it was slicked back deliberately. I clean the mascara stains out from under my eyes. I mute Tim's Snapchat messages and then hide his chat, and then my breath catches.

Snapchat.

Susannah has her live location on her Snapchat, only because she can't figure out how to turn it off. She downloaded the app to stay in touch with me. I am the only person she talks to on it, and if she was trying to hide for some reason, she wouldn't even think of it. I feel energized as I realize that I am finally on to something. My fingers can't move fast enough as I click into her profile, blood rushing in my ears, an uncomfortable dizzying pressure building in my head.

There is her avatar, looming oversized on the cartoonish map.

Last seen: 16 hours ago.

I do the maths. That would have been soon after she left the cottage.

But it's the location that stuns me – a place that, until today, I had never heard of.

How? How is it possible?

Badger's Cove. Where a woman, who the police say is not Susannah, lies dead.

18

New York, April 2011

Susannah had struggled to extricate herself from the awards lunch – it felt as though there were faceless people pushing and pulling out of her, talking to her, asking questions – but here she is, pulling up outside Mount Sinai at last. The hospital is a sludgy brown concrete building at least fifteen storeys high. Her phone is blowing up with messages, but she can't focus on a word of them. David phoned a short while ago to say that Lucy was in surgery.

In the cab over, Susannah couldn't figure out if her sense of deflation was solely because of how worried she was about Lucy. She suspected that she'd be feeling flat regardless. She had told herself that winning the award would be a vindication, a triumphant response to all the doubters – not least, herself – but experience tells her that reaching one milestone just means obsessing about the next one. Because this goes deeper than winning awards – it's about how she values herself. And whatever value she might have as a writer, after today she can't rate herself highly as a sister. She will be making this up to Lucy for the rest of her life.

Inside the building, perched on the eastern border of Central Park, a faceless man points Susannah towards a lift that leads up to the emergency room where the others are waiting. She dreads entering the ER, and this terrifying new chapter of her life. She feels her heart beating fast as the lift door opens. She spots Tara and David almost immediately.

Tara is sitting with her head between her hands, wispy curls scrunched up between her fingers. David is rubbing her back slowly, absent-mindedly, his eyes fixed on some point just beyond the nurses' station.

He sees Susannah, comes over, wraps her in a hug and whispers 'well done' into her ear. Upon hearing these words, she breaks down. How stupid she has been. How irrelevant it all was. How selfish, how awful, not to run to her sister straight away.

Tara clearly feels the same way.

'Of course, you're going to make this all about yourself. This is your fault, Susannah, your fault! You promised Mum you'd look after her. You gave her your word!' Tara roars.

'I'm not making this about myself! I'm allowed to be upset, Tara, Jesus Christ. And you're one to talk, aren't you? You weren't exactly keeping a close eye on Lucy yourself, were you? What was it you were so busy doing out on the rooftops of New York, exactly?'

Tara recoils and looks guilty.

Susannah knows she has hit a nerve. She is a novelist; it is her job to observe people. She sees Tara eyeing up her husband when she thinks no one is looking.

'You are full of shit, Susannah. I hope you enjoyed your precious day. Lucy could have been dead for all you cared.'

A nurse comes out from behind the station and heads straight to the two women.

'Folks, can we keep it down, please? There are other families here, and people trying to get on with their work.' As she motions around the waiting room Susannah realizes that their spat is a source of distraction and entertainment. All eyes are on them, a combination of shock and fascination on people's faces.

Tara mumbles an apology. The nurse gives them a final cautionary glare before returning to the station. Tara moves closer to Susannah and whispers into her face.

'One day, in your hour of need, you might just find that there is no one who wants to help you. You don't just *abandon* your family, Susannah.'

Having delivered her knockout blow, Tara takes off down a lino-covered corridor, leaving Susannah and David staring after her.

By implying that Susannah is doing the same thing she condemns their father for doing, Tara is hitting her rawest nerve. Evelyn has long since given up on her former husband. Lucy barely knows him. In fact, Lucy seems to think it's her fault he left. And Susannah can never bring herself to talk to him.

Tara is the one who keeps trying with Patrick, and the only one who seems to succeed in reaching him across the divide. But it was like this even before he left, when they were teenagers and Susannah went through her wild phase – though looking back, it wasn't that wild – while goody two-shoes Tara gave him something to brag about.

A part of Susannah wishes it could be different with her father. But neither of them can ignore what Susannah knows – stuff she should never have seen or heard when she was young. While Evelyn is philosophical, Patrick is self-righteous and resentful – still blaming Evelyn for everything. Since the publication of her first book, he has made a point of letting Susannah know that he's never read a word by or about her. Yet, and Susannah hates herself for this, she has always been envious of Tara's easier relationship with their father. It drives her mad that Tara knows this and uses it to get under her skin.

Susannah and David sit slumped in the waiting-room seats. For the longest time, they don't speak. She can't speak. She wouldn't know where to start. Then she hears him muttering.

'What, David? What are you saying?'

'He got away,' he whispers.

'Who got away?'

David runs a hand over his stubble, pulling his chin downwards in evident frustration.

'The bastard who did this.'

Susannah feels a dark unsettling heat rise within her, the likes of which she has never felt before. It vibrates from within her core and makes her hands shake. Justice must be done. It's that simple.

'You have to be kidding!'

'I wish I was. The cop – Officer Millar – had to leave when we arrived. He filled us in as much as he could. But he was off duty and said he would get someone to come in to us to answer any questions. He said they had a description and they were searching for the guy, but I could tell he didn't seem confident that they'd find him.'

'No! No, no, no. That can't happen. He can't get away with it!'

Susannah takes a few steps away from her husband, casting her eyes around for the bathroom.

'I need a second,' she says, walking away. At the end of the hallway, she finds a ladies' room. No sign of Tara. When she gets in, she checks the emails on her phone. She cannot believe what she is doing.

It was mere hours ago that she promised herself they would never set eyes on each other again, because she knew her future depended on it. She hopes she does not regret what she is about to do, and that her actions don't set into motion an even worse chain of events that could destroy their family.

19

I can hear my heart thumping as I stare at Susannah's last known location. Her phone must be off. I think of the last time I tried to find my mobile. I had left it in a late-night taxi home after a disastrous trip to see Tim. On the train back to Dublin I had drunk an entire bottle of wine out of a coffee cup so by the time I got into the cab, I was a mess. I located the phone via the Find My iPhone app.

I race up the stairs to Susannah's room. If I can get her Apple ID, I can maybe locate the phone, even if it is off. Susannah is a total neat freak, so things are perfectly in place. I tear up covers and blankets. I open every cupboard and pull open every drawer. Finally, under a pile of cashmere jumpers, I locate her MacBook, along with the *Sea of Mirrors* manuscript.

I wrench open the laptop and the screen lights up, straight onto her login page. *Yes!* I want to leap into the air and wave my fist. Despite Mum's multiple warnings about using the same password for everything, Susannah has admitted to me that this is exactly what she does. And I know her password because she lets me use her Amazon Prime account so I can get free delivery.

I sit on the bed and start to type. I think this is it – that I'm about to find her phone, find her, and bring an end to this day from hell.

But the login box simply shakes from left to right, denying me entry.

Shit.

I try again.

No dice.

'*Fuck!*' I shout, pointlessly, at the wall. I am deflated. I sit on the bed staring at nothing in particular. David and Tara will arrive any moment. Maybe they'll have some ideas because after my fleeting moment of inspiration, I'm stumped.

Idly I remove the manuscript from the folder and start flicking through it. When I looked at it yesterday my eye was drawn magnetically to my own name in the first few pages. I start scanning again, to see where this fictional Lucy appears next. I'm too addled to take in much, but it looks a mess – maybe this is what authors' drafts usually look like. I spot my name intermittently. Reading around it I see there's a storyline about a couple finding a body beneath the floorboards as they renovate their home. And there's something else about a woman trying to find out the real reason for her cousin's death a decade previously. The fictional Lucy has a lot on her plate.

And then I come upon something that makes my heart leap into my throat. It's a crossed-out name, with a new name handwritten over it. I flick on. In the pages that follow, the name is crossed out and changed over and over. But there is no mistaking the original crossed-out name.

Olivia Philips.

The dead woman in the cove.

20

New York, April 2011

Lucy opens her eyes and sees blue curtains gently blowing in a warm breeze. *Funny,* she thinks, *aren't the curtains in my hotel room green and heavy?* When she thinks of the hotel, she thinks of the snow. And when she thinks of the snow, she remembers. Falling to the ground. His hand, her neck. His breath, her scream. Blood, everywhere. Shock. Blue lights, unknown faces in hers. The police officer looking into her eyes asking: 'Are you OK? Can you hear me?'

She feels a hand on her left arm, and she turns her face to see who is touching her so lightly. Susannah, her face stained with streaks of mascara, her eyes bloodshot. In this one moment, what has happened hits Lucy with such a force that it knocks her breath clean out of her body. She reaches up to touch her chest and finds bandages sewn directly on her skin, and they criss-cross all the way up to the bottom of her face. The shock of this, combined with the pain on her sister's face, intensifies her own alarm to an almost unthinkable level.

Lucy sobs violently, her whole body wracked with distress. Susannah is on the bed then, her arms around her younger sister, telling her it will be OK, ignoring the sympathetic queries from the patients in the nearby beds.

As she feels the comfort of Susannah's embrace, Lucy begins to calm down. It was always this way for her. On one hand, it could be excruciating to feel other people's pain inside herself. On the other, something as ordinary as a hug flooded her with warmth, the infusion of love almost doubling up inside her. In her sister's arms, she settles enough to catch her breath. She feels a heavy ache across her chest and has a sense that strong painkillers are blocking the worst of the pain out.

'I'm so sorry,' Susannah says, opening her mouth to speak again.

But then the curtain is pulled back slightly. Tara is standing there, with David just beyond her. Lucy feels the tension immediately. Susannah doesn't look up but instead focuses on the drip going into Lucy's arm.

'Would you like a coffee?' Susannah asks Lucy, clearly looking for something normal to say.

'Yes,' Lucy says, and with that Susannah leaves through a different parting in the curtains so she avoids passing Tara.

Tara rushes over.

'I just need to go to the bathroom,' Lucy says, trying to disentangle herself from the drip, before realizing she'll have to take it with her. Tara and David are fussing over her and she tells them she's fine. She tries to put on the new dressing gown that someone left at the end of the bed. But of course, the drip is in the way. Tara helps put it over her shoulder on the drip side. She pretends not to be dizzy while making her way to the small bathroom at the end of the ward. She also pretends not to see the other patients' pitying glances.

When she gets into the bathroom, she looks in the mirror. She sees stitches overlaid on bandages overlaid on stitches and feels nothing. There she is, someone else, someone she doesn't recognize, someone different. It's a deeply unsettling feeling, but she knows what's happening. She is changed forever. She is meeting herself for the first time, the new Lucy. Will it be awful, this person, this future? Will things ever be OK again? Maybe it's the shock, but for now, there are no more tears.

When she's done, she leads the drip back across the ward but stops at the curtains when she hears David's voice, low and soothing. She peeks through and sees him and Tara, their backs to her, sitting facing the bed. Tara's head is down and David is slightly turned towards her. Lucy sees his hand move softly across Tara's back, feels the shiver of longing that passes through her sister.

Wrong, Lucy thinks. *All of it. All wrong.*

21

I watch as David's car pulls up outside the cottage. Sitting beside him, Tara has her hands over her face, as though trying to block out the view. From the kitchen window I see him turn to her. It looks as though he's asking if she's OK. I see David shiver as he rolls up the window, and feel a shudder run down my back.

Tara gets out of the car first. She's thinner than I've ever seen her, and not in a healthy way. Her face is gaunt and grey and her thin brown hair is scraped back into a tight bun. Her glasses look so big on her face. She looks like she hasn't eaten a square meal in weeks. She grabs a coat and bag off the back seat, then walks around to David. I hear her say, 'This place is cursed.'

David locks the car with a press of his fob and puts a hand on her shoulder. 'Come on, let's go in. Unless she arrived back in the last twenty minutes, she's not here.'

They haven't spotted me watching them.

I see Tara take a steadying breath and together they make their way towards the front door of the cottage. But as she passes the blue picnic table, Tara stops and stares at it, with a look so intense that it takes me by surprise. I know what it's like to have a tsunami of emotion crash over you – I know better than anyone else – and I feel it from her.

Tara turns her attention out over the wall, to the beach and sea beyond. I put myself in her shoes and I see what she sees. The beauty of the place; how the mouth of the sea opens right up to the slipway when the tide is in, snapping its jaws shut at the walls; how the strand belongs so completely to itself. The wind has picked up, turning the sea feral, each fresh wave violently tearing down the previous one. I'm seeing it properly for the first time.

'Tara,' David pleads, a hand on her back, as he reaches the front door. I walk over and pull it open.

'Hi,' I say, wondering: what happens next? Where is this all going?

When Tara looks at me, she seems taken aback. I realize it's been a while since she last saw me, and I see her sizing me up, feel her judgement when she takes in my clothes, my blotchy face, my unwashed hair. She hugs me, tight, and I let myself feel that moment of bliss. David, however, appears incapable of meeting my eye. He gives me a one-armed, half-hearted hug and stares around at the inside of the cottage instead.

Tara sits on one of the couches, holding her brown cardigan around herself. She, too, is sizing up the room. David sits beside her, his thigh grazing hers.

Again, I flinch. Seeing them together like this messes with my head. But that's a question for later, after we've found Susannah.

'What's that?' David asks, a sharp edge to his voice.

He's pointing at the *Sea of Mirrors* manuscript sitting on the coffee table. Seeing the crossed-out name of the murdered woman was mind-blowing. How on earth did Susannah know her? Does she have something to do with a murder? My first instinct was to hide the manuscript until Susannah reappeared and I could work out what was going on. But I realized this was too big a problem to keep to myself.

Before I can answer David, he says, 'Is that my manuscript?'

'Is that *your* manuscript?'

'Yeah, Susannah . . .' he pauses. 'Susannah took it from me.'

Hang on! Is *David* writing about me? Is *he* the one who knows Olivia Philips?

I am seized by anxiety as I grapple with the new idea. My

brain feels overloaded. The only thing I can think of is to grab the manuscript, say I'm not getting involved in whatever's going on between him and Susannah and run upstairs with it.

Oddly, this unexpected turn of events seems to clear the clouds in my mind. Downstairs with David and Tara, suddenly I felt uneasy. Tara was glancing all around the room like a ghost was going to materialize. And then David saying the manuscript was his. I need to figure out who I can trust. I need to take some kind of decisive action before it's too late. With every second feeling like a high-stakes game of poker, the pressure not to misstep feels enormous.

Realistically, I tell myself, *neither David nor Tara would do anything to hurt Susannah.*

But is this me letting my emotion get the better of me? Being blinded by loyalty? What am I missing?

I see Susannah's face in my mind and feel as though there's a clock ticking in my head. Time is moving on. Desperate as I am to know where she is, I'd settle for the knowledge that she's OK. There is a puzzle in front of me. I have a feeling that the answers to why we're here and what happened to Susannah lie in our past.

A voice in my head, one I rarely listen to that doesn't hold much sway, is saying: *What if it's a gift you have? What happens if you use it? What do you have to lose by trying?*

I decide to do what any decent detective would do. In my criminology course, we were taught to understand the reasons why criminals act the way they do. Cause and effect. God knows, I've spent years thinking about the consequences of things, going back over my mistakes, trying to figure myself out. Now I need to focus on the actions that have brought us all here, starting at the beginning.

Susannah mentioned being here with Tara when they were kids. I think of how miserable Tara looks sitting downstairs, as though this is the last place on earth she wants to be. Now I recall her comment to David when they arrived, that the place is 'cursed'. Such a strong word. I wonder why she would say such a thing.

Susannah brought me here for a reason, she told me so herself. Whatever it was, she was going to explain over dinner and she wanted Tara there to hear it too. And whatever it was, it was serious enough for a garda to turn up at the door and threaten her, to order her to leave town. Everything is connected and I need to find out how.

Instinct and training are telling me to go to the guards with everything I know. But if I tell the inspector I met at Badger's Cove about the link between my sister and Olivia Philips, will I make things even worse? Susannah was last seen at the scene of a vicious crime, and now she's gone. I don't think Susannah hurt the woman, but what if I am landing her in the middle of a murder investigation, and she walks in the door in an hour only to be arrested?

And can I trust the inspector with the information that one of his officers knows more than he is saying? If Jack Fogarty is rotten, do the other guards know about it, or would they cover up for him? Or will I be uncovering something rotten that could save my sister?

I have to make a choice. Reveal my hand and potentially forsake my sister? Or try to work it out on my own.

It's the link to the dead woman that tips me over the edge. I can't keep something as huge as this to myself. It would border on an obstruction of justice. And for better or worse, I choose to believe that Jack Fogarty is a lone bad apple.

My heart is fluttering as I ring the Dunmore East garda station and ask for the inspector's name. *Paul Menton*. I tell the garda on reception that I have information about the murder of Olivia Philips, but I will only talk to Inspector Menton.

When he eventually comes on the line, Menton listens

patiently. But he remembers me from the crime scene and I can tell he thinks I'm a crank. I can feel the insinuation in his exaggerated patience and his slow exhale. However, a call like this can't be ignored. I've set the wheels in motion, drawing a link between his murder victim and my own missing sister.

I know it was the right thing to do, but as I walk downstairs my heart continues to skip beats. David and Tara are now sitting on the opposing couches, both lost in thought.

The next step is to go back. There is a history in this cottage and a reason we are here. I take a deep breath at the bottom of the stairs, square my shoulders, go over to Tara and sit down beside her.

'Tara,' I say, a firm tone to my voice at last, 'Susannah said you came here on holiday in 1983 but have never been back. Can you tell me about that time?'

She looks at me suspiciously.

'Has she never told you how she nearly drowned?'

PART TWO

22

Dunmore East, April 1983

It's April 1983 on the strand, and the locals and tourists in Dunmore East are so busy marvelling at the unseasonable heat that no one notices six-year-old Susannah Brown is drowning.

Her parents Evelyn and Patrick are in the gently lapping water, not even four metres away. They are up to their knees, carefully steadying their youngest daughter, four-year-old Tara. She is kicking furiously in every direction, her eyes scrunched up in delight under her fringe.

It's 18 degrees in April and no one can quite believe it. By Irish standards, this is positively tropical. Evelyn holds her hand up above her eyes to block out the sun as she shouts to Susannah to come in a bit closer.

'Susannah, stop messing around,' she says, almost absent-mindedly. She glances at her but does not notice that her daughter is slowly going under.

Susannah's arms do not flail. She does not shout – she can't – her mouth is just under the water. It is taking every ounce of her diminishing energy to keep her head up and take tiny sips of air, which sound like little 'pops' from her mouth. She doesn't know what is happening or why she can't seem to move closer to her mother. The terror she feels is in her eyes, but dazzled by the sun, no one sees.

At the edge of the surf a local farmer, Johno, watches a trawler in the distance heading towards the harbour. He always wanted to be a fisherman, to spend his days out in the vast blue sea, but the farm was handed down through the generations and he was the only remaining son. His life has been mapped out for him and his days have fallen into a predictable rhythm. He tries to make sure he is grateful for what he has, tries not to dwell on what might have been if he had been free to make his own choices for himself. And yet, at this moment, gazing out towards the horizon, he is thinking about how trapped he is.

His gaze drops closer to the shore and he feels the girl's eyes on him. In an instant, he knows. He shouts, jumps into the water and pummels his way through the waves. He splashes past a couple with their child, drenching them as he passes. They look at him, shocked, confused, half-smiling at the dark-haired man who seems to be losing his mind.

Amusement turns to panic as soon as Johno scoops the girl out of the water. It all happens so fast. On the beach, people gather and peer out at the commotion.

As Johno carries the child out of the water a woman with jet-black curls bouncing wildly around her head races to meet him. He places the child on the damp sand. Her eyes are closed, her long brown hair splayed out around her head. Johno senses the girl's parents over his shoulder and throws them a cautious glance. They are frozen in shock, their younger daughter trembling, her mouth the shape of a perfect 'O'.

He tilts the child's head back and lifts her small chin before pinching her nose closed. Johno puts his mouth onto hers. Her father makes a sound as if about to protest but is pulled back by his wife. She is gagging, as if it is her who is drowning, and pulls a clump of her tawny hair from its roots. The child's chest does not rise underneath her Barbie t-shirt. Someone shouts for an ambulance; another voice asks if there's a lifeguard. But Johno knows there is no time to wait. As crowds gather, again Johno breathes air into her lungs. He places one hand on the centre of her chest and presses hard, avoiding her ribs. A trickle of water shoots from her mouth and flows down the side of her face.

'Thank God,' someone says, as Johno turns the child onto her side and watches her splutter and begin to shake and cry.

Johno is not sure how many minutes have passed when he feels himself being wrenched up, wet clay-like sand sticking to his knees and shins. It is the girl's father who has a hold of him. Tears are streaking down the man's handsome face as he embraces him, asking again and again, *How did you know? How did you know?*

Johno pushes him off gruffly.

'It's nothing,' Johno says, an angry croak in his voice.

The crowd is dispersing, the drama over. Other parents are holding their children just that little bit closer. 'There but for the grace of God,' one woman says, making the sign of a cross over her chest.

The child, now wide-eyed and in shock, is being wrapped in jumpers and cradled by her mother, who is shuddering and inconsolable.

'Please, it's nothing, nothing. She's fine, she's fine,' Johno hears himself say, keen to get away from all these eyes locked on him, all these hands slapping his back.

At his elbow, his wife Maggie – the woman with the wild black curls – tugs at his sleeve. 'Come on,' she says, 'it's OK, come on. The lifeguard is here. Let's go.'

Time to go. Too many people.

Maggie and Johno Fogarty rush away as a lifeguard sprints down the concrete slope of the boat slipway, an emergency kit tucked underneath his arm.

Back in the sand, Evelyn straightens up a little. Her arms are still wrapped around her daughter's sopping-wet back. She watches the couple hurry off.

Who are these people?
How did she not see what was right in front of her eyes?
How did he know?
Why did he seem so angry?
And how can she ever repay him?
But it's too late. They're gone.

23

Tara is recalling – haltingly, because she was so young at the time and she's struggling to remember the details – how Susannah nearly lost her life only metres from where we sit. I've never heard anything about this eventful family trip from long before I was born. I have so many questions piling on top of each other. By some miracle of self-control, I am tamping down my growing feeling of alarm.

Sitting here in the afternoon light, I think David and Tara can sense the shift in me, the switch from bystander to investigator – and that they are as much under the microscope as anyone else. David knows I've seen his texts from last night. And that if I read his manuscript – if it is his manuscript – that I know he has some connection with Olivia Philips.

As for Tara, she is well aware that I know how jealous she has always been of Susannah. Though she may not realize I copped that she was lying about her whereabouts earlier on.

I close my eyes and try to put my thoughts into a proper order so I can tell them what I know – that Susannah's last seen location was the murder scene, and that I've been in touch with the gardaí. I'm building up to telling them when we hear heavy footsteps, followed by a sharp rapping on the door.

David pulls himself to his feet, opens the bolts and swings the door open. I see two figures standing back, as if to be ready for whoever might open the door. Inspector Menton and a young detective.

Tara rises from the couch, her hands moving slowly up her thighs. As the men come into the room, she puts her glasses on, puts them back on top of her head, and pulls them back down again. Her head tilts to one side and her brows are knotted together. She is a picture of fidgety anxiety.

Menton addresses me first.

'Are you Lucy Brown?'

David steps in front of me, a protective arm stretched between me and the inspector.

'Have you found my wife? Jesus Christ, tell me,' he says, his pitch high. He does not sound like a guilty husband. He is every inch the desperate, pleading partner.

'I'm Inspector Paul Menton, and this is,' he says, turning to look for his colleague, who has just gone out to the patio to take a call, the way sidekicks always do on TV detective shows.

'Never mind,' he says, turning his attention back towards us, his eyes shining with the light of suspicion. 'Who are you?'

'I'm David Murtagh. These are Susannah's sisters, Tara and Lucy. Do you want to sit down, Inspector?'

Menton accepts the offer and fastens his eyes back on me. He produces a document from inside his jacket.

'This is a search warrant for this property. Who's the legal owner?'

My mouth drops open. David splutters. Tara is raking her left hand through her thin curls, scratching her nails off her scalp, and I feel a heavy finger move across mine.

'My mother. Evelyn Brown,' Tara replies.

'And where is Evelyn Brown?'

'In Dublin,' I say.

'Please inform her that a search warrant has been executed.'

'I'll ring her,' Tara says.

Inspector Menton gestures towards David and me, and orders us to sit.

Tara is back in under a minute to say that Mum has been told about the search.

'She's on her way. She was in Wicklow at an event with her clients, so she won't be long,' Tara says.

I notice she says nothing about her consenting. I'm not surprised it was a quick call. I'm sure that as soon as Tara mentioned Susannah's disappearance in Dunmore East Mum pressed 'End' and grabbed her car keys. If she's coming from Wicklow, she should be here in two hours, less if she breaks the speed limit. I wish she had got the news some other way.

Menton's detective begins searching the kitchen.

'As you're aware, the body of Olivia Philips was found in Badger's Cove this morning,' he says. 'I received a call from yourself, Lucy Brown, at 2 p.m. this afternoon informing me that the last known location of your sister's phone was around 9:30 p.m. at Badger's Cove last night.'

At this, David's and Tara's heads swivel towards me, their mouths hanging open. I was literally about to tell them, but with the inspector getting there first it looks like I am the one who's up to something.

'We conducted a search based on your phone call and retrieved your sister's phone,' Menton says.

I gasp. I can't help it.

'Where was it?'

'Smashed up and floating in the water, not far from where Ms Philips's body was found. We are currently analysing her phone and Ms Philips's phone, which was on her person. Her last call was to a Susannah Brown. So, this begs the question – where is Susannah Brown?'

I'd laugh if it wasn't so serious. This is the very question I have been trying to get the gardaí to take seriously since this morning. However, I can see that my call has backfired. Menton seems to think that Susannah is his top suspect, and that either we are hiding her, or she's on the run.

Susannah is many things – selfish, secretive, sometimes even shifty. But she's not a killer.

'As I told you on the phone, she ran out of this house last night and hasn't come back. Before she did, one of your officers stood at that door threatening her. And today the very same garda comes to take my statement, pretending that he doesn't know her. So, my question to you, Inspector, is have you spoken to your detective?'

Before Menton can reply, David jumps in.

'Spot on, Lucy! Who is this guy? Have you questioned him?'

'Rest assured, Mr Murtagh, we will be speaking with Detective Jack Fogarty and will investigate all leads thoroughly.'

I hear a low splutter from Tara. Even without seeing her, I can feel a buckling sensation inside me. Glancing back, I see her steady herself on the back of a chair. But she says nothing.

This has been most revealing.

First, Inspector Menton says he *will* speak with Jack Fogarty. So, he hasn't spoken to him yet. Which suggests Fogarty has gone AWOL.

Second, Tara knows something about Jack Fogarty.

Third, David is either an Oscar-worthy actor, or he doesn't have a clue where Susannah is. I've known David a long time, and I don't think he's that good a performer.

I don't want to be here when they begin to turn this place upside down. I'm also furious with Inspector Menton. I thought I could work with the gardaí to get to the bottom of this but how could I have forgotten? I am an outsider. And my call has given him his best, and possibly only, lead into the murder. The way he looks at us is accusatory, and it makes me want to get the hell out of here.

'We are not under arrest. You have no right to detain us,' I say.

'Listen, love. You barely made it a wet week in the force before shitting your pants. Zip it with the amateur-hour crap. The last known call of a murder victim was to someone who was staying in this house, who was at the scene of the crime, and who has just done a disappearing act. So, I will conduct this investigation as I see fit. You'll do as I say, and you will not impede this search either.'

'Don't you speak to her like that!' David says.

'I'd urge you to keep a calm head, Mr Murtagh.'

This has been another revealing exchange. I can ignore Menton digging into my background and mocking me – because his rapid breath and sweaty palms have given him away. He is under the spotlight and he hates it. The story is at the top of every bulletin. The media will be swarming – reporters arriving by the hour; TV cameras, Irish and British, setting up outside the station; the podcasters are probably on their way. He's scrambling for answers.

Just then Menton's phone rings. He glances at the screen and then holds a hand up to the three of us – as if to say 'don't move' – before going outside to take the call.

Tara, who has been behind me, comes closer and stands right beside me. She leans in to whisper in my ear.

'I know him.'

'Who?'

'Jack Fogarty.'

Her voice is tremulous, her eyes are focused on the ground. Despite the gravity of the situation, I feel a thrill at having read her so accurately.

I whisper back, 'From where?'

'Lucy, we have to get out of here. All of us. Now.'

24

Dunmore East, April 1983

Evelyn Brown feels as though her world is bathed in gold. She has never felt more at home, anywhere, than she does in Dunmore East. She feels the grit of the sand between the soles of her feet and the smooth soles of her black pumps. If she licks her lips, she can taste salt so bitter it makes her mouth water.

But however mellow Evelyn feels, her two warring daughters are making a determined attempt to pierce her moment of serenity, their voices rising in volume inside the hotel restaurant as she queues to pay for lunch. Susannah screams that she needs to go to the bathroom this very second, while Tara is so overtired and exhausted from the sun that she just wobbles on the spot, sobbing next to her sibling. Meanwhile, the entire restaurant watches on disapprovingly. Evelyn knows – they didn't come to hear two bawling brats, thanks very much; they came here to enjoy lunch and a drink by the sea.

Evelyn knows she needs to pay quickly and get the hell out, but the woman ahead of her in the queue is whispering urgently to the waitress at the till. Evelyn can't hear the conversation over the wailing of her children and the hubbub of the busy room.

Susannah accidentally stamps on Tara's foot and the four-year-old goes into such a convulsion that she is briefly silent. Her face is a colour somewhere approaching purple and Evelyn can see she is about to explode with the kind of howl that makes a parent feel like they are seconds from being pushed off a cliff, or perhaps seconds from willingly diving over.

Feeling a rising panic in her chest, Evelyn leans around the woman in front of her to find out what's happening. The woman has a head of wild springing black curls, and she is desperately scrabbling around her purse. She is so red-faced that it extends all the way down her neck, back and arms.

Something clicks in Evelyn. She has seen this woman before. She's the woman from the beach yesterday. She was with the man who saved Susannah's life.

She grabs the woman into a hug like they are old friends. 'Oh, thank God I found you! Thank you so much for lending me the money earlier. I was so stuck. I owe you big time.' She sticks out a crisp ten-pound note.

The other woman blinks, tears swimming in her eyes, and Evelyn says more pointedly: 'No, really. I can never truly repay you.'

Susannah's head swivels between the waitress, her mother and the strange woman with the dark hair and the sad eyes.

The woman mumbles something in response, but Tara's screams drown her out.

The waitress, with the weary air of someone who has already done a full shift and doesn't have time to mess around, whips the note out from between the two of them.

'OK, Maggie, you're settled,' she says, handing the change over to her. She turns expectantly as the woman hurries away, reaching out to Evelyn for her bill.

Evelyn hands over another ten-pound note. She tells the waitress to keep the change. With her daughters in tow, she follows this woman – Maggie, was it? – out to the front of the hotel. From this vantage point, nestled high on the side of the cliff, they have an elevated view of the strand below. The roar of the sea reminds the girls they are on holiday, and they suddenly forget their woes and peel off, running circles around the outdoor tables where other families drink ice-cold cider and eat smoky burgers.

Maggie is standing up against a stone wall by the side of the building, her hand resting on a blue iron rail that sits atop it. Evelyn gently places a hand on the other woman's shoulder.

'Hi, again. Are you OK?'

'Oh, yes. Thanks so much for that, I've never been more mortified,' she says, avoiding Evelyn's eyes.

'Are you kidding? That's my daughter over there who nearly drowned yesterday on the beach. Weren't you with the man who saved her?'

Only at that moment does Maggie seem to remember them.

'Oh, my God, yeah. Right. Yeah, that was Johno, my husband.'

'So, yeah. I know who owes who. There's no amount of money that could ever repay that.'

'Oh, I did nothing. It's my husband who's the hero.'

Evelyn detects a hint of sarcasm, but then thinks she's hearing things.

Maggie returns her gaze out to the bay, giving Evelyn a chance to size her up. Not that there is much to size up. Maggie is small and lithe and, in a word, exquisite. Her eyes are dark and round as coins, her black lashes unnaturally long, and she radiates magnetism.

Evelyn feels dumpy next to her. *If I sat in this woman's lap,* she thinks, *my thighs would probably crush her.*

The thought makes her hyper-aware of her body, and she begins pulling at her sleeves, feeling a familiar guilt. The exhaustion that came with the birth of her two children is still with her. It has been a while since she made – in Patrick's words – 'an effort'.

'Do you have kids?' Evelyn asks.

Maggie, appearing to have forgotten where she is, sounds surprised when she answers.

'Oh, yes. I have two. Katie and Jack. Four and five. A real handful, just like your girls.'

'You're kidding! Isn't that something.'

Another awkward silence stretches between them.

Evelyn tries again.

'Why don't you and your husband come over and let us make you all dinner this evening. We're staying right over there.' Evelyn points to a thatched cottage just 30 metres away.

'You're staying there? How did you even know how to rent them? I live here and I never even knew they were . . .'

Evelyn waits for the rest of the sentence, but it does not come.

'Oh, my husband Patrick. He knows everyone. Well, at least he thinks he does. Please come over, the girls would love to make some new friends. Actually, *I* would love to meet new friends – I'm sick of the two of them.'

The women laugh and seeing an opening, Evelyn speaks again. 'Please, come,' she says, trying and failing to keep the desperation out of her voice. 'The view from the house is something else. You can see the whole beach. We can have a glass of fancy wine, some mammy time. Patrick only ever picks the good wine, or so he says. Though honestly I wouldn't know. My mother says I'd lick it off a scabby leg even though I don't drink that much, except this one time I got drunk in front of her and she never lets me forget it. I just don't get the time, what with the girls. Sure, who am I telling, you know all this yourself.'

Evelyn stops herself there because she is rambling. Too much time solely in the company of children will do that to you. But she sees a flicker of something in the other woman's eyes, interest or even excitement.

'Well, it's not like I have any other plans. Some evenings I sing down in the local, but it's closed tonight. And I suppose it is the Easter break. OK, so. We don't live too far away. I should warn you though, Johno is not a talker.'

'Each to their own, I say. What time would suit you?'

'Well, Johno will be doing the milking till after seven. By the time we're ready, it'll be close to eight when we get here. Is that OK, with the girls' bedtimes?'

'Absolutely fine. Like you say, they're off school. I leave them up late on holiday hoping that they'll sleep late. Sometimes it works.'

'OK, see you around 8 p.m.'

Evelyn is delighted with the turn of events. She will pull out all the stops for this family. It's the least she can do.

One day in the future, Evelyn will identify this as the moment in which her words, and her words alone, changed the course of their lives, and unbeknownst to her, the lives of her daughters.

25

Gardaí are swarming all over the cottage and to compound matters, I see camera people at the entrance to the enclave. Dunmore East is a village so journalists were bound to pick up on the garda activity here. We are under instructions not to move from the couches. I'm trying to figure out a way to get us out of here so I can talk to Tara and David discreetly, and without it looking like we have something to hide. Now I have to factor in the media too.

Tara is still beside me on the couch, shivering, her eyes clamped shut. She looks pale and clammy and I'm worried about her. I want to ask her about Jack Fogarty, but I can't. The fact that Inspector Menton has yet to speak to Fogarty has left me suspicious. Why aren't they tracking him down as a matter of priority? With his colleagues all around I can't mention him.

David is taking a different tack with the gardaí, peppering them with questions. 'What were the messages on my wife's phone? How did they know each other? Is anyone going to tell me what the hell is going on?' Of course, he's getting nowhere.

I let him rant and rave because it gives me a chance to do some homework on my phone while waiting for our moment to escape. The fact that it hasn't occurred to me to do so till now says a lot about my frazzled state of mind.

Olivia Philips was a very big deal in the UK. Probably here too if I watched reality TV or knew anything about classical music. She rose to fame playing the piano on one of the best-known TV talent shows in the UK, and although she didn't win, her talent and beauty resulted in a record deal. She was the cool modern face of classical music.

I read with a mounting sense of panic. Not only is Olivia a British darling, but so is her mother, Joan Philips, a soprano who has performed in places like the Royal Opera House, the Sydney Opera House and La Scala. On my earphones I listen to her tell Sky News that the 'Dublin Murder Unit' will be taking over from local gardaí. There is no such thing as the Dublin Murder Unit and while the Garda National Bureau of Criminal Investigation may well be on the way, it will only be to assist local detectives. Nevertheless, it's more pressure. This is huge. It can't be much longer before Susannah, herself a well-known writer, is mentioned as a person of interest. Something like this – two beautiful, successful, artistic women, somehow connected in a murder – will be catnip for the media.

On the screen Joan looks blonde, lithe and poised. But she has the bewildered look of someone who has not yet absorbed the reality of a devastating loss. 'Olivia went to Waterford all the time. She said she found it peaceful by the sea. The police in Ireland say they have a definite line of inquiry but they need to move faster. They need to find the animal who did this,' she says, finally breaking down.

There's loads more online about Olivia and her family. She grew up in Blackheath in south-east London, the location of a concert hall with world-class acoustics where Olivia was able to practise. But I don't have time to fall down rabbit holes about Olivia's family. I have my own to worry about, especially my missing sister.

Just then Tara leans over and looks at me imploringly. 'We need to talk,' she whispers.

'I know,' I whisper back, 'but we can't here.'

Tara starts shivering again. I can feel the couch shaking and finally have a flash of inspiration. I hoist her up by the arm and drag her over to Inspector Menton. Being so much taller,

I seem to loom over Menton and I can feel how disconcerting he finds it. I get that from men a lot.

'Inspector, Tara has diabetes and hasn't eaten all day. Look at her, she's shaking like a leaf. It won't look good if she collapses and the guards end up having to explain why they put so much pressure on the innocent sister of an innocent woman.'

The word 'No' is practically bursting out of him, but whether Tara is hamming it up for effect or it's genuine, she is properly shuddering now. Menton's forehead creases into a frown.

I know he's wavering, so I plough on, sounding far more confident than I feel.

'Look, the Strand Hotel is just over there. We will go the back way to avoid the cameras,' I say, indicating 'we' as Tara, David and myself. 'We'll be ready to go to the station once we've eaten. Mum should be here by then. You can talk to us then when you've figured out what exactly it is you're looking for.'

Menton glances over to the hotel, not 30 metres away.

'Doyle!' he shouts.

One of his uniforms scurries over.

'Bring these three across the road, through the back door, away from the cameras. Wait with them until we are ready to bring them to the station to take their statements. Don't let them out of your sight.'

This Doyle fella looks terrified, as if it's his first day on the job, and my heart softens for him. He leads us out the back door and down a dusty concrete passageway with high walls that link the back entrances of all the thatched cottages. The sky is overcast now, making it seem darker and later than it is.

We slip out onto the road which, to the left, winds down to the beach before lifting back up to the Strand Hotel, which is tucked into the side of a cliff. Doyle points towards the hotel, as if I can't see it myself, the baby-blue building lit up with dim bulbs where clueless and unburdened people are drinking and socializing.

I would love to make a run for it up the hill beside me, but how guilty would that make us all look? And what would that even achieve?

We glance at each other and make our way to the hotel, all our minds spinning, the sea whispering its secrets as we pass the strand. It would be beautiful if things weren't turning to shit.

Although the air is crisp and we are not dressed for it, I lead us to an outdoor table located the furthest from all the others. It is wedged against a wall, and beyond that wall is a steep drop down to the beach. The garda, Doyle, sits with us. This will not do.

Tara takes her seat last, pulling her cardigan around her before standing up again abruptly, saying, 'I think I'm going to be sick.'

Doyle grimaces and says, 'I'm supposed to keep you all together. Please sit down.'

Tara goes to heave and he jumps back. She runs inside, leaving the bewildered garda staring at her back. I was hoping to talk to her first, but I'll have to go with the cards I am being dealt.

I sigh and say, 'We're not the flight risk, Garda Doyle. We don't have a car, she does.'

It's a lie – I know David drove them here – but it has the desired effect. David and I are left alone.

26

Dunmore East, April 1983

'Jesus, woman, calm yourself. You'd swear President Hillery himself was coming over. What's got into you?'

Evelyn slams a stainless-steel wine bucket down on the wooden table outside the cottage, regretting it immediately. The apology tumbles quickly out of her mouth.

'Sorry, sorry, Pat, sorry. It's just . . . this is the man who saved our daughter's life. I just want to say thanks. I want them to enjoy this evening.'

A pained expression crosses his tan face: he hates being called Pat, and his ego is wounded. His damn pride. *It will be the undoing of us*, she thinks. She tries to avert his incoming bad mood, a sour tidal wave that cannot be stopped, only managed.

'Oh, don't get like that, please, love. We owe this man a huge amount, but it doesn't mean you're less of a father. Right place, right time, that's all. You had your hands full with Tara. What were you to do? Sure, I didn't even see what was happening. How on earth I didn't, I'll never know, but anyway . . . all's well that ends well.'

She senses the air still a little. It's obvious what happened yesterday has got under his skin. He runs a hand through his thin black hair and flicks an angry glance in her direction. She always thinks he looks like a shark when he does that. It's the way his nose flares and his eyes narrow, like he is about to go in for his prey. She found it attractive when they first met. Not so much anymore.

'Everything I do for this family, do you appreciate it at

all, the hours I put in? Working is not easy, you know. Look around you. All I ask for is a little respect. Is that so much?'

Thankfully, the girls run out at this moment, each holding seashells, each shouting: 'Mammy, Mammy! Listen to my one, you can hear the sea!'

'No, listen to mine!'

'No, mine first!'

Evelyn picks the two shells out of their hands and puts one to each ear.

'I can hear two seas. Wow, two seas, listen, take turns,' she says, thrusting them back.

A familiar feeling of dread fills up her chest, stretches down through her torso and sits heavy in her abdomen. She wants to make a good impression with Maggie and Johno. Evelyn smooths down the tablecloth – it's her mother's best polka-dot cloth – and checks that there is enough ice in the bucket and that she has picked the best wine – not for her, she doesn't taste a difference, but Patrick will want them to put on a good show. That's why she must pack table linen, glassware, a wine bucket and the good canteen of cutlery – the various accoutrements of 'civilized' dining – when they go on holiday. Patrick likes the idea of crossing paths with other businessmen, of being able to entertain. The likes of Maggie and Johno are not what he has in mind though, hence his spiky humour, but he knows he can't really object.

She makes sure there are no smudges on the glasses, checking her watch as she does so. They are ten minutes late.

Even the weather is playing ball. There's just one wispy cloud high in the sky. It's April, so the sun will set soon. In its wake it has left an incredible pastel kaleidoscope. Up top, the sky is a clear baby blue, turning even cooler below before it meets a peach, then light pink, then inky purple horizon. Then below the horizon line, the sea reflects it all, mirroring the same colours backwards.

She can feel it: there is promise in the air.

Evelyn wipes her hands down on her apron, realizing as she does so that it is covered in ketchup from the dinner she made for the girls. In her haste to make things perfect, she hasn't checked her own appearance. That is not unusual: she often forgets about herself.

She hasn't so much as brushed her tangled hair, which is pulled back into a messy bun at the nape of her neck.

'Watch the girls,' she says, rushing past Patrick, whose head is buried in the *Irish Times*.

'Where are you going? They'll be here any moment,' he calls after her.

He rarely reads newspapers but he went out and got one so he can create the right impression. He wants to seem successful and worldly, the sort to immerse himself in current affairs. It's a far cry from the threadbare house he grew up in, with only his uncle for company, in North County Dublin.

Evelyn runs across the big open-plan kitchen. She takes the stairs two at a time and bounds into their small double bedroom, wrenching open the wardrobe door. A beautiful musty smell hits her. The smell of holidays – other people's stuff. She finds a floral green plissé dress that she knows she'll be shivering in later, but she pulls it on regardless. No matter what way she tugs it, her belly seems to bulge. After Susannah, it never went back to the way it was. *It'll have to do*, she decides, when she hears the crunch of tyres on gravel outside.

She rakes a brush through her unruly hair. It just falls back into its usual puffy shape, so she twists it a few times and clips it up high on her head. One last glance in the mirror. She hates her nose. It's too big and long and when she was younger her classmates used to call her 'horsey'. They stopped that when her brother Adam threatened to give them all a black eye.

Evelyn shuffles over to the small window, craning her head out as far as she can to see beyond the protruding thatched roof. Next to their spotless Toyota Land Cruiser she sees a battered old car, covered almost completely in dust and dirt. She cringes a little. She hopes it doesn't make them feel awkward, all this showiness, the stink of money in the air.

Evelyn hears two small voices, two new children, and the rumble of an unfamiliar male voice. She applies a layer of mascara and dabs some cream blush on her cheeks. She feels instantly better and briefly wonders why she doesn't do this more often. Then she remembers – there's never any time.

She takes a deep breath and walks downstairs as nonchalantly as she can.

27

In the dusky gloom, I can feel David's sadness, his confusion, his worry, his fear. All understandable emotions. But there's no time for sympathizing. More important, I can't let them overwhelm me. Tara will be back with Garda Doyle shortly. I need to clear things up.

'David, we don't have much time. I need answers. What were those texts about on Susannah's phone? Did you write the manuscript Susannah brought with her? But most of all – and, David, forgive me – did you hurt Susannah?'

He raises his arms and goes to rise, as if in protest, but I push him and his arms back down into the seat and remind him that there's no time to lose.

I wait a moment and I see his eyes well up. He brushes the tears away with the back of his hand.

'It's a bit awkward,' he says, biting his lip.

I wait.

'A few days ago, my emails were open on the computer in the office. Susannah spotted an email from her agent.'

'What's the problem with that? Don't you often handle stuff for Susannah?'

'This was different. It was an email to me, about my work.'

'Your work?'

'Yeah. This is why I didn't want to tell you any of this. Being blunt, I still don't want to tell you, Lucy. This is personal and is going to embarrass her. She's proud and she always wants to be this beacon of strength for you. She'd hate you knowing this.'

'She might be dying somewhere, David. There are more important things than pride right now.'

'Summer might have been about to drop her. She had stopped responding to Susannah recently. You know her books never did as well after *The Broken Bay*. There was huge pressure on Susannah to deliver the goods after she won the award. But she could never hit those heights again. She changed publisher but it didn't improve things. She was seriously worried about being dropped not just by her publisher, but by Summer.

'But the thing is, I've been writing a book of my own. I was a writer before I met Susannah, and . . .'

'Go on,' I say, when he hesitates, 'spit it out.'

'When I first met Susannah, she was stuck with a major aspect of her book. It was something she had been grappling with for months, she said. That's why she was at the retreat, to riddle it out. I read her script and saw the answer straight away. I'm good at that sort of structural stuff. Anyway, I made the suggestion, she tried it and boom, it worked. *Shadow Play* obviously became a huge debut. I helped her then with *Her Perfect Lies* as well. She got paranoid about doing it without me and shut me out of *Under the Echo*. It tanked, but honestly, Lucy, that wasn't because I was hands-off; she was just trying too hard to be different. I did a lot on *The Broken Bay* but, again, it was just helping her resolve some technical problems.

'As well as the writing, after the second book was published the amount of admin was too much for her to handle. Though she had an agent, there was always stuff coming in from foreign publishers, or media requests that bypassed the publishers, or invitations to festivals and panels. I sort of became her right-hand man. I enjoyed it, but looking back, I stopped a good chunk of my freelance work because I didn't have time, and I think I got a bit bitter as time went on.

'Things came to a head in New York. We had a big row about the arrangement, if that's what you'd call it. After that, there was no more collaboration. She never talked to me about her writing, and I never asked. I continued to take care of some of the admin, but I never commented on any of her books. It's something we should have talked about, but it was just too painful to go there.

'Then last year, I had an idea for a novel. The thing just poured out of me. It felt amazing. I finished it and I sent it to Summer a few months ago. She had never stopped pestering me for a novel. That's what Susannah found in my emails. Summer sent an email with the subject line, "At last! I'm gonna make you a star!!!" She was really excited because she had two publishers already interested.'

Just for a moment, I can hear the excitement in his voice, despite the dire situation.

'And Susannah flew off the handle?'

'Yeah,' he says, 'she did. Said I hadn't been honest. Accused me of kicking her when she was down and stealing her agent. Said the two of us could have done much better if I had shared ideas with her over the last few years. She was so furious that she took my hard copy, which was sitting on the desk, deleted the original on my computer, and even said she had deleted the emailed copy, so only she had it. It was ridiculous, of course. Summer has it. But Susannah can get like that in arguments – the red mist descends.

'I was in a rage myself when I texted those messages you saw. I feel sick at the thought. What if they were my last words to her?'

He sobs into his hands, and I pat his back awkwardly.

'What my book was about didn't help,' he mutters. 'I feel terrible about that too.'

'What was it about?'

'A married couple who give each other one "exception" a year. It ends up with the husband killing the wife.'

He's gone from gentle sobbing to actual weeping and I am mortified.

'Jesus. Right. So, *Sea of Mirrors* is not yours?'

'No. My novel is called *The Exception*. *Sea of Mirrors* must be her latest.'

'And you've no idea who Olivia Philips is? You have nothing to do with Susannah's disappearance?' I ask, more reasoning it out to myself than anything else.

His tears turn to snotty rage. 'Jesus Christ, Lucy! How can you even ask?'

With perfect timing, Garda Doyle returns with an ashen-faced Tara.

Over his shoulder I see Mum's car pull up in front of the cottage. I notice the squad cars have disappeared, and with them the waiting media. I breathe a sigh of relief that she doesn't have a camera in her face. Yet even from here, I can hear that she is shouting.

I take off, fast, in her direction, the others in hot pursuit behind me. It takes less than thirty seconds to reach Mum. She's at the front door, her way blocked by a garda.

'What is your name?' she asks Mum, whose shoulders are slumped and who has one hand clamped to the doorframe to steady herself.

'You are testing my last nerve,' Mum says, breathing hard.

'This is my mother, Evelyn Brown,' I say. 'She owns this house. Inspector Menton wants her here.'

As if by magic, at the mention of his name the front door opens and Menton materializes, a supercilious expression on his face.

'Mrs Brown – please come in.'

It's as if he's welcoming her to his humble abode. Mum is having none of it. With a sudden burst of energy she barges into the middle of the room and scrutinizes everything – the few remaining gardaí, the sealed bags, something in the corner that only she seems to be able to see. Then she turns back to Menton, still in high dudgeon – and quite frankly, I'm here for it.

'Why are you searching my cottage? What do you think you're doing? My daughter is missing, and a woman is dead, and you're here rooting around my cupboards? Have you lost your mind?'

Even Menton wilts a little under the full glare of her anger. He invites her to sit and talk. As she moves towards the table, she glances around and clocks me watching her. The fury in her eyes stops me in my tracks.

'You better tell me what you're doing here, Lucy,' she says.

28

Dunmore East, April 1983

Maggie Fogarty stands at the bottom of the stairs in the cottage, agog. She clutches a bunch of wildflowers in one hand, a dusty bottle of wine in the other and gazes all around. She wears a pale grey cotton dress cinched in at the waist.

Maggie is rapt. 'This place . . . this view,' she says, a little breathless.

Maggie has the sharpest feeling that she somehow belongs here, in this house. Inside her chest it feels like someone has just struck a tuning fork and it hums and hums. A current has come alive in her and she can't identify what sparked it, the house or something else.

Patrick looms over her, taking the bottle of wine and pretending to look impressed. Maggie did not have a chance the previous day, on the beach, to get a proper look at him, what with all the commotion. She sees now that he is handsome, tan with broad shoulders, dark eyes, an imposing but slightly awkward presence.

They all turn to look at the four kids, who are scoping each other out tentatively in that way that small kids do on first meeting, giving each other the suspicious side-eye.

Susannah sighs, breaking the ice. 'OK, come on, come on, I'll show you the toys,' she says in a world-weary voice that makes the adults laugh. She goes up the stairs, and they follow like ducklings behind the mother hen.

'She'll cause a revolution one day, that child. Either that or she'll get herself in terrible trouble,' Evelyn says, before turning her attention back to the others.

She is trying very hard, Maggie thinks. She doesn't know whether to be put off or to feel complimented. In Evelyn's over-the-top friendliness, it doesn't take Maggie long to sense underlying loneliness. That much she can identify with. Being a mother *is* lonely.

'Come on, outside, everyone,' Evelyn says, leading the adults exactly as her daughter had done with the kids. At the picnic table, she lights a few candles, being careful not to step into anyone's space.

Maggie has been so busy taking in the house and their hosts that she has barely paid attention to what Johno is making of it. But she knows he hates this kind of stuff, schmoozing, meeting new people, drinking wine. He works the land, tends to the cows, sees the odd few fellas in the local bar for a pint, comes home to his wife and children. She glances at him and he, as always, is trying to fly below the radar. His brown and grey hair flies in every direction, including directly upwards. *Why won't the man ever go and get a bloody haircut*, Maggie thinks. At twenty-eight, he is only two years older than her but already has silver streaks in his hair, which he blames on the stress of the farm and hard outdoor work. At her insistence he put on a shirt, but he hasn't worn it in so long that there's a whiff of mothballs and it's strained at the buttons in a way that Maggie finds embarrassing.

He is rubbing his hands back and forth on the knees of his jeans, muck caked deep underneath his fingernails. It would probably take an industrial appliance to get the filth out.

Evelyn goes to pour wine for everyone but Patrick stops her. 'You always pour it arseways, let me do it. There's a particular way, you see.'

Maggie smiles at him across the table. She loves a Dublin accent, even if some of the locals call them 'dirty Dubs'.

Making an effort to look unbothered by her husband's criticism, Evelyn smiles brightly and says she will get the charcuterie from the fridge.

Charcuterie, Maggie thinks, smirking on the inside. *It's called ham and cheese around here.*

She catches Johno's eye and then flicks her eyes down at his hands. Taking the hint to do something about his fingernails, he asks to use the bathroom, leaving Maggie alone with Patrick. She takes it all in – the cliffs, the sea, the house. Maybe this is exactly what she needs – new people, an adventure. Things have been far too quiet lately for her liking.

At the kitchen sink, Evelyn splashes water on her face. She can't seem to tamp down the anxiety thrumming through her. The girls are still upstairs showing off their elaborate dolls' house. It is suspiciously quiet. Nothing good ever comes of children being this quiet.

Behind her a man clears his throat. She spins on the spot to find Johno Fogarty standing awkwardly, hands in his pockets. He is glancing around the kitchen, his face blank.

'Oh, hi. Can I get you anything?'

He picks a piece of lint off his arm, choosing not to look at her directly.

When he speaks, his voice is gruff. 'You OK?'

She considers lying, but then realizes it has been a while since anyone has asked her quite so genuinely how she is feeling. So, she goes for it.

'Well . . .'

He looks up now and for the first time she sees his eyes, the colour of the sea in springtime, blazing and vivid. There is something in the way he looks at her that makes her feel suddenly rooted to the spot.

'I find it hard to make friends, I go way over the top trying, then I get anxious that I've gone over the top. I end up in this loop, over and over, wondering what people are thinking of me, but thinking they must be thinking terrible things. I overthink everything. And then I overthink the overthinking.'

His face has softened and she keeps going – she can't seem to stop.

'Basically, I'm crazy. Exhausted. And crazy. And maybe a bit lonely.'

Evelyn braces for mockery, but instead she feels her cheek twitch and realizes she is copying Johno, who is smiling for the first time since she met him. A big, broad, unexpected smile. It suits him. It transforms him.

They both laugh, quiet at first, but louder the more they try to hold it in.

He stops and sighs, and says, 'Me too.'

29

I want to tell Mum everything I know before she speaks to Inspector Menton. I don't want her thinking I've been hiding things from her – though that's exactly what I've been doing. I reassure myself that it's just been a matter of timing. I wanted to pick my moment to tell her what was going on.

It took me a second to realize that what seemed like rage when she looked at me was actually fear. Her breathing was so fast and her stare so intense that I struggled to answer her question about what had brought me here.

I was about to say, *I don't know why I'm here*. But then I wondered why she didn't ask why Susannah had been here. Or how we got in. She seemed to be focusing on the wrong thing.

Menton's forever-ringing phone takes him outside again and gives me the opportunity to give Mum the heads-up. When I get to the bit about the garda I saw today being the man who had threatened Susannah at the door last night, she stops me.

'What was his name, this man who showed up twice?'

I'm struck by the deadpan way she asks, as though she already knows the answer.

'Jack Fogarty,' I say. She rocks back and forward slightly, her eyes set right ahead, her face expressionless.

'What did he say to you?'

'What do you mean?'

'What exactly did he say?'

'Last night he told her to leave, or else. Today he just said that if she didn't show up by tonight to ring the station. Mum, Tara says she knows him. Do you know him? Does Susannah?'

'Yes. He knew the girls as kids,' she says. With that she marches over to Menton, who has just walked back in.

'Where is Detective Jack Fogarty? Are you aware that he threatened my daughter last night?'

The uniform gardaí posted at front and back doors seem to perk up. I can feel their energy shift. Hearing their colleague's name mentioned in connection with the chief suspect is quite the scoop.

'We are currently trying to ascertain his whereabouts,' Menton says, grudgingly. He steers her out of earshot – surprisingly she lets him. He lowers his voice right down. Even though I can no longer hear, the body language is unmistakable – Menton is trying to placate Mum and she's having none of it. Why he hasn't hauled us off to the station for questioning yet, I have no idea. It just compounds my belief that he is terrified of the press, and probably of his superiors. He must be hoping to find some kind of smoking gun in the cottage.

David and Tara didn't follow me and Mum into the house. They're sitting at the picnic table, both lost in thought. I check the clock on the wall and see the time has just passed 4:30 p.m., which means Susannah has been missing for nineteen hours now. Though it won't provide much warmth, I pull her rain mac from the wall. As I step out the front door, David gets up and comes towards me.

'Is she OK?' he says.

'Better than I expected. She's giving the inspector a hard time.'

He goes back into the house.

I bury my hands into the pockets of Susannah's mac and find a pack of cigarettes. That gives me an idea. Tara lies about it, but I know she has the occasional cigarette; I smell it off her on stressful family occasions. It's time for her to come clean. It's time for everyone to come clean. Now that I have eliminated David as a suspect, I need to be able to see my sister with clear eyes too.

I go over to her, holding up the pack of cigarettes. When I sit down she practically snatches the box out of my hand. I light a cigarette for her, and she inhales that thing like it is fresh air. I have never seen her as stressed in my entire life.

'Are you having, or have you ever had, an affair with David?' I say.

She looks at me sadly and my hand automatically goes to my chest. Dear God! It can't be true?

Tara opens her mouth to talk but closes it again and purses her lips to take another deep drag. I'm sick of playing games with people who are lying. I'm going to wait this one out.

'I suppose you could probably always tell that I had feelings for him. That's been the way since I first set eyes on him. There was a time when I thought something could happen – there was a kiss that I made a big deal of, in my head. I held on to it like it was a lifebuoy when things were bad at home, and sometimes they were very bad. I used to escape into fantasies about the imaginary life I would have with David. But the answer to your question is no. David is a good man. Too good.'

A tear rolls down her cheek and she swipes it away.

'Why did you lie to me about where you were this morning?'

'What? I, I, I . . .'

'No lies. Just truth.'

She inhales deeply and then expels a long plume of smoke.

'I've been cheating on Myles.'

I am not at all surprised. They've been like strangers for years and I've never understood why they stick together in that awful house as it disintegrates around them. It's an oversized pile in the middle of nowhere, lashed up during the property boom.

'No shit,' I say.

'You knew?'

'Not really. I'm just not surprised. Who have you been seeing?'

'Whoever I pick up. After the first time, a guy in the hotel bar in Donegal, it was easy. Surprisingly easy. And, I might as well be honest, it's a lot of fun.'

'Er, how many?'

'No idea.'

I'm not even sure why I asked, 'How many?' It's not like I'm judging Tara. I just feel sad for her. Though – and I don't think it's my imagination – I can feel the burden of her secret lift now that she has shared it. It's in the way she tilts her head up to exhale the cigarette smoke, as if also exhaling the pressure and guilt.

And out of nowhere I cop why she hasn't left Myles, and why this is how she's handling her terrible marriage. She doesn't want the past to repeat itself. She wants a different life for her children. She wants to break the cycle, even if it breaks her. She doesn't want to end up like Mum and Dad.

'Where were you last night and this morning?'

She points her left arm out, towards the Strand Hotel.

'The Strand?'

'No! I was in a hotel much further up, where the Three Sisters meet.'

'The what? Where?'

'The Three Sisters rivers? The Barrow, the Nore and the Suir? No? All of this area, from Cheekpoint – where I was, around eighteen kilometres up – to here, in Dunmore East, is where those three big Irish rivers meet and exit together to the sea.'

The synchronicity of this is not lost on me. Tara sees me hesitate.

'It's a coincidence that I was nearby, Lucy! You can't seriously think I had anything to do with this? I hate this place. I avoid it. I told David where I was. I'd been drinking late and I couldn't drive, so he came and picked me up on his way.'

Intuition tells me she is speaking the truth. It's nothing to do with my unusual perception. It's simply that I know Tara well and the story rings true.

After finding out so much about my sisters' marriages in the last hour or so, I feel like a therapist. But I feel something else – and it's cringey to admit it in the circumstances – now that I'm getting answers and making progress, I feel alive for the first time in ages.

This shouldn't be a revelation, but it is. All the time spent with Tim when I knew I wanted to break it off but I couldn't bear to cause him, and therefore myself, pain. All the evenings spent watching TV or scrolling Instagram because Tim preferred me being in, or I didn't want to go out myself. All the invitations I ignored. Of the many things missing from my quiet life, I can see that this is the most important – purpose.

Now that I've started, I don't want to stop. My mind is in overdrive. Fragments of what I've learned over the past twenty-four hours swirl in my head. But one thing jumps out: what Susannah said yesterday about Mum and Dad having a fight and Mum returning to Dunmore East 'to get some space'.

'Tara, what did Mum and Dad fight about that made her come back here?'

'I don't know much about the second trip. But there was a bad fight when we were here in 1983.'

30

Dunmore East, April 1983

The land cruiser dominates the winding rural road. Patrick, who has both the sunroof and the top buttons of his blue check shirt open, takes a sharp turn and slams his foot on the brake.

'Jesus, Mary and Joseph,' Evelyn cries, a hand on her chest, her eyes flying to the two girls in the back.

They came *this* close to colliding with a massive tractor, its gigantic tyres looming up over the top of their bonnet. Patrick whips off his silver-rimmed designer sunglasses to get a better look. Sure enough, it's Johno, descending from his driver seat high above.

The two girls resume their bickering. Evelyn shushes them as Johno sticks his head into Patrick's window, tanned arms resting on the frame of the window. He's at ease in a way that he wasn't last night. *We are on his turf now*, Evelyn thinks.

'Goin' the wrong way, I'd say,' he says, his eyes resting momentarily on Evelyn, who looks away quickly. It is not a small flutter that she experiences high in her chest. Her heart actually thumps. *What in the name of God*, she thinks as she gazes out to the fields beside her.

Patrick shrinks back into the leather seat a little, muttering about Evelyn and her stupid map and how women have no sense of direction.

'She couldn't find her way out of a paper bag, this one,' he says, jabbing his thumb in his wife's direction. The laugh he's expecting from the other man does not come.

'Turn back. Take a left at the crossroads. Fourth house on the right,' Johno says, slapping the roof of the car and turning back to his tractor. He shouts over his shoulder as he gets back up into the cab, 'Careful with the bends in that yoke, you can't see a thing with the hedges around here.'

When he's out of earshot, Patrick turns to Evelyn and says, 'I know I should be grateful, but that man grinds my gears. All that intense silence and staring last night. Has he nothing to say for himself at all? Is there anything going on up there, that's what I'm wondering. Is he simple?'

Evelyn pretends she doesn't hear this as he reverses into a small clearing to turn the car.

In the back, the bickering is reaching ear-piercing levels.

'Shush now, girls, be nice to each other,' Evelyn says.

'Mammy, tell Tara to leave me alone!' Susannah says. Her little sister is sobbing silently beside her. Tara hates car journeys and always tries to cling to Susannah, who has no interest in comforting her. The more comfort Tara seeks, the more forcibly Susannah rejects her.

'Maybe this was a bad idea,' Evelyn says.

'Well, it was your idea. Too late now, he's seen us,' Patrick says, ignoring Johno's advice and taking the crossroads with another rough jerk of the steering wheel. 'And what in the name of God are you wearing?'

Evelyn looks down at her outfit – a high-neck baby-pink dress that stops just above her knee. It covers her arms to her elbows. Modest and tasteful, at least that's what she thought when she put it on earlier.

And was this *her* idea, to come here? She does not remember suggesting a day two.

Last night had gone well in the end. She was so used to the girls' constant fighting that simply having children playing without screaming and bawling was a relief. Susannah found a pliant new best friend in four-year-old Katie. The two spent the evening on one of the bunk beds styling a doll's hair, Susannah telling Katie the facts of the world as she knew them.

Tara and Jack took turns playing hide-and-seek until they tired themselves out and fell asleep beside each other on the couch. The only hiccup was when Tara woke up disorientated and, upon going up to the bedroom, realized that Susannah had let Katie fall asleep beside her in Susannah's bed. It precipitated a tearful breakdown on the stairs as Tara cried that Susannah never let *her* get into the top bunk beside her. It sometimes broke Evelyn's heart to see how very desperate Tara was for her sister's love and attention.

Out on the patio, with the tide edging closer as the sky turned darker shades of blue, the wine flowed and the initial tension loosened. Evelyn would not normally drink so much – in fact she usually didn't drink at all – but Maggie knocked back the wine at a great rate, and she tried to keep up.

Of course, the person who spoke longest and loudest was Patrick. He had several stories he liked to tell in company. These included the story of how he managed what he called his 'clothing empire'. While he said it with a wry chuckle, the incidental details about the challenges of supplying suiting for prominent politicians and lawyers, and smart dresses for their secretaries, were designed to impress. It was, he implied, very highbrow – Dublin's answer to Savile Row. And of course, that put him on first-name terms with some very influential people.

The bragging was wasted on Johno and Maggie, which made it more excruciating. Johno's face stayed impassive, and she was sure he thought Patrick was full of hot air. Maggie played it differently – dialling up the level of fascination and prompting him to say more. 'Do you really think so, Patrick?' Evelyn was sure it was an act.

Evelyn had once been dazzled by Patrick's air of sophistication. But the truth about him was both tragic and banal. Patrick was orphaned at three. His mother had dropped him to pre-school, come home and climbed into bed beside her husband who was off work with the flu. By the time they woke up and realized their house was on fire, they were trapped. His father was an electrician, and the suspicion – never stated – was that he had messed up something when he rewired their home. Patrick ended up living with his father's uncle Edward, the only one who could take him. It was an austere upbringing, as Edward, an elderly bachelor of a strong religious bent, had taken on the child out of duty rather than affection and had no interest in nurturing him. At fifteen, after his inter cert, Edward had told Patrick it was time to work for a living and had him go into one of his tailoring businesses as an apprentice. When he died, not long after Patrick turned eighteen, it turned out he had left him the three shops.

It was not long after that when Evelyn met Patrick, and her heart went out to him when she heard his story. It took a long time for her to see how much it had damaged him, resulting in an obsession with class and status. He had gone off to register their first child, Susan's, birth and come home with a birth cert on which she had become Susannah. There was no discussion about it. He declared that it was more 'appropriate'. Appropriate for what she had no idea. Around the same time, he became 'Patrick', though she'd known him as 'Pat' for two years by then. Occasionally 'Pat' slipped out and earned her a furious glare.

Evelyn had learned to ignore when her husband started doing his captain of industry act around strangers, sharing his insights on the importance of entrepreneurship. But last night the drink had removed her normal filters. The words tumbled out before she could even register them herself.

'Don't mind him. He didn't start it. It was his dad's uncle's business before he died. It's three small shops and the third one is about to close. I wouldn't even be so sure about the first two, with all this talk about the recession only getting worse.'

She couldn't believe she had spoken so bluntly. She would normally never talk out of turn like that. She blamed the wine.

He glared at her for a split second and gave a tiny shake of his head. Then his face fell back into a smile, but as he spoke the small bones in his jaws were clicking. 'Don't mind Evelyn, she hasn't the first clue about the economy.'

Maggie laughed and looked away. She had almost certainly seen the look that Patrick had given her so Evelyn was grateful when Maggie asked how he was managing, what with inflation and the high taxation. She seemed very well informed, Evelyn thought. And then realized she had said that out loud instead of just thinking it.

'Well, I was on my way to becoming a store manager in town. Alas,' Maggie said, elaborating no further and swilling her wine around the glass.

When she saw that both Evelyn's and Patrick's faces were blank, she put her glass down impatiently and said, as if it should have been obvious, 'The marriage bar! When I married Johno, that was the end of that. I was twenty years old with my whole career ahead of me but no, I was married, and sure I may get back into the kitchen and let that job go to a man. As if me selling knickers was going to upset Father Reilly. Come to think of it, Father Reilly probably would have a stroke if I mentioned knickers around him. Though he's probably thought about them plenty, dirty old bastard.'

Evelyn flinched. She had never heard anyone talk like that about a priest. If her God-fearing mother could hear this, she would be appalled and probably rebuke Maggie forcibly.

She wasn't surprised to see an enraged look on Patrick's face. He leaned over the table towards Maggie, and she was waiting for him to chide her for talking about 'a man of the cloth' as she just had. Patrick could be conservative like that.

To her amazement he said, 'But what are you now, around the same age as me? Twenty-six?'

Maggie nodded.

'I thought the marriage bar was a thing of the past. Didn't they do away with all that nonsense when we joined the EEC?'

'Not in the private sector, not in the companies around here. They seem to like clinging to the good old days,' Maggie said, knocking back a big glug of wine and reaching for the bottle.

'That seems short-sighted – businesses need to retain good workers. I know that myself.'

Two thoughts kept swirling around Evelyn's head. This conversation seemed so grown-up. Despite having kids, she still felt nineteen, not twenty-five. The second was how seriously Patrick treated Maggie's opinion. Evelyn knew that if she had slagged off a priest, or complained about the marriage bar, he would have been quick to tell her she didn't know what she was talking about. Yet Maggie could hold forth and there was no blowback. If anything, he seemed to relish debating with her. It made Evelyn feel smaller than ever, facing the fact that her husband saw her as intellectually inferior. No one asked Evelyn about her job because her job was to stay at home and rear the children. The difference between her and Maggie was that she was happy to do it.

Throughout this, Johno was silent. Mostly he kept his gaze out to the sea. It was almost as though he wasn't there. He didn't even flinch when Maggie gestured around her at the cottage and the charcuterie and the wine and said, 'I mean, this is the life I should have had. You can't do it on one farm salary, though.' A flush of embarrassment lit up Evelyn's cheeks, both on her behalf but also on Johno's.

As the evening wore on, the conversation moved onto easier subjects. Patrick brought out a radio, put on WLR FM and there was dancing to 'Down Under' and 'Billie Jean'. Well, dancing by Maggie and Patrick. Maggie produced an Instamatic and took photos, pictures Evelyn hoped she would never see. What a state they must have looked.

For Evelyn, the end of the evening was a bit of a blur, but when the dancing started, she knew better than to join in. She busied herself inside, checking on the kids, instead of making a fool of herself, even though she really wanted to dance.

Somewhere in that haze, she had apparently invited herself up to the Fogartys' house today, though she doesn't remember asking and it doesn't sound like her at all.

She had experienced the worst hangover of her life that morning, not helped by the row that had happened behind the bedroom door when their guests finally left.

That's a blur too, thankfully. As the screaming in the back of the car reaches fever pitch, and the tyres crunch over the mucky stones in Maggie and Johno's driveway, Evelyn pulls the sleeves of her pink dress over the purple bruises on her arms.

31

Tara said she didn't want to risk anyone hearing what she had to say about a fight in 1983, so she shuffled me from the front of the house around to a narrow side lane that divides two cottages, where we stand now, both shivering.

She lights another cigarette and in the lane its orange tip moves wildly from left to right and up and down, reflecting her agitation.

'Remember, Lucy, I was only four. I remember bits and pieces, but so much of it is just snippets.'

'That's fine,' I say, trying to hide my impatience with her cloak-and-dagger attitude. This is typical. To the outside world Tara seems like the most timid of the Brown girls, but she's actually the family's biggest drama queen. She could start a crisis with only herself in the room. Mostly this is amusing but I am exhausted, and I have never been as aware of the passage of time as I am now. I just need her to get to the point.

'Well, for what it's worth – somehow, and I don't know how exactly – after Susannah nearly drowned on that holiday, we ended up getting friendly with the family of the man who saved her. Johno Fogarty. There were two kids in the family, about our ages – a girl, Kate or Kathy, or something like that, and a boy, Jack. I remember Jack more clearly than anything that holiday.'

Jack Fogarty.

She stops here, casting her eyes around herself as if he is about to emerge from the shadows. *Hurry the hell up*, I want to say, but don't.

'He was . . . weird. I just remember even at that age thinking he was really weird. One evening we went to his parents' house. I remember how fixated he was on Susannah. There was some incident between them and we suddenly had to leave. And when we got home, things turned physical.'

'Physical? Physical between who?'

Tara presses her lips tight together as though she's trying not to cry. She looks down at the ground and crushes out her cigarette with her shoe.

32

Dunmore East, April 1983

Maggie and Johno's house – small and built of brown brick – is adjacent to their farm. The windows are covered by net curtains. At the front door are discarded different-sized wellington boots, all covered in thick clumps of muck. Jack and Katie are first out of the front door, hopping up and down at the car windows, excited to see their two new friends.

Maggie follows close behind them, drying her hands on a tea towel.

Evelyn's heart sinks.

Maggie is also wearing a light pink dress but the colour brings out her dark features and she looks glowing and radiant. On her, Evelyn knows, the pink blends with her skin tone, making her look washed-out. Maggie opens the passenger-side door and greets Evelyn with a hug, like they're old friends. Apparently, she's decided it's her turn to make the effort today.

She rushes around to the other side of the car and wraps Patrick up in an even warmer hug. He hands her a basket of small gifts that Evelyn had put together from their kitchen.

'Oh my God, so thoughtful of you, Patrick! And this is the fancy stuff too, thank you very much.'

'Oh, it's nothing,' he says, delighted with the attention.

'Come in,' she says. 'Now, it's nothing like your place so don't be too disappointed. In fact, it's a pigsty compared to what you're used to. But I've made us a little table out the back, and the sun is shining again, so we'll take what we can get. Johno will be back in a while.'

Evelyn follows the group in, taking in the details of the house in much the same way as Maggie had done the evening before. It is rustic and homely. In the kitchen is a massive stone hearth with a black stove in the centre, and one long sooty pipe leading up out to the sky. In the middle of the room a sturdy and large farmhouse table is scattered with colouring crayons, toys and half-finished sandwiches. There is an air of happy chaos. She adores it.

Back in their semi-detached home, Patrick insists on everything being immaculate. Keeping the house clean is one of her most important jobs, as he sees it, and it's one which she resents ever more with every passing year. It is impossible to keep it clean with two small children, but God knows she tries. Maggie, on the other hand, clearly just embraces the madness. How liberating that must be.

Maggie leads them out a back door to a long, unkempt garden dotted with wildflowers. The field dips right down at the end, giving way to another field and beyond that, in the near distance, the blue vastness of the immeasurable sea.

'I love it,' Evelyn says. She means it sincerely.

'You don't have to lie, it's OK. It's a mess. It always smells like cow shit. The roof will cave in any day. Nothing works. But hey,' Maggie shrugs, pulling out plastic chairs for them from behind a long table covered in a red-and-white cloth, which looks brand new. There are four wine glasses laid out.

'This looks splendid, Maggie,' Patrick says, bestowing upon her his most charismatic smile, hand on the hip of his light blue chinos, tufts of black hair streaking out of his navy shirt.

'It's nothing,' she says, smoothing down her dress as if she were bashful.

Susannah starts tugging at Evelyn's arm, saying 'Mammy' repeatedly until she gets her attention.

'What is it?'

'Where's the man?'

'What man?'

'The man,' she repeats, annoyed.

'Do you mean Johno, Jack and Katie's dad?' Maggie says, fishing ice-pops out of a bowl of ice. She hands them out. Susannah nods.

'He'll be here later. He is milking the cows, and he'll be finished soon, OK?'

Susannah goes uncharacteristically quiet and looks thoughtful for a moment. Then, without another word, she tears off down towards the end of the garden shouting at the others, 'Last one to the end is a poop!' Susannah, since very early on, has shown she has her father's sense of self-belief and feels she has all the best ideas. Evelyn hopes her confidence will last.

The adults laugh and Maggie pours the wine, making sure to start with Patrick's glass, which she fills right to the top.

Even though Johno is a man of few words, the dynamic is different without him. Evelyn feels cut out of the conversations between her husband and Maggie. After going inside to use the bathroom, she finds herself sitting at the kitchen table watching Katie and Tara drawing. She helps them sort through the crayons to find the pink ones. Jack comes in with a bloodied knee and says his mammy said to show her where the plasters are kept. Susannah is behind him, hopping from one foot to the other. Once he's fixed up, the two of them race outside again. As Evelyn watches the girls draw their pictures, she feels more like a babysitter than a guest. Katie presents her with a page, blue eyes wide in anticipation of approval. Evelyn runs a hand through her curls and holds up the drawing with her other hand. For the work of a four-year-old, it's surprisingly good. It's a drawing of her family – Mammy, Daddy, Jack and Katie. When Evelyn tells her how fantastic it is, she beams. Her shyness and pride melt

Evelyn's heart and she scoops her in for a hug, to an angry glare from Tara.

After twenty minutes or so, the two girls get bored and run back outside to play. Evelyn returns to Patrick and Maggie. An empty bottle of white wine and a freshly opened bottle of red sit in front of them.

'It's an interesting proposition, and I'm not just saying that. You'd make an excellent manager. You have leadership qualities, I can see that,' Patrick declares, taking a big gulp of the wine.

'What's an interesting proposition?' Evelyn asks. She tries not to act put out, but the way Patrick acts around Maggie is getting under her skin. He opens his mouth to answer but a screech from the end of the garden stops him.

The four children run as fast as their small legs will take them.

'*Maaaaaammmmmmmy!*'

Surprisingly, it is Susannah howling and not her younger sister.

'Jack said he's going to kill me!'

'It was a joke!' Jack says, looking like a small drunk indignant man. Tara and Katie are on the verge of tears.

Maggie throws her eyes to heaven, and pours another glass of red.

'One more hour of play, and then: bedtime,' she says. This sends the kids running in the opposite direction, the intended effect. Still, though Evelyn knows they're just kids, Jack's words give her an uneasy feeling. Why would a little boy be talking about killing anyone? He looked more angry than ashamed when Susannah told on him. She wishes Maggie had explained that it wasn't a kind thing to say and had encouraged him to say sorry to Susannah.

After a while, Tara returns to the adults' table and sidles in beside her mother.

'What is it, sweetheart?' Evelyn says.

'Susannah won't play with me. Everyone is leaving me out of the game.'

Evelyn often worries about how sensitive Tara is and thinks she will have a job on her hands to toughen her up as she gets older. She brings her inside to choose a book and then settles her into a chair at the table outside.

An hour later the kitchen is bathed in light from the sunset outside, as well as from a few mismatched lamps. Evelyn pulls up her sleeves and begins scrubbing the dinner plates. She is annoyed. She can't help it. Johno hadn't turned up by half seven and Maggie said there was no point waiting, she'd put something away for him. Over dinner Patrick and Maggie kept talking about business and the economy and made no effort to include her in the conversation. It seemed she was there to divide out the children's sausages and chips and make sure they all got enough.

She shakes one of the plates aggressively and it slips out of her hands and crashes back into the sink, breaking cleanly in two.

'Let me help you with that,' comes Johno's deep voice as his arm reaches around her into the sink to remove the broken plate. She freezes. She hadn't heard him come up behind her.

For a moment, they just stand there, neither of them moving or speaking. With wet hands, Evelyn pulls down her sleeves. She can feel herself blushing as she turns towards him.

He wears a flannel shirt and filthy overalls. His broad forehead is both tanned and burnt red and is creased into a frown. His light blue eyes had been fixed on Evelyn's upper arms.

He crosses the kitchen to a bin but his smell – sweat and graft, not unpleasant – lingers. She closes her eyes, feeling embarrassed and scared. And secretly, in her heart, excited.

He returns and stands next to her at the counter and folds his arms.

She has a sudden image of straddling him on the kitchen floor and she feels a lurch deep inside her.

'Where did you get those bruises?'

'The kids are very rough.'

'No, they aren't,' he says.

She knows he is looking at her, but she can't look at him.

'You'd be surprised,' she says.

If she looks back, he might be able to see her thoughts – of lifting her dress off over her head, of pulling off his shirt, of kissing his neck and what his skin would feel like under her lips.

She turns back to the sink and starts washing the cutlery vigorously. Surely he will walk away now, leave her alone, alone with the thoughts of slowly removing her bra as she sits astride him, and leaning over to kiss him.

'*He* does it to you,' he says.

She doesn't want to lie but she can't tell the truth. So, she says nothing – scrubs, scrubs, scrubs and thinks of taking him in her mouth, and of the sound that he might make. She feels wet, and she knows she needs to stop right now, tell him everything is fine and go out and join the others.

'Evelyn,' he says.

And then he is inside her and it's all she can do not to scream out loud at the thought of it. The physicality of him. It's too much.

Another voice. Maggie.

'There you are, you're late.'

The spell is broken.

'What took you so long, Johno? I'm wrecked here with the kids running around; hosting people is hard on your own. I left you some dinner in the oven. Come on outside and talk to Patrick. You OK, Evelyn?'

Evelyn spins around, dishcloth in hand, and puts on her game face.

'I'm so sorry, I broke one of your plates. I didn't realize my own strength. I'll follow you both out, just going to run to the loo.'

Evelyn steps over kids' books and piles of toys and makes her way up the stairs to the spartan bathroom, where she thinks of Johno until she comes.

When she opens the bathroom door, Patrick is standing right outside, a murderous look on his face.

'We're leaving.'

33

I leave Tara down the lane to chain-smoke her demons away. Except her demons are now mine too. I need a moment, to absorb what she's told me and figure out what to do next. There is only one place I can sit alone in silence. I take the car keys Susannah left on the small table by the front door and go out to her car. I point and press the fob to unlock it, before remembering it was open when I checked earlier. I sit in the driver's seat and a trace of the scent she always wears makes me unutterably sad. I look to my phone for a message from her – but of course there's nothing. I didn't really expect there to be.

Instead, there are loads of missed call notifications, and a blizzard of messages from Tim. The most recent reads: 'I know your sister is trying to turn you against me. Your choice if you listen. May have to reconsider the rent arrangement, FYI. Maybe we can avoid. Call me ASAP.'

The bastard!

'I am leaving that hole!' I type. 'I don't want to hear from you ever again! Go fuck yourself!'

I'm surprised the phone doesn't combust, such is my venom as I type. I block Tim on everything. I feel euphoric. As if I have a new clarity about what's really important.

I turn to thinking about this terrible fight in 1983 that Tara described. Somehow, I always thought about our family having a 'before', when things were picture-book perfect, and an 'after' when they turned to shit. And a part of me has always believed that it was the 'oops' late arrival who was neuro-atypical and cried a lot and needed so much attention that changed everything.

I thought that with all my needs and demands I was the biggest burden in this family. And that I drove Dad away. He never showed up to my medical appointments as a kid or took much interest in my condition. When we were younger, he would put in an appearance for birthdays and Christmas, big occasions. But that was it. I've always felt there's a hole in my life where he should be.

And though I grew up in a home that was calm and supportive, especially when it was just me and Mum, with Tara and Susannah dropping in at weekends or coming for short stays, a part of me sensed that this was a remnant family, not the *proper* original family. Then came the icing on the cake – I managed to get myself attacked in New York, which devastated Mum and seems to have been why Tara and Susannah fell out for good.

Still, when I got the stitches out back in Dublin, Tara and Susannah put their fight on the back-burner. They were both there with Mum to support me that day. As I lay on the table, the nurse who pulled the long threads out of my chest and neck asked what the matter was, because tears were streaming down the sides of my face and ricocheting off the floor.

'They will be just like wrinkles one day,' she said. I think she was trying to be kind.

Though I had let him know, Dad didn't show up. By then he was working with the British Irish Commerce Association, advocating for businesses like his that had closed. He was also settled down with his new wife Nina, an Australian he'd met in London, and their toddler daughter. Him not turning up hurt more than getting all the stitches pulled out of my body.

Years later, after my meltdown in Finglas, I called him to tell him about it. I don't know why, but I gave him graphic details I didn't share, and still haven't, with Mum, Susannah or Tara. I guess I was looking to jolt him into a show of sympathy. Instead, he said, 'Well, I did warn you. You were never cut out for that job, Lucy. You should find yourself an easier job, look for a nice fella and settle down.' I hung up. He didn't try to ring me back.

All these years, I thought it was all my fault. Especially because he seemed to maintain a great relationship with Tara. And I have to admit I have always held that slightly against Tara and erred towards judging her and siding with Susannah because, like me, Susannah has a terrible relationship with him.

But Tara has blown the story I've been telling myself out of the water. Though her memories were fragmentary, she has painted a picture which tells me that this family was not particularly happy back then. The opposite, in fact. As she talked, I could feel my body reliving my two sisters' sense of dread that night, and I could feel every bit of their fear.

Tara told me how Susannah let her share the top bunk even though she wouldn't let her up any other night on the holiday. Susannah had wrapped an arm around Tara and told her everything would be fine, just as she always did when things got bad. This final throwaway comment was what really got me – *just as she always did when things got bad between Mum and Dad.*

This family lived a life before me. And now, I am starting to wonder if it was what happened in *that* life, all those secrets, that tore this family apart.

Not me.

Just as I begin to see myself and *my* life in a different light, I see my two sisters differently too. I don't know what came before me.

I'm not sure how long I sit in a slightly dazed state when there's a tap on the passenger-door window. I click the button to open it and David gets in, tears streaking down his face, his hand on his neck as though he can't breathe.

'He's killed her!'

'What?'

He's gasping for breath and can't speak.

Susannah is dead?

Other than the garda at the front door, I see no police, no activity. This doesn't make sense. I tell David to calm down, to breathe, but he just waves his phone in my face.

'Look at what I've found.'

He's breathless, his chest rising fast, his brown eyes wired. He hands me his phone, the screen open on something.

'It's an email from Jack Fogarty. Read it. He's killed her.'

All his intense energy radiates into my bones.

'Slow down, slow down!'

At first glance, what's on the screen seems to be an email from Jack Fogarty to Susannah, to both her work and personal accounts – it seems he doesn't care what David will make of it. It was sent yesterday afternoon, an hour after she and I sat outside the Strand Hotel drinking rosé.

'I saw you. I warned you before. You better get the fuck out of here.'

I recall the shocked expression crossing her face, and her sense of urgency about getting away from the hotel.

So, it was Jack Fogarty she saw outside the Strand and – and this seems like definitive proof – it was indeed he who threatened her at the door last night.

The bravado in Susannah's response astonishes me. 'I think you'll find that your threats won't work on me anymore.'

I only hope Fogarty hasn't decided to teach her a lesson.

34

Dunmore East, April 1983

It took just seven words to turn a bad situation worse.

I wonder where she got that from, Evelyn had muttered darkly after their hasty exit from the Fogartys' house the previous evening. She thought she had said it quietly. She thought wrong.

The car journey back to the cottage was filled with a simmering silence. She knew she would regret what she had said. When they got in, they sat Susannah and Tara down on the couch and asked them what happened.

Back in Johno's house, when Evelyn had opened the bathroom door, shame written all over her face, she thought that somehow her husband had read her mind and that the jig was up.

What she had not expected was for him to say: 'We're leaving. Susannah punched Jack . . . in the balls. In the balls, Evelyn! Repeatedly, he says. What kind of children are you raising? I've never been more ashamed in my life.'

As he stormed off down the stairs, she noticed the damp patch between his shoulder blades and got a strong whiff of stale sweat and red wine.

She had not thought him fit to drive home but said nothing. The journey was laced with white-knuckle tension.

In the cottage, Patrick said he wanted answers.

'He was being mean to me, and then he was mean to Tara,' Susannah said boldly.

'Is that true, Tara?' Evelyn had asked.

Tara's bottom lip started wobbling; fat tears rolled down her face. Patrick was standing by the stairs, his eyes black and narrowed.

'Just tell me what happened, and everything will be OK. Come on, girls. Tell your mammy.'

There was silence as both sisters gave each other the side-eye.

'Speak up or we're all going home tomorrow, and that's that,' Evelyn said as the silence stretched.

Tara pulled at a thread in her grey tights and began speaking in a whisper.

'Tara, speak up! We don't have all bloody night,' Patrick said, his fists balled up by his sides.

'I said . . . Jack pulled down his pants and showed me his . . . his . . . his . . .'

She motioned to her crotch.

There was a beat where time stood still before all hell broke loose. Patrick was suddenly upon them all, shouting into Susannah's face, demanding to know what happened, if this was true, if her sister was lying, what exactly happened, where it happened, *Did he touch you? Did he make you touch him?* And on, and on.

People out walking their dogs on the beach can probably hear him shouting, Evelyn thought.

Tara was crying so hard that she began to retch. She ran into Evelyn's arms but Patrick pulled her away again and ordered both girls up the stairs. They did as they were told.

Then he grabbed Evelyn by the collar and slammed her, face-first, against the front door. When she looked over her shoulder, she could see his teeth were bared. His eyes were dead. He then grabbed her by the arm, opened the door, threw her onto the front step and slammed the door shut in her face.

'Go and talk to those paedophiles and sort this out before I properly lose it,' he shouted through the door.

Evelyn sat outside at the patio table, unmoving. The hairs on her arms stood up. It was cold.

Much later in the night, Susannah snuck her out a glass of water and a chocolate animal bar. She lingered beside Evelyn waiting for a response. Though she was still petrified by shock, with a supreme effort of will Evelyn gave Susannah a one-armed hug and said, 'Where would I be without you?' She knew she sounded robotic. It was the best she could do. When Susannah went back inside Evelyn could hear that she left the door unlocked.

When the sky was brightening, and only the sea dared to lap gently on the shore, as if it were saying sorry over and over again, Evelyn headed inside and settled on the couch. She didn't cry.

She told herself in those small hours, *He has never hit me. He has only grabbed me in frustration.*

He adores the children.

It's hard for him. He is under stress. The economy is going down the tubes. He needs to let off steam.

I need to be strong for my daughters.

I will be strong.

Evelyn awakes to a kiss on her temple and the waft of freshly brewed coffee. She had fallen asleep on the couch, and it takes her a moment to remember where she is and why.

'Can't believe it's Thursday already,' Patrick says cheerily from the kitchen. He looks striking in a crisp black shirt. His skin is smooth and tan. He looks well rested. She hears the pop of the toaster and her stomach rumbles at the smell.

He brings her a plate of toast slathered in butter, the excess dripping all over the plate, with two boiled eggs.

'They should be the way you like them. You were really passed out there. Hmm . . . you don't look so great. You'll have to tidy yourself up for tonight, Evelyn. Maybe take a bit of time to yourself this afternoon. I'll bring the girls to the beach.'

With a mouth half-full of toast, she asks, 'What's tonight?'

'The gig. Session. Whatever they call it around these parts.'

Patrick is at the bottom of the stairs shouting at the girls to come down. They have clearly been waiting because seconds later they are down the stairs and hanging out of him, shouting with glee, still in yesterday's clothes.

'Maggie's gig, Evelyn. For God's sake, sharpen up. She's singing at an open mic or something, up there in the Spinning Wheel. You told her we would go. Why, I can't imagine, but we won't argue over it. They'll have to do something about that boy of theirs, though, I won't be letting that go. You'll have to have a word.'

Evelyn hopes it won't have to come to that. The whole thing, she's sure, was overblown. Kids are curious, she thinks – it's normal.

With great exaggeration, he drags his legs – one daughter hanging on to each – into the kitchen as if he is trying to escape them but is not strong enough. They cackle with laughter.

The resilience of children.

Had she? Had she told Maggie she would go to this gig?

Evelyn has a vague memory of Maggie shouting something about her singing as they sped off out the gate, but had she even had a moment to say yes?

Her own mother always told her never to look a gift horse in the mouth and so she drops it and busies herself with the girls' breakfast, completely forgetting about her own.

Evelyn is going all-out tonight. Hair spray. Lipstick. Eyeliner. Heels. Perfume. What she wants more than anything else is to feel good about herself, to feel valued. But most especially, she wants to feel desired. Because something has shifted inside her. Evelyn cannot believe the dreams she had in the small hours of the morning, that her mind is capable of conjuring such things.

In one dream, Johno slammed her against a wall, but not in the way Patrick might do. It was charged with longing. He had dropped to his knees and when she remembered what happened next, she felt that same lurching feeling somewhere low down. That was when Patrick had woken her on the couch.

And somehow, she does not feel guilty. Her entire life is a litany of guilt, so she refuses to feel bad about thoughts over which she has no control. As she applies another layer of lipstick she feels relieved that she saw Maggie earlier, so there shouldn't be any awkwardness over last night. Maggie had appeared unannounced at the front door of the cottage, two shamefaced children holding her two hands.

'What do you have to say to Susannah and Tara, Jack?'

He mumbled something into the side of his mother's leg, before being told to speak louder.

'I'm sorry. I was only joking. I'm sorry.' Then he started crying.

Evelyn thought it should have been her daughter who was apologizing. Violence was never the answer, and the kids were just being kids. Then she heard her words from last night. *I wonder where she got that from?* Not wanting to go any deeper down that particular rabbit hole, she accepted the child's apology and told Maggie that yes, of course, they would still be going tonight, and no, not to worry, there were no issues whatsoever between the kids.

If Evelyn worried about going over the top, she need not have fretted because Maggie has thrown the kitchen sink at it. Her curls are tamed into a sensual sheath of black silk. Her smoky eye makes Evelyn's purple eyeshadow-black eyeliner combo look like a juvenile attempt at a gothic look. Maggie wears a short plunging black cowl-neck dress. Beside her in a white frilly top and white jeans, Evelyn feels like a fussy poodle next to a slinky fox.

Still, three vodka and tonics in, she is starting to care less and less.

Evelyn, Patrick and Maggie are sat around a small circular table in the middle of the packed pub. They are enveloped in a cloud of smoke, Maggie making it her business to add to it by smoking one cigarette after the other. She is also throwing back handfuls of peanuts from a bowl in the middle of the table.

Johno is at the bar, where he has been since they arrived. He's talking to the owner who stands with arms folded over his belly, laughing heartily. Evelyn tries not to look at him, but she finds herself wondering if he is looking at her. Every time she stands up to get a round in, Patrick stops her and tells her to sit down, making sure to go to the bar himself and order the drinks without so much as a 'hello' for Johno. Some sort of stalemate has been reached between the two men.

'You're not still worried about the stupid stuff with the kids, are you?' Maggie asks, throwing an eye over her shoulder at the makeshift stage to see if it's her turn.

'What? No, no, no. Not at all,' Evelyn says.

'OK. It's just that you have a distracted look in your eye. I'm just saying it's natural for kids to be curious about each other like that. How else do they learn?'

Patrick clears his throat gruffly, which is his signal that the topic is closed, and he doesn't want to hear another word about it.

Of course, Maggie is impervious. 'Claire will keep a close eye on them – that woman should have been a nun.'

Maggie's neighbour Claire has the unenviable task of babysitting four children who had to be bribed with a load of sweets to let their parents out the door without going into meltdown.

Luckily, before Evelyn has to say anything a skinny teenager squeezes between the tables to tap Maggie on the shoulder. It is her turn.

As she makes her way to the stage, Maggie appears to be swaying her hips deliberately from side to side, flicking her glossy mane over her shoulder. She is like a pop star making her way to her rightful place under the spotlight.

Whatever Evelyn was expecting, it is not what comes out of Maggie's mouth. It's a raspy, deep, soulful wail. The hairs on Evelyn's arms stand on end. Maggie sings with abandon, her head thrown back, belting it out. Removing the mic from its stand and stepping off the stage, still singing, she makes her way around the room, stopping here and there to perform a line for a table, touching some people on the shoulder or arm.

Every person in the room has stopped talking, stopped drinking, stopped thinking. Maggie walks up to the bar and stops in front of Johno. He stands very still, pint in hand. She sings a lyric, asking him who is he loving, who is he fooling?

Johno takes a sip of Guinness as every man regards him with unreserved envy. He is inscrutable.

Maggie, unfazed by Johno being unfazed, makes her way back to the stage and delivers the final line of the song, as the pub rises as one to its feet.

Evelyn cannot even find it within herself to be jealous. To have such a talent is just awe-inspiring, and she tells Maggie as much when she returns to the table, cheeks flushed, drinks pouring in from men all over the bar, their wives and girlfriends none too impressed. Maggie is like a local celebrity. Even Patrick – usually averse to 'vulgar' displays, as he would regard an earthy performance like Maggie's – is laying it on thick.

'Is Johno going to join us?' Evelyn says suddenly, the drink loosening her up. The question has been on the tip of her tongue all night.

'What did you say?' Maggie shouts over the hubbub.

'Nothing,' Evelyn says, raising her glass to take a swig. But the glass is empty and five vodkas in, Evelyn realizes she is quite drunk.

Patrick leans towards Maggie to shout into her ear. While they're distracted Evelyn leaves the table, as if heading to the ladies' room, but instead she circles the edge of the crowded bar until she gets close to it.

Her heart sinks as she glimpses Johno's shoulder slip out the front door. On an impulse, she follows him.

The weather has turned cooler and there's a thick fog hanging in the air when she steps outside. It's pitch black. The orange streetlights are lit, though. They aren't far from the beach, and she can hear its rhythmic push and pull. There's a gloom over Dunmore East. She casts her eyes around for Johno. He literally just left ahead of her, but with the poor visibility she can't see him. She follows a shuffling sound until she finds herself at the slipway down onto the beach. The tide is halfway in.

She walks down the slope tentatively, wobbly in her high heels, the vodkas not helping. The mist and fog cling to her hair and leave a fine sheen on her skin. She hears the click of a lighter and sees Johno leaning in against the high beach wall. He's watching her and she feels self-conscious under his gaze.

As she walks towards him, she asks herself: *What exactly is it I want here? What am I doing?*

'What are you doing here, Evelyn?' he says, reading her mind.

'You're avoiding me. I mean us.'

She wants it to be teasing, but it comes out as an accusation. She never was a good flirt. Never had any practice.

She stands next to him, side by side, following his gaze out to the Hook Head lighthouse. The lights are warning them to go no further. Keep the ship far away. Her shoulder just about grazes his. A tiny current runs down her back, into her legs, into her feet, into the sand beneath her. He doesn't respond.

'Why are you avoiding me? You haven't said hello all night.'

'I'm not avoiding you.'

'Yes, you are.'

'No, I am not.'

'Then what's the matter?'

A moment passes.

'Him,' he says.

'Who?'

'Him.'

'Patrick?'

Johno steps in front of her. She goes to take a step backwards but is already up against the wall.

'Yes, him. How am I supposed to sit next to that man knowing what he does to you? I can't bear it.'

'It's not as bad as it looks, honestly. It's just a bit of grabbing. He has never, not once, hit me. That's the truth, I swear.'

Johno gives her a withering look. So his tone, when he speaks, surprises her in its softness.

'It's your life, Evelyn. I'm not trying to interfere. Sure, I don't even know you, like. And I'm not trying to be out of line here. But you're a good person. I dunno – I feel like . . . like you deserve better. A woman deserves better.'

What do those words mean? Is it a compliment? A come-on? Pity?

He sighs deeply and walks off towards the far end of the beach, which is dark, and at its furthest part even darker under the shadow of overhanging trees. Evelyn's heels have slipped all the way down into the watery sand and she takes them off and follows him in her bare feet.

When they get as far as they can go, he says: 'Sorry. It's not my business.'

Evelyn puts a hand on his shoulder and has a visceral flashback to one of her more unspeakable dreams. She wants to say something but no words come. He's leaning against the high sea wall, his eyes blazing even in the dark. It's a different kind of anger that he has. A virtuous kind. An unbearably attractive kind.

Evelyn throws her shoes up on a ledge and puts her second hand on his other shoulder. He looks more furious than ever but does not stop her – that's when she knows that he has felt it too.

I'm not going to do this all by myself, she thinks.

You shouldn't be doing anything at all, her conscience replies.

He puts his hand around the soft nape of her neck and brings her mouth to his. She feels like a cup being filled up with lust and craving. It's expansive, overwhelming, unthinkably intense. Just as she thinks she can't bear the pain or pleasure of it anymore, he pushes her off.

'Shouldn't have done that. Jesus . . . too many beers.'

He makes off into the gloom back towards the slipway, and she can barely believe her ears.

'You what?'

He turns on the spot and spits the words out at her. 'I. Am. Married. I know Maggie . . . she does go on, I know. Jesus, I know. But I do love her. We have children. We made a vow. Life is not perfect but there's no way I'm doing this. This is just madness.'

For the second time in twenty-four hours, she is petrified by shock.

'Tell them I've gone home. Maggie can get a lift with Claire and the kids from yours when she's ready.'

He goes to leave again but thinks better of it, and comes back to where she is standing, mouth agape.

'I'm sorry. If you ever need me, I promise to be a friend. But this . . . this I cannot do.'

Then he walks up to the road, starts his car and drives into the night.

Evelyn stands stock-still, the freezing water surging past her ankles, like she's no more than a piece of flotsam.

Back inside the pub, in an unlit storeroom, Patrick Brown hikes Maggie Fogarty's dress up around her waist and they fuck for exactly two minutes.

35

David is hunched over in a bizarre way. I realize he is probably starting to have a panic attack, and I wonder how I can stop his panic from taking me over too. I feel it closing in.

My sister could be dead. She really could be.

My hands begin to tremble, and tears spill down my face. We've let her down. I've let her down, getting lost in my own thoughts, my feelings about my life, my world, this family. He was right there in front of us all, and we've been wasting time interrogating each other. I just want to shake myself, and for a moment I struggle to get it together.

I need to snap out of it. I make a decision to focus on each small moment, each small action, and I hope that will be enough.

Now we have evidence they must look for Jack Fogarty. How can they not?

'Where's Inspector Menton?' I say.

'In Susannah's bedroom talking to Evelyn,' David says, his breathing ragged.

I close my eyes and try to block out his anxiety. It is so, so hard.

'Let's go,' I say.

We walk past the bouncer garda, and into the house. I stoop my head down as we make our way up the stairs.

Reaching the landing, I see the door of Susannah's room is ajar. I hear my mother crying. The sound stops me in my tracks. Then I hear Menton.

'Mrs Brown, please, take a breath. I need you to tell me exactly what happened in April 1983. I need to know what I am dealing with when it comes to Detective Fogarty. Time may be running out for your daughter. Tell me exactly what you know.'

David comes up behind me at the top step of the stairs. I glance over my shoulder. He's irritated that I'm blocking his way. I can see he's about to protest so I put a forefinger to my lips and shake my head. The universal language of *Shut the hell up!*

36

Dunmore East, April 1983

Evelyn has tried to outrun her guilt all morning, but she has failed. She awoke with a start around five-thirty, well before sunrise. Staring into the gloom of the bedroom, anxious and jittery, she could almost feel the last of the vodka leaving her bloodstream. Her mouth and lips were parched, her head was thumping, and she could see an aura in her peripheral vision. A migraine.

Everything about the end of the night was blurry. Stumbling home with Maggie, who chattered all the way. She couldn't remember a word she had said. Paying the babysitter and getting Maggie and her kids out of the house. Clumsily bashing into the girls' room to check on them. Then when everyone was gone, she crashed.

When she woke, Patrick's face was mashed into the pillow, a line of drool spilling from the corner of his mouth. She had never seen him as drunk as he was last night. By the time she made it back to the bar, he was slurring his words and being embarrassingly rude to Maggie Fogarty. Evelyn thought, earlier that morning, how typical it was – he could turn on a dime and after a few days of being buttered up, now poor Maggie got to see his dark side. Then she had pictured the swing of Maggie's hips as she took to the stage last night, and saw her serenading Johno at the bar, and her sympathy dissipated.

Patrick was so drunk last night that he hadn't even noticed Evelyn's absence. Normally he would get agitated if she was gone for even five minutes. That was the interesting thing about Patrick – he acted like the independent breadwinner but he seemed reliant on her presence. Even if it was just to have someone to control. He liked to keep an eye on her.

For good reason, she thought.

Would she have done it? Would she have done more than kiss Johno? How far would she have let it go?

The answer was clear but when she got near it, the guilt and shame rose up with such force that she thought she might either burst into tears or vomit. Evelyn had never known such despair, not in her worst fights with Patrick, not on her most tetchy days as a mother.

She would have done it.

And if she got the chance, she would still do it.

This was a new kind of horror – facing the reality that she was not the good woman she believed herself to be. Not the perfect wife, not the best mother, no angel. There was only one thing for it – stay away from the Fogartys.

It's hard to believe they've been in Dunmore East for nearly a week. Since Susannah's near drowning on Monday, it's been as if she's trapped in a fever dream. A dream that culminated in her chasing a local farmer on a beach in the middle of the night. What sort of insanity had taken hold of her?

She had turfed the girls out of bed at eight and marched them down to the beach. They had been up far later than usual and were cranky. Evelyn realized how out of it she still was when Tara started crying quietly, 'I'm hungry, Mammy.'

Breakfast! She had forgotten about breakfast. Great. Another thing to feel shit about. And had they even had a proper dinner last night? How distracted had she been?

Evelyn hugged Tara and Susannah in turn, and said she was very sorry, and she was a bad mammy, and they'd go home now and have a lovely big breakfast, and then maybe a treat. Back in the cottage, she made scrambled eggs, sausages and toast and afterwards gave the girls an Easter egg she had been saving since the weekend. She settled them in front of the huge box TV to watch *Bosco*. The high-pitched squeak of the puppet drilled through her aching head as she cleaned up.

Patrick remained in bed, which was extremely unlike him. Evelyn scrubbed the dirty plates and wondered what it would feel like to be able to do that to her own conscience.

Evelyn just needs to salvage this last full day of the holiday, go home tomorrow and steady herself. Release herself from the madness. Go to church. Make her confession. Take her punishment.

There was no use telling Patrick anything. Nothing happened – well, nothing beyond a drunken kiss – and he would only explode in a rage. As for her mother or brother, she couldn't say anything to them either. Margaret once told Evelyn she would have two roles in life – wife first and mother second – and that the three greatest virtues were dignity, service and loyalty. And while she and Adam were close, she couldn't bear him thinking badly of her.

Looking out the kitchen window, she pictured herself diving into the sea, sinking all the way to the bottom, staying there forever, cleansed of her sins, stripped of her shame, returned to the elements whence she came.

A sharp rap on the door wrenches her back to reality. She glances at the clock: 10:50 a.m.

Drying her hands with a tea towel, she opens the latch of the door and pulls it open. Johno. The lack of expression across his features makes him appear impassive, even vaguely annoyed.

'Oh, hi,' Evelyn says, suddenly aware that she looks like a dog's dinner in her faded black tracksuit. There are grease stains on her t-shirt from the fry-up. The mascara from last night is smudged under both eyes. Her teeth are unbrushed.

'Well,' he says, as if it is she who has turned up at his door.

Evelyn has no idea what he expects her to say. In the few seconds of waiting, she manages to notice the smoothness of the dark skin on his arms, the muscles under his brown jumper, the deep lines on his forehead, how very blue his eyes are.

She clears her throat. 'Umm, everything OK?'

He also clears his throat.

'Yeah. Maggie sent me. She wants to say thank you for last night.'

'No problem. Is that all? Do you want to come in?'

'No!' he says, with something approaching alarm on his face.

'Sorry,' he says. 'No, thanks. She was wondering if you want to join her and the kids for a picnic in the park by the cliffs. There's a playground.'

'Now?'

'No. Four o'clock.'

'Are you going to be there? Don't you have to work?'

He appears to be struggling with something. Then Evelyn realizes why. He does not want to go. And he does not want this picnic to happen. But it seems Maggie's force of personality has won the day again so he has no choice.

'Thanks, but we can't. We're going to Tramore.'

From the couch, Susannah pipes up – in her loudest, bossiest voice – 'That's a lie! We are not going to Tramore. Daddy said last night we could go on the swings today. I want the swings, Mammy!'

Evelyn turns back to look at Johno. The corners of his mouth are twitching.

'I'll be there,' he says, adding, 'You leave tomorrow, don't you? Sure, we couldn't let you go without saying goodbye. See you at four.'

And with that he turns, hops into his dusty car and takes off up the road. As she watches the car, the swell of emotion in Evelyn's chest feels like pure joy.

As she comes back into the kitchen, Susannah says, 'Why are you smiling like that, Mammy?'

'Never you mind.'

Tara, who has been watching carefully, says softly, 'I don't want them to come. I don't want to see Katie and Jack.'

Evelyn ignores her and floats back into the kitchen, the day suddenly brighter.

As ever with the girls, they run late. As the day wore on, Tara became more worked up, hanging out of Evelyn's sleeve, telling her that Jack doesn't like girls and Katie leaves her out. Susannah was unimpressed. 'Stop being such a cry-baby,' she told Tara. It is her command that the excursion go ahead. Susannah's forcefulness even won over her bleary-eyed father, who seemed to Evelyn to be too tired and distracted to protest against the plan, which was unlike him.

In the end, Evelyn had to resort to bribery again. She told Tara that if she went for just one hour, when they got home she would give her three of the fancy chocolates that were supposed to be for Daddy only. Evelyn was pretty sure there was whiskey in those chocolates but by then she no longer cared. Because tomorrow means a return to normal life and before then she wants to see Johno one last time. Just to say goodbye. Just to put a lid on this thing and then put it away forever.

Arriving at the park, Evelyn spots them immediately. Maggie is lying on a large tartan blanket. Jack and Katie are sitting next to her.

Katie screams when she sees them: 'They're here!' She is up within seconds, tottering over to Susannah, whom she idolizes. She starts chattering away about finding three spiders in the shed earlier that day. 'One of them was bigger than Daddy's hand,' she shrieks.

Tara clings to her mother's leg, eyeing the two girls with jealousy.

Jack watches them all with interest.

There is no sign of Johno. Evelyn feels like she has been kicked in the stomach. Had he been lying earlier? Playing with her emotions?

'Patrick, Evelyn! That was some night, huh?' Maggie says, dusting crumbs off her shorts. How is it that she can make basic khaki shorts and a white vest top look so good, Evelyn wonders.

Once crumb-free, she launches herself at Patrick with full force. For just a second, Evelyn sees her husband flinch. Evelyn thinks she should have warned Maggie about this: he is not great with over-the-top public displays of affection. Maggie then grabs Evelyn in a half-hearted one-armed hug.

'Come, sit, sit. Now I know the last thing anyone wants to do after last night is drink. But you know what they say, hair of the dog that bit ya. I brought cider. A local guy makes it and gives me free crates. Help yourself,' she says, motioning to a cooler box.

'Sure, one for the road,' Patrick says, lowering himself onto the blanket.

'Tara and Susannah, stay where I can see you,' he says.

The two girls tear off in the direction of the swings, followed closely by Jack and Katie, leaving the adults alone.

Evelyn sits awkwardly on the edge of the blanket, not wanting to take up too much space. She fans out her blue maxi-dress and pretends to be unbothered by Johno's absence. She is not going to ask where he is.

'How was the head today, Patrick?' Maggie asks, popping open a bottle of cider and resting the icy bottle against her tan leg.

Evelyn sees that Maggie has once again tamed her curls into soft ribbons. She looks fresh as a daisy, her eyes bright, her attitude relaxed. She leans back on her elbows and throws one leg over the other.

Patrick cracks open a cider.

'Ah, not too bad. Better not have too many of these, though. We can't hang around, we'll have to get ourselves sorted for the drive home tomorrow. Evelyn was meant to start the packing this morning, but' – he prods Evelyn with his foot – 'I'm guessing the hangover got in the way.'

'Hmmm,' is all Evelyn can manage. She pulls down her sunglasses over her eyes, training her darkened gaze on the kids.

'Ah, don't ye be rushing off now. Look how happy they are. The best of pals. They'll miss the girls. Especially Jack. He's taken a right shine to your Susannah.'

Maybe it is in Evelyn's head, but an awkward silence seems to descend. The park is surrounded by a line of tall Monterey pines and through the leaves Evelyn can see the vast sea glistening in the sunlight. In her awkwardness, she looks anywhere except at Maggie and Patrick. She scans the perimeter, noticing exits dotted here and there.

'What are down those steps over there?' she asks Maggie.

'Oh, they all lead down to different coves. On the left is Kittiwake's Rock. Further to the right is Badger's Cove. The steps are steep but when you get down it is so beautiful; there are rocks where you can climb all the way down and sunbathe right by the water. Little inlets where you can get up to bad deeds. Oh, there he is! Johno! Over here.'

Evelyn feels her pulse quicken. *Bad deeds* indeed. She turns herself around in the direction Maggie is looking. When she sees him lurching towards them, his hands pushed deep into his pockets, smudges of dirt on the knees of his trousers, she is overcome with a mix of shame, lust, longing and simple affection.

'Well,' he says when he reaches them, idling at the other edge of the blanket. Evelyn keeps her eyes averted, focusing again on the children, who are squabbling loudly about whose turn it is on the slide.

'I'll go and check on them,' Johno says, making his way to the small playground. Evelyn remembers realizing that he'd been railroaded into this outing, and has an urge to throw herself through the trees and off the cliff. Patrick and Maggie begin chatting about clothes or fabrics or something that Evelyn is not interested in. She reaches into the cooler, removes a bottle of cider, opens it and downs half in one go.

Briefly, she glances in Patrick's direction and can see he's been looking over at her, waiting to catch her eye. He shoots her a warning look.

After half an hour, the kids get bored of the playground and are back at the picnic blanket. Evelyn is on her second bottle of cider. As Patrick sips his he continues to watch her carefully.

'Daddy, Daddy, Daddy,' Susannah calls.

'What is it, Susannah?'

'Jack said there is a secret cave down there,' she says, pointing towards one of the small gates at the end of the sloping hill where they sit. The sea waits just beyond.

'Can we go? Can we go? Daddy, can we go?'

'Absolutely not. Too dangerous,' Patrick says.

'It's not actually. I pointed them out earlier, remember? That's the entrance to Kittiwake's Rock right there, which is a nice gentle slope down towards the sea, and then that's the entrance to Badger's Cove, further along the path there, which has a lot more steps,' Maggie says, pointing to a gate in the distance.

'You must see Kittiwake's Rock. The views are amazing. Sure, why don't you and I bring them down and let Evelyn enjoy her drink. Jesus, Evelyn, you're getting stuck into those, and there's you codding us all week that you don't drink.'

Johno, who has been tying Jack's laces, looks up and squints at Evelyn. As ever, his expression is inscrutable.

'Go on, so,' Patrick says, before adding: 'Evelyn, take it easy on those. We can't have you getting drunk in front of the girls. Again.'

He hauls himself up off the blanket and offers a hand to Maggie to help her up. The kids are ecstatic, leaping up and down, screaming about who will see the monster in the cove first, who might catch a jellyfish, who might see a whale.

Patrick, Maggie and the kids make their way towards the row of trees, stopping to open the gate at the exit sloping down to the cliffs. Johno and Evelyn are alone. She does not want to look at him or talk to him. She is smarting with the knowledge that he does not really want to be here and the sting of rejection from last night suddenly feels fresh.

To her surprise, he moves over to sit beside her, his warm arm grazing hers. The touch is electric.

She can feel his face turning to look at hers.

Tears begin to form in her eyes, completely unbidden, unwanted. *What on earth is happening to me?* she thinks. *Don't cry! Don't cry in front of him.*

He puts his left arm around her, scooping her in so that her head rests in the nape of his neck. God, that smell, that incredible smell of his, like freshly cut grass and sea air. She lets herself cry.

'I'm sorry about last night,' he says. There is a gentleness in his voice that only makes her feel more wretched.

She hiccups and makes a noise somewhere between a laugh and a sob.

'Why are you sorry,' she says, 'when I'm the one who forced myself on you? I don't know how I could have done such a thing . . . I'm so sorry.'

He releases his hold on her, letting her wipe her tears on the sleeve of her cardigan.

'Is that how you remember it?' he says.

'Is there another way to remember it?'

'Well, yes,' he says.

She looks at him straight in the face but he says nothing.

'You're going to have to elaborate. I know you're a man of few words but come on!' They both laugh.

'I don't know how to put this. Whatever it is that you feel – well, you're not alone. There's something going on which, to be honest, is new to me. What I did, I wanted to do. I knew you were coming over to me at the bar and I knew you would come out. I knew right well what I was doing. I knew it was wrong, and I did it anyway. Do I regret it? Yes. And no. But it can never happen again. I just don't want you going home thinking, I dunno, thinking . . . that it was your fault. Or that I'm annoyed. That's just how my face looks.'

They laugh again, the tension broken.

'You don't laugh much,' she says, teasing him now.

'I do around you.'

'I don't get it,' she says. 'I wasn't looking for something like this to happen. I don't understand why it's happened. And so quickly, too. Sort of out of nowhere.'

'Hmmm. Some things can't be explained. And that's OK,' he says.

Her heart is fit to burst. Sure, this is the end of whatever madness has taken hold of her. But she can let go of her feelings of guilt and shame and allow this to be a secret place she can go to when times are dark – the knowledge that once, a man like Johno Fogarty wanted her.

As she sits there, letting the thought sink in, she realizes just how close he is. And how empty the park is. How easy it would be to lean in . . . just one more time.

A scream pierces the air.

Evelyn knows that scream. She has heard it once before.

It's the scream that came from her mother's throat when she found her husband, the love of her life, collapsed at the end of the stairs, dead from a heart attack.

It is the scream of a woman who knows that something unspeakable has happened.

Evelyn and Johno race to the end of the park and down a concrete slope that leads to a grassy area overlooking the sea, which stretches below them at a long drop. Evelyn takes in the scene, confused and scared, unable to put the pieces together.

Her eyes flit left to right, frantic, until they land on Tara and Susannah. Pure, visceral relief. They are both wide-eyed and clinging to their father's legs. Near them stands five-year-old Jack, who seems to be staring into a hole in the ground.

Johno runs to his son and grabs him up.

He turns to Patrick.

'What's happened? Where's Maggie and Katie?'

Evelyn is taken aback to see tears running down Patrick's face. She has never seen him cry before, and the sight reinforces her sense that something terrible has happened.

'Patrick! Answer me! Where are Maggie and Katie?'

Patrick points into the middle distance, to a spot Jack's gaze is also fixed on.

'I, I, I have no idea how it happened. I can't even. I can't look. I didn't know it was there. She was there and then . . . she was gone. Maggie went down to get her. I can't look, Jesus Christ, I can't look.'

Evelyn and Johno edge towards the grassy plain that he has pointed towards. They come to a sudden stop beside each other. The ground has split open like a mouth. Way below, foamy water crashes off the cliff walls. The ground has opened into a sheer drop, easily missed if you are not paying attention. Johno falls onto his knees, clutching at the edge of the earth, peering down into the hell below.

The soft blonde curls are unmistakably Katie's. Half of her body – the upper half – lies over pebbles. Her legs float loosely from side to side as the water eddies around her. Leaning over her, Maggie's shoulders are heaving and after her frantic climb down the rocks she is gasping for air. When she lifts her face to take a breath, Evelyn can see that a halo of red surrounds Katie's head.

37

'That's the plot of her book.'

'What is?'

'What Evelyn just said about that day in 1983. That's the whole plot of *The Broken Bay*. I mean, it's the plot, more or less. I worked with Susannah on all the drafts, I remember all the details. I never knew there was a real-life inspiration.'

We are down on the beach. After Mum stopped talking, we crept downstairs and out the front door, I thought for some air and to get our bearings after hearing Mum's shocking story. But David kept walking, like a zombie, out through the front gate, onto the road and down the slipway to the beach.

'Are you sure she never hinted at something, David? Why would she keep that from you? From us?'

He says nothing for the longest time. He stares out across the water to the peninsula in the distance. He is not so much dazed, as I assumed, but deep in thought.

'There's something else,' I say. 'Spit it out.'

'This Jack Fogarty guy, I've been thinking about him all day, thinking his name is so familiar. Then I looked him up online when your mum was telling that story and I realized I've met him before. In New York.'

'*New York?* What on earth was he doing there?'

He runs a hand over his stubble, which is what he does when he's thinking hard.

'Tara and I were just about to go out to look for you,' he starts. He looks a little awkward. None of us ever get into the details of the day I got attacked.

'Go on,' I say.

'Susannah, Tara and I were at a pre-awards thing in the hotel. I saw Susannah standing at the bar talking to a sort of well-built fella. That was the morning we had the big row, so I left her to it. Then they moved off into a corner away from everyone, which was odd. They were talking intently, and she looked grim. I went over but the minute she saw me she plastered on a big smile and when the guy turned, he was all smiles too.

'It turned out he had nothing to do with the awards. He was some Irish guy who was over for a boxing match that she knew from home, or so she said. I was still raging with her, so I was just going through the motions of being the helpful husband. The last thing I remember was giving him her personal email address, so they could keep in touch.'

We think it together – we have to get that email.

'Damn – I don't have her password,' he says.

'Try LucyBrown77. Caps on the L and the B,' I say.

He looks at me curiously but gets out his phone. Since the password didn't work on her laptop I'm not hopeful, but it works.

Finally! I think. Maybe we'll get some answers now.

He searches for Jack Fogarty and an email appears from April 2011. I feel we're getting close to the truth, but I'm worried about what the truth will be. I have butterflies, and not in a good way.

I lean in close to David, as we read his screen.

You didn't like being cornered there, did you, Susannah? I'm taking it you never shared any of this with your glorified personal assistant of a husband? Maybe tell him your great novel *The Broken Bay* is one of the longest confession notes in history? Didn't anyone ever tell you that secrets are corrosive in a marriage? You should ask my parents.

> You know what I want. Dad's farm is being repossessed, and in my opinion, your family owes him big time. Your family ruined Dad's life, and mine. Because your family know the truth, don't they? It's obvious from the novel. You have some neck putting all that down and profiting from our misery.
>
> It's so freeing, writing an email like this, knowing you can never show it to anyone. I want €20,000, in four instalments of €5,000, by this day next week. I have attached the bank details.
>
> I didn't like your little threat there on my way out of the hotel, Susannah. You're not the one to be throwing them out. Don't ever show your face in Dunmore East again. I mean it. I will kill you with my own hands if you ever set foot there again. And tell your mother the same.

And there it is. More proof. A blackmail threat – though what Fogarty thinks he has over Susannah or our family isn't spelled out.

As David's finger hovers over the screen, I spot something. 'Scroll down. She replied.'

The reply was sent at 4:42 p.m. the same day.

'That's just after she arrived at the hospital. I remember she said she had to go off and make a call,' David says.

It's short.

> I will give you everything you want and more. But I need you to urgently call me. You can burn my body in a fire after, but please, ring me now, on this number. I need your help. You will be glad you called.

We lapse into silence. We hear the sea roaring in around us, the clink of glasses from the hotel behind us, a stray car passing, the helicopter still hovering in the distance, the crows screeching in the sky, the toll of the church bell, a foghorn sounding at the lighthouse.

Suddenly David looks up and I know he's going to ask the question I've been asked a million times before. Any time New York comes up, someone has a go.

'Lucy, why were you out that morning?'

I think now of all the things I've learned about my sister today – her self-doubt, her imploding career, the tensions in her marriage, the stuff she saw growing up. And I see a woman just like me: a woman with secrets and shame and pride and fear. So, I am not going to reveal that it was she who sent me out into the snow that morning.

'Why are you asking me this? How many times have I told you and everyone else, David – I fancied a walk. The more interesting question is what Jack Fogarty did after getting her email.'

Afterwards I heard that Susannah lit a fire under the NYPD. She never revealed what strings she pulled to get them to pay attention to my case. We all assumed it was through her publishing connections. But there it is – Jack Fogarty.

In the end, it didn't make much difference. The guy who attacked me got away. But at least the police came around to the hospital and stayed in touch, long past the point where either we or they expected a result. You wouldn't think a lowly Irish detective would have much clout, but I guess someone took him seriously.

All roads seem to lead back to Fogarty but it's still impossible to see what's going on.

I have a brainwave.

'Type in Olivia Philips,' I tell David. The brainwave doesn't lead to anything though – nothing comes up.

We have found out all we can. I get David to forward the emails to me. Inspector Menton needs to know all this. But first I need to speak to Mum.

Relief floods me when I hear Mum's voice on the phone. But before I can explain anything she shushes me.

'Lucy, listen to me. I'm in the garda station clearing up a few things. One of you better ring your father tonight and tell him what's happening. But more importantly, I need you to listen carefully to me now. Stop interrupting and listen. Don't go trying to investigate this, OK? Leave this with me now. Go back to Dublin.'

38

Dunmore East, April 1983

Maggie's screams rise up from below, carried up in a horrifying echo that bounces between the cliff walls. The words 'It's an emergency. Do something' form inside Evelyn's head, but she's struggling to comprehend what's happening and can't seem to act. The whole situation is surreal.

On a clearing of high rocks to her right Susannah and Tara, red-faced and crying hysterically, cling to their father's legs. He is grasping both of them by the back collars of their t-shirts.

They're fine, thank God. They're fine.

Johno is knelt over a grassy patch of ground to her left, as if prostrated in a call to prayer.

Evelyn feels the intensity of the sun bearing down upon her as she tries to get her brain to work. She hears footsteps racing down the path behind her and she turns to see a man in yellow Lycra cycling gear advancing towards them.

'What's happened? I heard screams, is everything OK?'

Evelyn tries to speak, but all that comes out is a croak. She clears her throat.

'Go!' she says. 'Get help. A child has fallen. Run! Call an ambulance. Tell the coast guard.'

It's a miracle that she could even string that much together.

When she turns back, she sees that Johno is shuddering on the ground, his face in the grass. She races over and drops down beside him. She wraps her arms around his back and kisses his face. He doesn't stop her. Johno reaches out his left arm and wraps it around her, and together they face the ground, Evelyn sobbing now too.

After a moment, she glances over her shoulder and sees a look in her husband's eyes. His brow is furrowed, and his grip has loosened slightly on the children. A piece of a jigsaw falls into place for him, but it's a game he did not know he was playing.

'Evelyn!' he says. It's a command, not a question.

She turns back to nestle her face into Johno's shoulder to whisper in his ear.

'The ambulance is coming. Help is coming.'

She untangles her body from his and walks over to her husband and daughters.

'Mammy, stop! Stop!'

Evelyn bends down low to look her daughter in the face, wiping away the tears falling off Susannah's long eyelashes.

Patrick, now ten metres ahead, shouts again at them to hurry up. He is dragging Tara by the hand. Knowing that her daughter has witnessed something so traumatic, Evelyn defies him, more worried about this uncharacteristic behaviour from Susannah than his demands.

'What is it, sweetheart? Don't cry, Susannah, everything will be OK.'

Susannah is trying to get the words out, her eyes screwed shut, her fists clenched by her sides. But the sobs continue to wrack her small frame. Evelyn puts two hands onto her bony shoulders to try to steady her. Evelyn knows that there is something to this, something beyond the indescribable terror that is still playing close to where they stand.

By now, Patrick has stomped his way up the path towards the kissing gate that leads onto the main road and is making his way down the steep hill towards the cottage.

Evelyn shushes Susannah again, trying to get her to move

along. She wants to shake her, to tell her that they need to move, to please stop crying and start walking.

Susannah whispers something which Evelyn thinks cannot be true. She must have misheard. Evelyn shakes her head as if that will release the words into the air around her and make them disappear.

'What?'

Now she does shake her daughter's shoulders. She tells Susannah to look at her when she's speaking.

'What did you just say, Susannah?'

As much as Evelyn wants to wish them away, she cannot deny the gravity of the words when they're repeated.

'I pushed her. I pushed Katie. I didn't mean to.'

'You what? No, you didn't. You didn't, Susannah. Don't be ridiculous.'

It's just the two of them now, under the hanging branch of a Monterey pine, with only a stray crow as their witness.

Now that she's said it, Susannah's sobs have turned to hiccups.

'Will Katie be OK?' Susannah asks.

'After you pushed her, did she get up? Susannah! Did she get up?'

Evelyn is frantic, disbelieving, her heart pounding in her chest.

'No, Mammy, she fell over the edge. And then she was way down on the ground, and she wasn't moving.'

Evelyn feels herself fall over the edge — over the edge of one life, into the terrifying depths of a new one.

What should she do with this information? She hears the judder of a helicopter in the distance, and with a sickening lurch in her stomach Evelyn realizes that these are the rescue workers who will winch Katie's lifeless body back up onto the cliff. She has her answer.

Evelyn grabs Susannah's hand and runs from the park.

As she does, she leaves the truth to perish on the cliffs of Dunmore East. She tells herself she will never look back, never return to this ill-fated place. But somewhere in the deepest part of her, she knows that this is a lie.

39

I am staring at the phone. Does Mum seriously expect me to go back to Dublin? With Susannah still missing? Does she think I'm a kid who's out of her depth? That I need to be kept in the dark while the grown-ups sort things out?

I don't know whether to be upset or annoyed.

'I need a drink,' David says. And then, pointedly, 'Alone.'

Him too?

'What the hell, David? Have you lost your mind? This is not the time for a few pints.'

But he's already fifteen strides ahead of me, weaving his way towards the hotel. He's almost running, as if he has to get away from me.

I can feel my system going into overload. I tell myself to keep it together, but whatever composure I was able to summon earlier seems to have left me. No amount of deep breathing can ward off the waves of panic and confusion flooding me.

I spot David at the end of the hotel bar, a whiskey already in front of him. He's engrossed in his phone. I approach quietly from behind just in time to make out what he's typing – THE BROKEN BAY. An email opens and he clicks on an attachment. Then he starts flicking through a long document – reading a few lines then moving on. It's hard to figure out what he's doing, but it looks like he's reading the end of every chapter.

I return to the hotel lobby and approach the front desk. The receptionist who comes over to me has concern etched all over her face. Seeing my reflection in the mirror behind her, I understand why. There are black bags under my eyes and my skin looks almost grey. The stress of the day has aged me by years.

She directs me to the ladies', and I take refuge in a cubicle. I find *The Broken Bay* on my Kindle app and I do exactly what David's doing, skipping past the descriptive stuff to get to the cliffhangers at the end of every chapter.

I read until the floor falls out of my world.

Why did you come back here, Susannah?

40

Dunmore East, April 1994

Evelyn Brown has stepped off the bus from Waterford Town to Dunmore East. Her face is covered with raindrops as she leaves the stuffy warmth of the bus and steps into the bracing air.

The water is all the way in, bashing against the sea walls in a gale so fierce it whips her hair up around her face. There is not a scrap of sand in sight. It must be high tide. A low fog hovers above the water. Evelyn can feel it settling onto her skin, damp and heavy. The high cliffs pin in the strand like they used to. Protective. Secretive.

Through the gloom, she can just about see the occasional murky beam from the Hook Head lighthouse, which sits on a peninsula that juts out in the distance. Each one feels like a warning.

If you didn't know better, you would think it was the depths of winter. There is not a soul in sight. Even the bus was empty, the seats damp, the windows fogged up, mucky footprints dirtying the floor.

Rose-tinted glasses must be a real thing, she thinks, because this is not how she remembers it.

She tells herself that she is not sure why she has come back after so long. She tells herself it's a coincidence that she has decided to come here, of all places. But the truth cannot be escaped – after all, she's ended up practically owning the house they stayed in all those years ago, even if she has resisted coming to see it. It was always a decision to keep a link between herself and Dunmore East, even if she's never admitted it properly to herself.

The eleven years since she was last here have been unrelenting. The business failing. The shops closing. The dire state of their finances.

A substantial inheritance from her mother had eased the financial pressure in the last few years – they could pay off some debts, catch up with the mortgage payments – but nothing could lift the depression that had settled over their household. Patrick blamed everyone and everything for things going wrong. Never himself.

About two years ago, shortly after he had wrapped up the administration of their mother's estate, her brother Adam asked Evelyn to imagine her life if she was alone and could do whatever she wanted. Without thinking she said she'd live somewhere like that thatched cottage by the sea in Dunmore East, the one with the gorgeous view she'd always raved about. Two months later Adam arrived over to say he'd used his share of the inheritance to buy the cottage in both their names. It had seemed like a pure fluke, but the elderly owner had been trying to offload it for some time as it needed a lot of work and renovation, work which Adam arranged to have done. Handing Evelyn the keys, he said it could be her 'getaway' house if she ever needed it. He didn't need to spell out what he meant – he'd never liked Patrick. Adam went travelling, met an Australian and it looked like he wouldn't be returning. Her plan has been to get a local estate agent to let out the house now that most of the work has been completed, but she hasn't got around to arranging it.

Of course, all these years Evelyn has also carried Susannah's secret. For her daughter's sake she's thankful there has been no lasting damage. While Susannah is a handful, it's a combination of personality, hormones and the terrible atmosphere in the house. Evelyn knows she'll be all right. She's confident she alone remembers what Susannah told her that awful day. Which was all the more reason to never set foot in the place again. And yet.

She has nothing but a small, tattered rucksack. Gone are the days of fancy handbags and brand-new clothes and she is completely fine with that. That life was never for her anyway.

Evelyn is not even sure what's in the bag. She packed it in a fugue state, throwing in the first things that came out of the chest of drawers, the nearest toiletries from the top of the dresser. She walked out the front door and as if by magnetic force, she finds herself in the place where she was last truly happy, where she once tasted a love so sharp it changed the colours of her world forever.

It's over between her and Patrick. It must be. She'll figure out what to do about the girls. She just needs time. Or space. Or something.

Her heart aches with the loneliness of it all. Her face has been a slick of tears all day. Nothing is quite connecting. *It's a breakdown*, a voice says. *You're having a breakdown. You have broken down.*

And in her heart, she knows why she is here. It doesn't matter that it doesn't make sense. It just matters that she is feeling something.

She has come back for him. She has come back for Johno Fogarty.

41

It is clear as day that the child in her book is Susannah at six years old. A six-year-old who pushes a local girl to her death. Did Susannah really think it would never catch up with her?

Jack Fogarty told her never to come back, and she defied him. The fact that she ever returned here, or would ever want to return here, is inexplicable.

Is that why she brought me here? To tell me this terrible secret that she had kept all these years?

Though maybe it wasn't a secret. When I told Mum about Jack Fogarty appearing last night, and about his threats, none of it seemed to surprise her.

The scale of trauma and tragedy that my family experienced before I was born feels devastating. But I don't feel lucky not to have known it; I just feel very lonely.

As if on autopilot I leave the bathroom cubicle and make my way to the sink. I fill the basin, lean over and splash my face with handfuls of cold water. Then I hold my cupped hands, full of water, to my eyes – as if to flush out what I have read. I squeeze soap out of the dispenser. I scrub my hands meticulously, fingers and thumbs going round and round, lathering the backs, between my fingers, under my nails, going down to the wrists. I scrub aggressively, as though they will never be clean again.

If Susannah's choice to return to Dunmore East is astounding, then the same goes for Mum. Uncle Adam bought her the cottage, and from her attitude all through the years it's obvious she wishes it were anywhere else on earth. But discovering that she came back herself after what happened, it's baffling. Susannah mentioned it was after a fight with Dad. I didn't think it was that big a deal. Now I'm sure it was a very big deal.

My hands shake as I pull open the bathroom door and I walk out of the hotel in a daze. I walk the short distance to the cottage, the sea spitting at me as I pass the slipway.

I find Tara standing at the kitchen sink, running cold water on her wrists – another Brown woman trying to scrub herself clean. I call her name but she doesn't turn.

'I know what happened here in 1983. I heard Mum telling Inspector Menton,' I say. 'I know what Susannah did to that girl. And it's all in her book.'

Her shoulders slump and her voice is hardly louder than a whisper. 'What happened was an accident. Susannah . . . well, she was just a kid.'

'I can't understand why she wrote that book. She might as well have invited Jack Fogarty to come after her. And as for why she came back now . . .'

Tara remains silent.

'And there's Mum. I can't figure her out either. She's had this house as long as I can remember and not once has she ever wanted to come here. If anything, she seems to hate the place. And still she ended up coming here when she had some row with Dad?'

'It wasn't just a row, Lucy. I avoided giving you a straight answer when you asked earlier, but now that you know everything else, you might as well have the full story. Mum and Dad's awful fight the time we stayed here – well, it wasn't the first one. And over the years the fights got worse, especially when the businesses closed. Really bad. Mum could do nothing right. One day, Dad hit her. He knocked her out. Susannah saw him do it. The minute he left the house, Mum threw some stuff into a rucksack and ran out the door. She came here – maybe because she had this place. That's all I know.'

42

Dunmore East, April 1994

The years haven't been kind to Johno. As if reading her thoughts, he scrunches up his heavily lined face and says: 'Forty soon. A hop, skip and jump from fifty. All downhill from here.'

Evelyn laughs, she can't help it.

She missed his dry humour, his staccato way of talking.

She has recently turned thirty-six and she can't say she has fared all that well herself. It's been a challenging few years. It's on the tip of her tongue to tell him that the girls hate each other more than ever, if that's possible, and with teenage hormones the fights are epic. Katie would have been around the same age as Tara and, luckily, she stops herself in time.

If it feels surreal to be in Dunmore East after all this time, it feels even more surreal to be sitting face to face with Johno Fogarty at the dining table in this cottage. How she has fantasized about a reunion. The conversations she has had with him that he has no idea about. She wonders if he ever thought about her, down through the years. There were times when she visualized him so intensely that she believed wherever he was in that moment, he must have felt her gaze on the back of his neck. But now that he's actually in front of her, she's not sure where to start.

The gales have picked up and they blow high-pitched whistles through the small windows, turning the air lonely and blue. Rain belts against the back door.

Johno has his hands cupped around a steaming mug of

tea. Drinking alcohol together would be too dangerous, they both know that. He keeps his gaze on the floor. They feel like strangers.

'Why am I here, Evelyn?'

'I see you're in no mood for the small talk. Nothing new there,' she says with a laugh that she instantly regrets. It sounded pathetic and girlish. He waits for an answer and she clears her throat before speaking. But no words arrive. And so, he asks again.

'What do you want to talk about?'

'Us?'

A flash of emotion crosses his face, and he jerks his head back.

'Are you serious? You just can't be serious. *Us?* Where is your husband?'

'I've left him. I thought—'

'You thought what?'

He is up out of his chair, pacing the room, driven by a manic energy that keeps her glued to the chair. He just paces and paces around the small room, breathing furiously.

Evelyn tucks her hair behind her ears and tries again. 'Is it because Maggie—'

He closes the distance between them and is suddenly right up in her face, eyes bulging. She doesn't remember him being like this. In the short intense time she knew him, Evelyn had seen him angry. She had seen him scared. She had seen him cry. But now he seems undone.

'Don't you dare mention her name. You have some nerve. You've lost your fucking mind,' he growls.

For just one second, Evelyn thinks he is going to hit her, and she surrenders. It's an instinct. Then his expression softens, and it crosses her mind that he is going to kiss her. This thought lights up every fibre of her being. He bites his lip. She registers the smallest gesture.

Please, please, please.

But the air turns icy, and he turns away, taking just three strides to get to the front door before he pauses and speaks over his shoulder.

'After everything that happened. That you could come here and think . . . That you would ever think. Don't call me again. Don't show your face around here. Go home.'

He slams the door so hard that a plate slips from its stand on the bureau and smashes into pieces on the concrete floor. After this she sits in silence, her heart aching like it has been punched.

43

I'm getting out of the car near the entrance to Badger's Cove. It's shortly after six o'clock but this day feels like it's gone on much longer. What I think I'm going to find out here, I have no idea. After Tara told me about the time Dad hit Mum, I felt as though I could hardly breathe. I ran out of the cottage and just drove around in Susannah's car. I cruised around mindlessly for ten minutes, before deciding to come here, to get as close as I can to the last place I know Susannah was . . . the word 'alive' pops into my mind, and my heart plummets again.

Instinct and training tell me there is no such thing as coincidence. And the fact that a horrific thing happened in 1983 involving my family, and then metres away, decades later, my sister disappears – and it's all on the same night a woman is murdered – well, there must be a connection. I guess I'm hoping to find an answer, or a clue, to where Susannah may have gone. As I'm about to make my way down my phone rings.

'Lucy, where are you?' Tara says. 'Where have you gone?'

'For a drive. I needed to get away for a bit. And I needed to recharge the phone. So, killing two birds.'

'You need to come back,' she says, an unusual tone of command in her voice.

'Why? What's happened?'

'Nothing. It's just—'

'What?'

'Mum rang from the garda station. She asked me to go up and gave me her car keys. She made me promise that I'd bring you back to Dublin.'

Despite myself, I laugh.

'If she thinks I'm leaving while Susannah's missing, she's wrong.'

'Lucy, I honestly don't think there's much you can do. And Mum's worried sick.'

'Tara, listen to me. It's simple. Until Susannah comes back safe, I'm staying put. I don't exactly have anywhere else to be.'

'Well, that's very good of you, but it's not as if Susannah broke her back looking for you all those years ago.'

She has actually gone there. *Jesus!*

'Tara. Listen to yourself. It's hardly the time to bring that up.'

In her sharp intake of breath, I can hear that she's stung, and I feel bad. I never join in her digs at Susannah and I know she resents it; she thinks I'm taking the side of the undeserving sister.

'Anyway, you'll have to break your promise to Mum,' I say. 'I'm not resting until we find Susannah. And, you know what, I think that deep down you're worried too.'

There's a moment of silence and I wonder if she's gone off the call. And then I hear a deep exhale, as if she's trying to regulate her breathing to avoid crying.

'I am, Lucy. I really am,' she says, her voice thick with emotion.

'What else did Mum say? Why have they taken her to the station?'

'They want a full statement on what happened in 1983. Menton seems to think it might be linked to everything else.'

'Yeah, that's what I was thinking too. But how?'

'No idea. I guess when he heard that the child who died in '83 was Jack Fogarty's sister, he figured he better cover all the bases. Mum told me he read out Susannah's last few texts. Remember he told us Susannah's last call was from the woman who was murdered?'

'Yes?'

'Well, he gave Mum a lot more detail. He said there was a text from Olivia around ten past nine last night, something about how she couldn't go into the cottage, that she had changed her mind. Susannah asked Olivia to come back in a text, and then tried to ring her but it sounds like she didn't get through. A short while later, I'm not sure how long, Olivia rang her, and that was the last call.'

So that's probably who Susannah was texting just before she left the cottage: Olivia. I let out a low whistle. How on earth did these two know each other?

'Lucy, I can't make you leave Dunmore East. You're an adult. But we don't know what we are getting caught up in here.'

'Don't you want to find her? Don't you want to help Susannah?'

She hesitates, and then says, 'Yes. Of course I do.'

44

Dunmore East, April 1994

Evelyn is meeting Johno in a deserted pub at a crossroads, in what feels like the middle of nowhere. It has taken her an hour to find it. She leaves the rental car in a dusty yard around the back and walks in the side entrance, pushing open a heavy door. The carpets and furnishings are a faded shade of red and the place smells of damp and stale beer. It hasn't been updated in at least twenty years.

Johno sits at a table in the furthest corner of the bar, hunched over the racing pages of a newspaper, his back to her. She can see how his shoulders jut out through his mossy green jumper. When he was in the cottage she hadn't noticed how thin he has become.

There is only one other customer in the pub, an elderly man in a green cap, a tobacco packet in front of him. His elbows are propped on the counter, and he is talking quietly to a tall barman with a handlebar moustache who acknowledges Evelyn with a flick of the eyes.

She glances down at what she is wearing. Jeans, runners and a grey jumper. Designer stuff, relics of her old life. As she approaches Johno from behind, she places a hand on his right shoulder, making him jump.

'Sorry. Just me,' she says.

He grunts.

She takes a seat opposite him. He says nothing but keeps his eyes — those light blue eyes she has thought about so often — directly on her.

'What changed your mind? About meeting up, I mean. You seemed so angry the other day.'

Evelyn had got up to find a note under her front door with just the time and the name of this pub on it. Although she had never seen Johno's handwriting before, it was obviously his. An unbothered scrawl.

In the two days that had passed since he had stormed out of the cottage, Evelyn had time to think. She had been planning on leaving that morning, realizing that what she was doing was crazy. Of all places to seek refuge, she picked the most dangerous. But when she saw his note, she threw caution to the wind.

In the pub, Johno chooses not to answer her question about his change of mind. He has an entirely different question for her.

'What did he do to you?'

The directness of his question, and lack of an answer to her own question, throws her. The barman glances over and she seizes the opportunity, asking for a double vodka and a Guinness for Johno. He has an empty water glass in front of him. She has no idea who is looking after the farm, but he does not protest, and she is glad.

Evelyn busies herself fetching the drinks from the bar. She sits down, takes three mouthfuls and feels her shoulders tighten as the alcohol hits her bloodstream. Then she lifts her eyes from her glass to look at him. He hasn't touched his drink yet. He is not going to let this go.

'He punched me.'

Johno drinks half of his pint in one glug and says: 'That bastard.'

She doesn't know why, but between the pent-up tears and the madness of being back in Dunmore East with this man, she splutters out something between a laugh and a cry.

'What?' he asks, but the corners of his mouth are tugging upwards, and it fills her with something that feels like hope.

'You always hated him,' she says, dabbing the corner of her eye with a small white napkin.

'I did. I do,' he says.

'Thank you,' she says.

'Thank me? For what?'

'For not judging me. For not saying "I told you so". For not looking at me like I'm some kind of weak idiot for staying this long. No one understands how hard it is. I've tried to hold my family together, against the odds.'

'I'll stop you there, Evelyn,' he says, 'because I have another question for you.'

Evelyn is slightly startled that he's taking control of the conversation.

'Did you really think we were going to sit here and have drinks, and not talk about what happened?'

'You're right. I'm sorry. Ask me anything.'

For the first time she sees trepidation in his eyes and fear etched into his deep frown lines.

'I don't need to ask you anything, Evelyn. I think I need to tell you some things. Things you probably don't know. About what really happened that day.'

Christ! she thinks. *He knows. He knows about Susannah.*

He says that they need to get away from listening ears, so it's best if they talk in her cottage. Now she must wait to find out exactly what he knows.

Evelyn and Johno are at opposite ends of the couch, pretty drunk, unwilling to leave each other again for the time being. There has been no significant physical contact, despite the heat off their skin. They are just talking.

They are on their second bottle of wine and the clock has struck one. Thursday has given way to Friday, day to night, tide to tide.

She is still absorbing what he has told her.

'Somewhere deep inside, I think I kind of knew there was something between them. But I was so caught up in the strength of my feelings for you, I didn't properly pay attention,' Evelyn says.

'Yeah. Same here. Did I think she was flirting with Patrick? Yeah. But that was just Maggie. She'd flirt with a lamppost. I hated it.'

'So, tell me again, so that I have this straight,' Evelyn says, extending her cramped legs along the couch, touching the side of his body. He does not flinch.

'Did they sleep together? What was it exactly? How far did they go?'

'The way Maggie told it, it was the full works. Aaargh, she wouldn't tell me when or where. I tried to find out but you don't know what she was like after Katie died . . .'

He trails off.

Evelyn lets those words linger in the air. The pain of the loss is still so raw on his face, etched into the deep-set lines around his eyes. It seems to envelop him, this cloud of grief.

'It never leaves you, you know,' he says, gazing into his glass of wine.

'I can only imagine, losing a child like that. My mam passed away three years ago. Cancer. I know it's nothing like what you're going through, but I miss her every day. It must be hard for you – this time of year, springtime, the anniversary of her death, seeing all this rebirth?'

Johno nods sadly and then says in a mock cheery voice, 'So! Yes. Our partners were having it off together when we were feeling like the worst people in the world over a drunken snog in the fog.'

She laughs but when it echoes back to her, it sounds hollow. It was more than a drunken snog to her, that night on the beach in 1983.

'I think I know where they did it!' she says, the pieces of the puzzle suddenly slotting into place.

'Oh?'

Johno reaches for the wine on the table, pouring himself a generous measure, and then refills her glass too.

'The pub. Where Maggie sang that night. When I got back from the beach they had gone from fawning over each other to there being this weird awkward atmosphere. I remember thinking he was annoyed at her.'

'Hmmm. You might be right there.'

'I know Patrick and that was a sign of guilt, only I was too drunk and too guilty myself to pick up on it. Think about it, it couldn't have happened any other time. That was the only time they were alone before – you know.'

He takes an unsteady breath.

'The days after what happened are a blur,' he says. 'Gardaí. Neighbours. The guards wanted to talk to ye, by the way, but ye had gone and we told them there was nothing to tell. There were funeral arrangements. Maggie went to pieces. She was out of it for the funeral itself, like she wasn't there. It was awful. She wouldn't speak, wouldn't even hug Jack. The poor lad has suffered terrible these last years.

'I couldn't get it fully out of her what happened on the cliffs. She said one minute she was talking to Patrick, the next, Katie was gone. I couldn't understand it. Katie had played around that park and down on those cliffs and coves before. And I'd always warned her – "Katie, watch your step" – because of the way the ground can split open like that but sometimes you can't see it with the high grass and that. It just didn't add up. I kept at Maggie. I kept asking. I kept saying, "Maggie, tell me the fucking truth." I just knew she was lying.'

Johno clenches his fists up on his lap. This anger is new. The previous version of Johno, the Johno she knew in 1983, was measured and easy-going. And while she can understand his anger, it unsettles her, because she can see that this rage is never far from the surface. She is, after all, vigilant about such things.

'Anyway,' Johno says, 'Maggie cracked one day. Lost the plot entirely. Was laughing in my face, calling me an idiot, asking how I couldn't see it. She'd been havin' it off with that fella from Dublin and wasn't I some twat for not knowing.'

'Why did she tell you that, as in, at that moment?'

'From what I can gather, she was having some conversation with Patrick about their affair, or whatever you might call it, when it happened. They could have been kissing for all I know. But their eyes were on each other and not on the kids.'

Evelyn holds her breath. This is dangerous territory.

'She said that she saw Jack running towards where Katie was, and then there was a scream, and she had fallen. Can you believe she would say such a thing?'

'What? What was she insinuating?'

'That Jack pushed his own sister to her death, though she never said it in so many words. I have never told him what Maggie said. It would destroy him. I know my lad would never do such a thing. Not to his own sister. They fought, yes, but that's what kids do. Had he pushed her before? Yeah, sure. But come on now.

'I knew it was over for us when she started at those kinds of insinuations. We might have been able to get over, you know, Patrick. But this? No way. Insanity. Woman had lost her marbles.'

Evelyn feels dizzy and discreetly takes a few long steadying breaths before asking what happened next.

'Maggie moved back in with her mother in Waterford. She just wanted out. I could never understand it. Imagine – leaving me and Jack four months later? We went from a family of four, to a family of just two boys. Her mother died a few years later, in 1988.'

'What is she doing now?'

Johno gives a weary laugh.

'Well. Ya won't believe it. She's running her own clothes shop. Apparently, the economy is about to take off again, from what the papers say. She's got what she always truly wanted. Her freedom. Her precious job.'

'Don't you ever see her?'

'I used to drop Jack up to see her but it hasn't happened in a good while now. He's sixteen. Moody, angry. It goes both ways – they don't have all that much time for each other. She blames him for Katie's death but it's no one's fault but her own. Too busy cavorting with that piece of shit rather than keeping an eye on her kids.'

There's silence again.

'Sorry!' he says.

'No need to apologize.'

Johno looks at her with questioning eyes, a smile on his thin lips, his eyes a little dulled from the alcohol and the weight of the conversation.

'What?' she asks.

'It's just a surprise to be here with you like this. It looks like whatever drew you back here has affected me too. The last couple of days I was watching out for you around the village, telling myself that if I didn't see you it meant you had listened to me and gone back to Dublin. But the truth is . . . I hoped the opposite. I was finding excuses to drive past this place and when I saw the light on last night, I put that note under your door. I suppose after eleven years I had all these questions. And to tell you the truth, I've got very cut off from the world. I always felt we had some kind of connection. Even after what happened, I never forgot that, or what it felt like when you held me in your arms after Katie died.'

Evelyn is surprised and moved by his honesty. She wants to take him in her arms again but before she can move, he gives her a shy smile and says, 'What did you think of me the first night you met me?'

'Well, that wasn't the first time I met you, was it? The first time I met you, you were on your hands and knees breathing life back into my daughter's lungs.'

She feels a stab of guilt but manages to conceal it.

'Oh Jesus, I had forgotten that. How did I forget something like that?'

'So yes, my first impressions of you were – well, I thought you were a hero. And the way you looked at me that night, the first night we were all together, over in that kitchen there. It was like you saw me. The actual me. And there was something instantly physical, that I simply could not name – I just wanted to be around you.'

Her feet graze the side of his thigh again. She wants to run her hands along the inside of his legs, and it takes some effort not to do so.

'I thought you were just perfect,' he says.

'Perfect!'

'Sensitive and kind and beautiful, inside and out. A great mother. When I realized what he was doing to you, I swear I could have wrung his neck with my bare hands.'

There it is again. That violence that is so very unlike him, or at least the him that she thought she knew.

But in this moment the only words Evelyn cares about are *kind* and *beautiful* and *perfect*. Because all she has ever felt is insecure and underwhelming.

'Imagine if we knew then that eleven years later we would be sitting here like this,' she says, 'not single, exactly, but not fully attached anymore. What on earth would we have said?'

Johno shifts on the couch so he can look her straight in the face. He puts his wine glass on the table.

'Well, it would have made some things much easier.'

'Like?'

There is an electric charge running through her, a wire sizzling, a static closing in. The air feels heavy, loaded, alive. She feels like she is crossing a bridge from one side of her life into another, and in many ways she is. He runs his hands up her shins and over her knees.

'Like this,' he says, reaching her thighs.

He rises from the couch, pulling her up by the hand.

'Come on,' he says, leading her up the stairs.

PART THREE

45

It's wild and vicious down here across from Badger's Cove, the sea assaulting the cliff walls relentlessly. The wind whistles through the long grass. I am standing on Kittiwake's Rock, looking across to the edge of Badger's Cove where Olivia Philips took her last breath. There's only a few metres of water separating these two beauty spots, like two open arms embracing the sea. From what I can see, the body is gone, but the scene remains taped off. There's no one around, though. The area has been dusted and tested to within an inch of its life by now, I imagine.

When I realized I wouldn't be able to access Badger's Cove, I walked back along the path and almost couldn't believe my eyes when I saw a sign for Kittiwake's Rock, a place I had only just read about in Susannah's book, *The Broken Bay*. In her book, this is where a terrible thing happened. I made my way through that gate and down the concrete sloped path to a clearing. How much devastation exists between these two swimming spots. I am standing on a cliff that juts out, jagged rocks all around me. In the evening light, darker than it should be thanks to some very ominous-looking clouds, I see the harbour twinkling just across the way.

If I continue slightly right the rocks slope down like stairs, eventually giving way to the sea inlet that feeds into a little swimming spot. It would take maybe one minute to swim over to Badger's Cove. To my left is a small expanse of grass, where a sign sticks out of the ground. Warning – sudden drop.

Just metres away I see that the ground gives way. Stepping cautiously, I go a little closer and see that the earth splits open, jagged cliff walls forming a narrow, plunging V-shape. It's as though a thin slice has been taken out of the cliff wall. I can't see the bottom, but I can hear the loud churning water crashing off the rocks beneath. This must be where Katie fell all those years ago. It's possible that her death is the reason for the sign.

Being in the spot where Susannah was possessed to do something terrible – a deed that haunted her to such an extent that she admitted to it nearly forty years later, even if she camouflaged her confession as a novel – makes me think of her with a fierce compassion that is entirely new. Always it has been Susannah minding me.

Pictures flash in my mind's eye like a film montage – Susannah's smiling at me as she lifts me into the kid's seat in a supermarket trolley. Or cleaning my bloody knees. Or advising me how to stand up to bullies in school – and arriving to deal with them herself one day after classes. And holding my hand after I had been dumped for the first time, at fifteen, declaring, 'Boys are trash, you're a superstar.' Not for a second did I think she was anything but powerful. But she has been living with this secret. And now, perhaps, it has put her in danger. I can't give up on her.

I try to remember all the apps on her phone. Gmail – there was nothing in her emails about Olivia Philips or Jack Fogarty beyond what David found. Instagram – I try logging out of my Instagram and into her account, but two-factor authentication means I can't get in. WhatsApp – without her phone, I can't get into her WhatsApp.

She has a Twitter account, but it's one she set up years ago because her publisher encouraged her, and she barely uses it because she thinks the internet is full of crazy people. It's a long shot, and I type her password more in hope than expectation – it's so long since she set up the account, she was hardly using the same one then – but, amazingly, I'm in.

I bypass the handful of notifications to go straight to her direct messages. I scroll up and down, trying to identify something that looks significant. I open a few before I hit gold – messages there from someone called Ophelia with only an egg for a profile. The first was sent over a month ago.

'Hi, I hope you don't mind me contacting you here, but my name is Olivia Philips. This is a temporary account! I was wondering if you are the Susannah Brown who was in Dunmore East in 1983?'

'Why do you want to know?'

'It's kind of mad. I'm trying to track down my father.'

What?

'What makes you think I would know him?'

'Because he's your father too.'

46

It has started to drizzle, but it comes at me sideways and blurs my vision. A woman's scream makes me jump in fright. In a moment of insanity, I think it is Olivia. Then Susannah. I swing wildly from left to right, trying to find the source. Then I hear it again and cop myself on. It's just a fox, stalking through the fields behind me. Spooked beyond words, I race back up the slope and out the gate back into the park.

After Olivia dropped her bombshell, Susannah sent her mobile phone number and the DMs ended. As I hurry up a narrow path, I google Olivia again. She was thirty-eight. And the pieces are fitting into place. The reason Susannah wanted me here. The four places laid out for dinner last night. Susannah, Tara, me, Olivia. The sisters' reunion that no one saw coming.

And this proves that Susannah had no intention of harming Olivia Philips. I need to tell someone, but I'm not sure who. David? Tara? Mum? Menton? I'm still dithering when a call comes up from David.

'David, what's going on? Where are you?'

'Your mum rang me,' he whispers. 'She said if I found Jack Fogarty, I'd find Susannah. She said he's been questioned but he has an alibi and was released. I waited outside the garda station till he came out and I followed him here.'

'You followed him *where*?'

'To his house.'

'OK, and what's he doing? Is she there?'

'Two other gardaí have arrived. I think they're up to something, Lucy. What should I do? I want to run in there and wring his bloody neck. I know he knows where she is.'

'Do NOT go into the house. Do not leave the car. Send me a pin for your location. I'll get Tara and come to you.'

'No! Just you!' he says, his whisper more urgent now.

David's sudden allergy to Tara baffles me – they seemed fine earlier. But I'm not going to waste time thinking about it in the middle of what might be a life-and-death situation. I decide to ignore him and go back to the cottage to get Tara. I don't know what we're dealing with, and I want her by my side. We have to find our sister. And our best hope now is for Jack Fogarty to slip up.

47

When I get back to the cottage, I find Tara with her coat on, scooping her handbag off the couch. A blast of rain comes in behind me as I stand in the front door, looking at her quizzically.

'Where are you going?' I ask.

'I have to get back to Mia and Mark, I've been gone since last night. And it's time I talked to Myles about . . . everything. I'll use Mum's car to go over to collect my own. She can pick it up at the hotel as soon as this is sorted.'

I cannot believe what I'm hearing.

'*Sorted!* Tara, have you lost your mind? This is not a double-booking crisis in one of your hotels. Susannah is missing! And she disappeared at the same time a woman was murdered. And she was talking to the woman before she died. And it all happened in a place you visited as a child. When she seems to have pushed a little girl to her death. Who happens to be the sister of one of the local cops. Who threatened Susannah just before she disappeared. This is not going to get *sorted*!'

I'm practically shouting at her, but she regards me with an air of detachment, as if she's the adult in the room who has evaluated things sensibly and isn't going to be swayed by her overwrought little sister. I can see what's going on. She's thinking this entire situation is Susannah all over – creating a big fuss, grabbing everyone's attention – and she'll swan in tomorrow, all sweetness and light, and wonder what the fuss was about.

I calm myself down slightly but there's no escaping the incredulity in my tone.

'What happened to wanting to help your sister?'

Tara casts her eyes downwards, exhaling a barely audible whistle through pursed lips. Evasiveness.

'Look, I'll come back tomorrow if she still hasn't shown up. I have to go now – I want to catch Myles before he heads to bed.'

'What the hell has got into you? Even now, with Susannah's life in danger – and I think it is – you can't just let the past go? I know you've never forgiven her for behaving like a diva in New York. But you're not proving anything by running out on her here. If anyone is entitled to bear a grudge it's me. But it was just one of those things that no one could foresee. Even if Susannah hadn't asked me to go out and pick up cigarettes, I probably would have gone out for a walk. Maybe the things that happen to us were always meant to happen to us.'

In the stress of the day and the heat of the moment, the words tumble out of my mouth unfiltered.

'You went out because of the smokes?'

Shit! This is the exact opposite of what we need right now. The exact opposite. This will give Tara fuel to hate Susannah for another eleven years. All because I couldn't keep my mouth shut.

But where I expect anger, there is just shock. And instead of a rant, there's a stunned silence.

Tara backs into the kitchen and sits at the table, her pallor white. It's as if she's deflating like a balloon – I can feel it mirrored in my own body, a flattened feeling. All her conviction about leaving has gone.

I put my hand on her shoulder.

'Tara, can we please put all this stuff aside, just for now? Can we focus on finding her before it is too late? You can yell at her all you want to when we've got through this.'

'Sure,' she whispers.

I want to tell her about the Twitter messages, which I'm still getting my head around, but she needs time to gather herself.

'Take ten. Call Myles and let him know you're staying on here. Let work know you have to take a couple of days off. Have one of those bananas, have two – you look like you're going to faint. I'll be waiting in the car.'

As I walk towards the car and open the door, I have the strongest sense of déjà vu. Except, I realize, it is not my scene I'm reliving but Susannah's as she walked away from me yesterday outside the hotel, opened her car door and bent in over the front seat. Before leaving the table, she mentioned needing to scribble something in a journal.

I do exactly what she did and lean in over the front seat and scrabble around. And there, tucked in between the centre console and the front seat, is a small leather-bound notebook.

48

I told Mum about Olivia. She didn't seem surprised or angry with Dad at all. I guess she doesn't give a damn anymore. She was more fixated on telling me what not to do – not to speak to Dad (as if I would), not to bring Tara or Lucy into it, not to go to Dunmore East. If anything shocked her, it's that I wanted to go there – so no hope of getting the keys to the cottage.

In everything I have read so far, this is one of the most astonishing things in Susannah's journal – Mum has known about this for weeks. No wonder she hotfooted it here the minute Tara called her. She'd already have been out of her mind about Olivia's murder, knowing the connection. Hearing Susannah was also here, but had gone missing, would have freaked her out completely.

Susannah's need to write down everything means that I finally have some answers. Olivia was adopted in the UK by a famous opera singer, Joan Philips, and her husband. I think of the TV clip I'd seen of Joan earlier, her face a mixture of rage and devastation. Olivia told Susannah her parents, especially her mother, were pushy and controlling – to the extent that Olivia developed carpal tunnel syndrome because of all the forced piano practice. So, there was a dark side to her fame and success.

Talking about her adoption was taboo in the family, and Olivia was so busy she put the idea of searching for details of her birth on the back-burner. That was until she found her adoption certificate and details of the Irish agency that arranged it. Olivia admitted to Susannah that she knew what she was doing searching her mother's room for her birth cert for a form she was filling out, rather than asking her for it as she usually would. She had some inkling that her mother had a lot of stuff hidden away. Even if she hadn't quite admitted it to herself, she must have been ready to find out.

Olivia said nothing to her parents. She contacted the agency and they were able to contact Maggie and she agreed to meet Olivia. In fact, she really wanted to see her.

Olivia was elated. She told Susannah that all her life she had been forced into a mould that wasn't a fit. She hoped that meeting her birth mother would help her figure out who she was truly meant to be. She met Maggie in Waterford town in the summer of 2019 and over the following months they struck up something close to friendship. It was a joyful time for both of them. But Maggie would never talk to Olivia about her birth father. All she ever let slip was that he was 'a fella from Dublin' and it sounded like it was a one-night-stand. Olivia knew Maggie was divorced and had a son – and had been married when Olivia was conceived – so she was taking her time drawing out Maggie.

> And then Covid-19 hit. Maggie got it early and came down hard with pneumonia, which got progressively worse until she was in hospital on a ventilator. She wasn't allowed any visitors. Olivia said there was no sign of her son, or any other relatives. Poor Olivia had to sit outside in the car park talking to her on a phone held by a nurse. That's how Olivia saw Maggie die.
>
> Despite knowing her only months, Olivia says she felt closer to Maggie than to her mother in the UK – less pressurized, more accepted. It was terrible for her after – her life felt really empty. The lockdowns gave her time to think and she became obsessed with finding out more about who she was. She wanted to know who her father was but she had

nothing to go on until she was clearing out Maggie's apartment, which she had inherited.

She found photos inside an address book and one of two little girls had two names on the back, 'Susannah and Tara Brown – April 1983, Dunmore East'! She sent me a screen grab of that and another picture, one of Mum and Dad dancing around a table in Dunmore East, though Mum looks like she's kind of just standing there, and Johno Fogarty sitting in a corner. And the two of us standing on the stairs.

Reading Susannah's journal, I wish I could see these pictures myself, to have just a glimpse into this world I never knew existed.

The penny dropped with Olivia when she saw the date. April 1983. Nine months before she was born. She did a bit of digging and sent me a Twitter DM. We met in the Westbury yesterday to make a plan. In two weeks, I'm going to get Lucy and Tara down to Dunmore East. Going back to where it all started might shake things up. I'm tired of all the secrets and lies – I have faith that between the four of us, we can throw open the windows of this family and let in some air!

I admire Susannah even more now – that she wanted to stop hiding, to finally confront the past. I've been hiding from my own past these last few years, so I know what it feels like to duck and dive.

Clearly, so does Dad. I already knew he wasn't a model dad, and from what I've heard in the last twenty-four hours, he was far from being a model husband either. I am not surprised to hear that he would sneak off behind Mum's back like that.

I put my hands on the steering wheel and exhale gently. My mobile rings. David again – I can't believe I'd forgotten about his vigil outside Jack Fogarty's.

Before he can say a word, I give him the headlines – Olivia is Susannah and Tara's sister. Susannah intended to reveal all.

'She never told me any of that,' he says flatly. 'Why wouldn't she tell me?'

'I don't know, David. But I had no inkling either if that's any comfort. But if the cops are insinuating that Susannah had something to do with the murder, this has to be proof that she didn't. This woman was her half-sister. I'll have to bring this to Menton – but can we even trust him?'

'I wish I knew.' David sighs.

'Anything happening there?'

'Just Fogarty drinking beer with two pals from the station. He hasn't drawn the curtains so I can see them in the kitchen. I guess he needs to let off steam after a tough day at the office, the bollocks. Give me one good reason why I shouldn't go in there and rip his head off.'

'Because if he knows where she is, he might lead us to her.'

David sounds unconvinced as he hangs up.

Tara finally arrives out and as she hops into the passenger seat, she's all questions. 'Has David been in touch? Has Jack Fogarty stirred yet? Have ye thought about what we'll do next?'

It seems like she gave herself a good talking-to in the house. Given what I'm about to impart, I'm glad she's more together. I bring her up to speed on David's mission outside Jack's house, and then I repeat the story I have just learned about Olivia for her.

'Jesus! Dad? Maggie Fogarty? What a car crash!'

'I know, Tara. It's a total mess. That holiday seems like an earthquake, with all these . . . aftershocks. Speaking of which – here's another one. Did you know Jack Fogarty was in New York when we were there?'

'What? No! That can't be right – where did you hear that?'

'David said you were all at a reception in the hotel that morning and he saw Susannah arguing with some guy in a corner. But when he went over, they both acted as if there was nothing up, said they knew each other from Ireland. He put two and two together earlier that Jack Fogarty was the guy. We got into her Gmail account and found emails they sent each other later that day. What's weird is that he seems to have gone from threatening her to pitching in to find the person who attacked me.'

Tara's eyes are wide, her mouth open.

'He threatened her?'

'Yep. It's all in an email. I'll show you.'

I hand my phone to Tara so she can read Jack Fogarty's email. I lean in beside her to reread it. A line jumps out: *Dad's farm is being repossessed, and in my opinion, your family owes him big time. Your family ruined Dad's life, and mine.*

'That bit about his father, Tara – what's his father's name?'

'Johno Fogarty.'

'Could he know the truth about Katie?'

'He was there on the day, but he was sitting off with Mum, so he didn't see what happened. I don't think so.'

'What about *The Broken Bay*? He'd have recognized the story and might have put two and two together – maybe that's why Jack was worked up that time in New York.'

'I barely remember Johno, but he didn't seem the reading type. I doubt it.'

'Maybe Jack told him?'

'It's possible . . . I guess.'

'Let me try something,' I say, reaching for my phone. I log in to the Irish land registry website. The site has details of every property in the country, very handy for gardaí. As I hoped, my garda login still works. I type 'John Fogarty' and select County Waterford. Within moments I have a plot of land and a postcode. I google the postcode and up pops the last house in a terrace overlooking the harbour.

'Fasten your seatbelt,' I tell Tara, 'we're making a detour.'

49

Johno's house is in darkness and there was no answer when I knocked on the door. Tara and I are standing in a tiny patch of overgrown weeds beside a rusty fence, peering into his front room through the crack where the curtains don't meet in the middle. Gulls squawk overhead and the wind whips through the sails of the boats, slapping the halyards off their sodden masts.

'He's not here, Lucy – let's go,' Tara says, turning on her heel to leave.

'Not so fast,' I say, grabbing her by the elbow, and stepping away from the window. 'Think about it. What if Jack Fogarty told his father what he knows or what he thinks he knows? And what if Johno Fogarty saw Susannah here and decided to avenge his daughter's death?'

Tara looks at me like I've lost my marbles. I realize I might be clutching at straws. If Jack Fogarty had imparted such huge news to his father, he would surely have told Menton by now and the guards would be on their way. On the other hand, I know Fogarty is capable of blackmail and extortion, so it might not be a big leap to keep quiet about his father being on the warpath.

'Let's look around the side.'

A rotting wooden door opens easily and we're in a small yard with barely room for Johno's two large bins. His back-door is a flimsy glass and PVC affair. I try the handle but, of course, it's locked.

'What the hell are you doing?' Tara says as I pump the handle.

I look for something I can use to crack the door open with but the tiny yard is empty, so I take off my coat and wrap it around my elbow.

'Lucy! No! Let's just go to the gardaí!'

I ignore her pleas and tell her to stand back. I smash in the glass, turning my face away from the flying shards. I reach in and find a key on the other side, twist it around and the door opens.

'You've lost your mind,' Tara says as she follows me inside. I feel a rush of adrenaline and, again, a sense of purpose I haven't had in ages.

The inside of the house is surprisingly dark, especially given the fact we are still an hour or so away from sunset, so I look around using the torch on my phone instead of searching for a light switch. Even in the poor light I can see it's shabby and filthy. The lino is peeling where it meets the cupboards. They have no doors and haven't been cleaned for a very long time. The room smells of tobacco and dried-out teabags. Beside the sink are more than a dozen empty whiskey bottles. The house is silent except for the ticking of a plastic wall clock.

I move from the kitchen into a sitting room. In the pre-sunset gloom, as the weather continues to worsen, the glow of the harbour lights comes through the gap in the flimsy curtains, giving the room a spooky feeling. There's a small television, two dark couches that look older than me and a scattering of newspapers on the floor at the end of one of the couches. There might have been a carpet once but now there's just concrete.

I stand very still, straining to hear if there is any movement from upstairs. Nothing. Going to the door into the hallway, I look back at Tara, holding a finger to my lips to signal for her to be quiet. There's no need – she's shaking her head at me, as if imploring me not to go any further.

The stairs are narrow and steep, and I take them slowly, Tara breathing hard from the bottom. When I get to the second step from the top, the stair creaks so loudly that Tara jumps, and I feel like I've been given an electric shock. But still, no response from the house.

As I stand on the landing, to my left I can see into a bedroom with an old wardrobe on one side and a double bed on the other, the mattress half-covered with a sheet and a flat pillow. From the bathroom, I can hear the steady drip of a leaking tap. To my right, there's a closed cupboard. I launch myself into the bedroom but there's no one lurking in the corners, and no one hiding behind the shower curtain in the bathroom either.

'There's no one up here,' I call down to Tara.

'Can we get out of here now? This doesn't look good, breaking into someone's home.'

I descend the stairs and look at her – a mistake because immediately I'm picking up on her inner turmoil. Until now, apart from the odd creaking floorboard making me jump, I was calm. One look at her and I feel my heart pounding faster, and my anxiety levels rising. I close my eyes a second and breathe myself back into my body.

'You OK?' she whispers.

'Yes,' I say, and I am. The controlled breathing's working. I open my eyes and focus on the sitting room again, searching for clues. Clues to what, I don't know, but my gut is telling me this man is involved. Despite her reservations Tara has her phone out and has also started looking around. She stops in front of the mantelpiece.

'Wow!' she says.

She is bent over, looking at a photo.

'He looks so old now,' she says, holding it up. In the photo, Johno is at the hull of a small boat, holding up a massive fish, his eyes scrunched up in the sunlight, his expression sour. The boat, the *Dunmore Rogue*, looks as battered as this house. On a shelf just above the TV I see another photo. It's of a younger Jack Fogarty and Johno Fogarty, side by side, casting off in a much newer-looking *Dunmore Rogue*.

My garda training to the rescue again, I log on to the public marine traffic website on my phone. I scan the coastline around Dunmore East, my finger hovering over the little green and red dots that represent boats. The *Dunmore Harrier*. The *Donna Grouper*. The *Billie John*. And there, just over five nautical miles away and moving into the Passage East harbour, is the *Dunmore Rogue*.

Tara is watching me and shaking her head vigorously. She knows exactly what I'm about to say.

'We have to go to Passage East, Tara. David has Jack Fogarty's house covered, we've checked here, we have to follow every lead.'

'It's the gardaí who investigate leads, Lucy, not us.'

'But are they? Are they investigating? I know you think I'm on some kind of one-woman mission to reclaim my dignity, but I promise you, I'm only interested in finding Susannah. And every second counts.'

'Shit!' she says suddenly, pulling me away from the window.

I turn and see flashing blue lights, flying down the harbour road towards Johno's house.

'Tara, get out the back, now!'

'What! I'm not going without you! Don't be stupid. Come on, Lucy, let's go.' She's hissing at me, trying to pull me out through the back of the house.

'Tara, listen,' I say, putting my hands on her shoulders. 'We have one minute max here. Go out to the car. Get to Passage East. I will deal with this.'

Just as I think she's going to run out the back door by herself, she grabs my arm and drags me into the kitchen. I glimpse two garda cars whizzing around the final bend towards this row of houses. We step out the back door and slink out the side gate but suddenly find ourselves confronted.

'Get down!'

We drop to the ground. I turn my head and see a plainclothes officer with a gun pointed at us waving someone in our direction. I see shoes, look up, and Inspector Menton is staring down with cold fury in his eyes.

'What in blazes are you doing here?'

His rage reverberates through my nervous system; this is the angriest I have seen him. My eyes move from Menton to someone just behind him. Jack Fogarty. To my surprise, Menton turns from me, and he and Fogarty run around the back of the house, followed by two other gardaí.

'Get up,' says the plainclothes officer, prodding us towards the house. When we get inside, I grab Tara's hand and shuffle towards the front door. But as I get close, it bursts open and I am knocked to the floor by whoever is coming through it with force.

It's David, and he's done something very stupid. He pounced on top of Detective Garda Jack Fogarty and tried to pummel him right in the face. But of course he did it in front of four other gardaí, and now he is having his ass hauled into the corner of the room. Thankfully he didn't manage to punch Fogarty, because the last thing we need is him being charged with assaulting a garda.

'You threatened to kill my wife!' David is shouting, his face contorted, the shadows of the room making him look deranged.

I can't blame him for being furious, after everything he has learned.

'What is he doing here?' I say to Menton, nodding at Jack Fogarty. 'Surely he is a suspect and should not be involved in this investigation. And what exactly are you doing to find my sister?'

'Pipe down or I'll have you in cuffs,' Menton says, while scanning the kitchen. From the growl in his voice, I believe him.

A garda comes down the stairs and says to him, 'It's clear.'

Jack Fogarty slumps down into one of the shabby couches, leans over and puts his head in his hands.

'What have I done?' he says. 'It's all my fault. All my fault.'

50

Jack Fogarty gives me his phone, his hand shaking, tears falling down his face. The depth of emotion welling up inside him builds inside my body. I can feel the tempest rising, the tears ready to spring from my own eyes before I have even read what he is going to show me.

But I can't let someone else's emotions pull me under. I root myself. I imagine that I am connected to the core of the earth. I accept his feelings. I just accept them, to see what happens. I let them run through me like water. Like breath. I don't just *try* to accept them but I actually do, maybe for the first time ever. And somehow, it works. It actually works. I am ready for whatever is coming.

'I was in the house with some of the lads from the station when I got it,' he says, referring to what's on the screen. 'I called the inspector straight away.'

I see an email sent from Johno to Jack, time-stamped 6:25 p.m., just under an hour ago.

> I saw your email to that girl Susannah yesterday. I thought, now what is this about? I went looking. Read the older ones. And then I found that book on your shelf, and I found out what happened to Katie. My own son, a liar. After everything we have been through. And you took her money? Who are you? Now it's all fucked. I thought the girl would be OK. But I just heard the news on the radio. She's dead? And it's your fault, and the Brown girl's fault. It's over. It's too late for me. I never wanted it to end this way. Bye son.'

There was another email from Johno just beneath it, by way of an afterthought.

> Did Evelyn Brown know all along? She did, didn't she? You can tell her she deserves it. An eye for an eye. Daughter for daughter. She can search the woodlands behind the old house for her precious girl, search the place where I nearly wasted away after my girl died.

In my mind I see a terrible image of my sister, dead in a woodland. The horror of it makes me dizzy and unstable. Why are the gardaí still here? Why aren't they searching? I turn, ready to launch into a tirade at Inspector Menton, but he has his mouth up to a walkie-talkie, already mid-flow.

'All remaining officers who are not already at the Wood Walk near Coxtown Cross, make your way there now. I repeat, all remaining officers,' he says. When he sees me open my mouth to speak, he puts his hand up, and I see the sweat glistening on his palms; I feel his heartbeat as if it were my own.

'*You* will stay here. Detective Fogarty, you come with me. Detective Quigley, you keep these two here,' he says, pointing at Tara and me. When I try to interrupt him again, he literally shushes me, and barrels out the front door.

I look back over my shoulder and see Jack Fogarty rise from the couch, but his body is sagging, like a man defeated. I have so much to ask him, but so little time.

'Why did you help me? In New York?'

He stops in the doorway.

'I couldn't say no. And in any event, it didn't make much of a difference. She thought I might have some sway, and I tried. But it was really her putting in all the effort. She pestered the detectives into getting a move on. She was just more persistent.'

'It sounds to me like you had every reason to say no to her.'

He keeps his eyes on me, unsure, hesitant.

'Yeah. I thought they would have told you.'

Told me what?

'But then when I went to the cottage to take your statement earlier, I realized . . . wow, this girl has no idea,' he says.

'Told me what?' I say.

But I know. I just can't face up to it. I've been dancing around it all day. And I'm still dancing.

He wrings his hands together and says, 'I swear to God, I had no idea that Susannah's disappearance was linked to the murder. I genuinely thought she left town last night after I warned her to get out of here. I never wanted Dad to know any of this. He was up in my house to collect a new fire extinguisher I'd bought for the boat. The laptop must have been open on the counter. Of all the bloody things. He's been through so much, you wouldn't believe. It would have destroyed—'

Menton shouts for him, so that's the end of that.

Once more I say, 'Told me *what*?' but too low for him to hear. I'm not ready for the answer. The backs of my legs have started to shake. I know the answer. If I'm honest, I've known it deep down since Susannah mentioned Mum returning here when she was revising for the Leaving. It's simple arithmetic.

51

The Passage East harbour is tiny: there are only eight boats docked, each tethered and bobbing wildly in the choppy sea. The wind has picked up further, and the rain pelts me thick and fast. Behind the black clouds, the sun sets. I am speeding along the wall of the harbour, checking out the names of the boats, aided by the glow of the yellow port lights.

I know the gardaí have it wrong. After Jack Fogarty and Menton left, Detective Quigley, the plainclothes officer, told me that after his daughter died Johno had taken to walking the length and breadth of a woodland near his farm in a fog of grief. His 'afterthought' email is misdirection and they've fallen for it. I saw the *Dunmore Rogue* moving towards the harbour at Passage East on the map. I'm convinced that's where we'll find Johno.

Escaping Quigley wasn't hard. I said I needed to head up to the bathroom. He stayed with Tara, who looked as though she was about to jump out of her own skin, and more likely to make some sudden move. I pushed the bathroom window open, squeezed out – all the time cursing my size, but then glad of it when my feet touched the top of a wheelie bin – and I slipped around to the car.

I'm drawing closer to the final boat – the *Dunmore Rogue* – right at the end of the harbour peninsula. For a second, I stop, steadying myself against the sodden harbour wall. My heart is palpitating, squeezing into itself and then bursting into irregular beats. I feel weak: I haven't eaten today. I try to tamp down my anxiety.

What if I'm wrong? If I am there's no plan B and I have no

clue what's about to happen. I take another breath and walk towards the boat, hoping an answer will somehow materialize.

As I close in on the boat, I see him. Johno. It must be him – the square shape, the jutting jaw. He looks exactly as he does in the photos in his house. If circumstances were different, I would want to take my time to study him. But he is about to untie the boat from the deck so I have to act fast.

With my heart in my mouth I march up to him, like a woman who knows exactly what she is doing. Inside my pockets, my hands are clammy and shaking and I feel as though I might get sick. I wonder if he can hear the tremor in my voice when I shout out to him.

'Excuse me, sir, the harbourmaster needs to see your registration.'

The roar of the wind drowns me out, so I have to shout a second time. He is bent over, pulling the rope in, just about to leave the port. It's an effort for him to stop what he is doing and stand up straight. He looks old. It makes me wonder if he is capable of this at all, if we've misunderstood his emails. And if I've got it wrong to think he's up to something on his boat.

Well, you were fired as a garda, after all. The voice of doubt is never far away.

'What?'

His face is gaunt, and he looks at me with heavy suspicion.

'I said, he sent me over, the harbourmaster. He says he needs to see your registration.'

'My licence?'

'Yes, exactly, your licence,' I say. I have no idea what I am talking about and I pray that I don't look as uncertain as I feel.

'At this hour of the night? Why the hell would he be looking for it at this time? I was only stopping for fuel. I don't see you asking anyone else here, do I?'

'Well, sir, that's because there is no one else here. He gave me strict orders. There's a lot of gardaí in the area investigating a murder down in Dunmore East. He is adamant about checking licences. I'm just carrying out orders. You'll be on your way when he sees it's you, sir, I promise. There won't be any issue.'

I'm hoping a little deference throws him off the scent.

Johno's face turns dark, and he scrutinizes me for a moment. He squints so he can see me better, and I can feel my heartbeat in my wrists, in my legs, in my feet. This whole situation is mind-blowing, on so many levels.

'Fuckin' unbelievable,' he says eventually. 'Where is he? He usually comes down himself.'

'He's hurt his leg. He's in the office over in the fort because of the weather,' I say, referring to the town's bastioned fortress that I passed earlier, and where I saw a small office block with some lights on and cars parked outside.

It's just lie after lie. Standing there with my wet hair plastered against my face, I redouble my prayers. And, as if in answer to those prayers, Johno eventually re-ties the rope. He hops up onto the pier with an agility that surprises me – not so rickety, after all.

I plan to rush back to my car to avoid making him any more suspicious. Now he's bearing towards me and he comes up close, making as though he is about to walk around me. But when we are shoulder to shoulder, facing in opposite directions, he growls into my ear.

'Do I know you?'

Shit! Think!

I'll have to fake it – treat him with Susannah-style sassiness.

'*Excuse me?* No! Do I know *you*?'

He narrows his eyes. He's so close to me that even in the poor lighting I can see small purple liver spots on the side of his face, tobacco stains on his mouth. He grunts and slopes off towards the fort. I walk a short way behind him, faking nonchalance, but it's hard to stroll casually in the driving rain when your heart is pounding like a jackhammer.

When he is at the top of the pier, and I am not far behind him, I point him off towards the fort while I walk in the direction of my car. He stops and watches me for ten seconds, seconds that feel like ten minutes. I stand next to someone else's car, pretending to be on the phone. When I'm sure he's gone, I run back to the boat against the wind and rain and clamber onboard. I scramble around the slippery deck and spot what looks like a hatch to below deck. I pull it up and an intense stale waft of fish nearly knocks me sideways. I try not to retch.

As I peer in, I let my eyes adjust to the darkness below. My heart thumps right up my throat when I hear movement behind me. But it's just the sails whipping against each other in the wind.

I steady my breath. *Move quickly*, I urge myself, as I climb into the depths below. When I get to the bottom rung, I hop down onto the floor and whisper: 'Susannah?'

52

'Susannah, are you here?'

I'm squinting in the dark, waiting for my eyes to adjust. I have to crouch because of my height and plant my feet wide apart so that I don't fall over as waves bash against the boat, tipping it from one side to the other.

And then I see her, in the corner, lying curled up. I gasp and scrabble my way over to her. Her mouth is bound. For a moment I think that she is already dead, but her eyes begin to flutter and through the tape over her mouth she makes a small sound that comes out as an 'mmmpph'. Her eyes begin to roll. She's bordering on delirious.

I turn on the torch on my iPhone, shining it at my face so she can see that it is me.

'I've got you! I've got you!'

I rip the tape off her mouth and untie her wrists. We embrace, arms wrapped around each other.

'I'm so glad it's you. I'm so glad it's you,' is all Susannah croaks out.

'Sssshh, save your energy. We need to get you off this boat, he'll be back any minute. Can you stand?'

She wobbles to her feet, but the sea swell knocks her off balance. I'm hunched over, my legs still wide to keep us upright, and I catch her before she hits the floor. I pull her more upright, trying to figure out how the hell I'm going to get us out of here. I have minutes at most.

I drag her limp body across the room and press her up against the slim ladder with all my might. When I hear her struggle to draw breath, a terror seeps into me, because I too find myself struggling for air. This is not the moment to give in to my condition. I accept what Susannah is experiencing. I let it wash through me. I accept it.

I push her up the ladder, her feet slipping off the rungs constantly. Finally, I get her to the top, but she loses her grip and slides back down to the bottom rung, and we are both knocked off our feet and onto our backs. That's when I hear it: footsteps on the deck above.

I put a protective arm around Susannah. I am not letting this man take us off to God knows where, to do God knows what. I am getting us the hell out of here. As I clamber upwards, I hear the motor roar and once again I am pulled backwards with the force of the motion.

'Oh, shit,' I say out loud, checking on Susannah, who is now on her knees on the floor.

'He said he's going to take me out into the middle of the sea. He said he's going to shoot me first, and then shoot himself, and that by the time anyone finds us, it'll be too late,' Susannah says, her voice croaking.

'Susannah, save your strength. Try to be quiet,' I whisper.

I rack my brains. *How* am I going to get us out, when she has so little energy? Thinking on my feet, I kill the iPhone light in case he opens the hatch and sees it. I send Tara our live location, hoping the gardaí will realize their mistake. I also send her a text – 'Below deck in boat. She's here. Got here just in time. He doesn't know I'm here yet. Send help.'

I'm scanning around, looking for inspiration. I see a makeshift bed across from us in the cramped space, empty food wrappers, empty tobacco packs, empty bottles of Jameson. He's obviously been living here. Between this place and the house, it looks like a grim existence.

Susannah whispers but I struggle to make out what she's saying.

I crouch down and wrap an arm around her, trying to warm her cold body.

'What did you say, Susannah?'

'I saw her being killed.'

'Olivia?'

'Yes,' Susannah says, her eyes black and unfocused and looking into the nothingness.

'Jesus! What happened?'

'It's because of me.'

'I'm sure it's not, Sass.'

'But it is!'

'Shush! Be quiet, Susannah! We can talk later!'

'It doesn't matter, he's going to kill us! And it is my fault! I was the one who brought you to Dunmore East to meet with Olivia.'

The motor stops. We hold on to each other's arm. He must have heard us, I think, cursing myself for not being quieter. The hatch door opens and his foot appears on the top rung of the ladder.

'There's a shotgun in the corner,' Susannah whispers, shaking violently now, her teeth chattering.

I know if I let that man down here, and if he sees both of us together, that he could kill us. So, I rush up the ladder as quickly as I can and push him back, catching him off guard. The push knocks him off his feet entirely. I scramble to my feet up on the deck and try to get my bearings.

But he is quicker than I could ever have imagined, because he spins around onto his front and begins crawling towards me. For a second I have an out-of-body experience – as if I'm watching a horror movie in which a deranged gaunt old man is clawing his way across a drenched and rocking boat.

I don't know whether to try and kick him in the head or run, but my feet can't gain purchase on the slippery deck and when I take a step behind me, I fall backwards onto what feels like glass. I am lying against the window of the bridge of the boat.

Rain splatters against my face and before I can understand what's happening, Johno has pulled me back down. He slams me face-first onto the deck, and then he gets up and holds me in place with his foot. This strength is completely unexpected. My cheek is pressed against the cold wet deck, until my head is wrenched up by the roots of my hair and I feel something snake around my neck. A rope.

Johno wraps the rope once, twice, around my neck.

'Tryin' to fool me, were ya? The harbourmaster, was it? You people are all the same. Fuckin' liars!'

Pure blind panic, that's what I feel, as the oxygen leaves my body and lungs. He's going to choke me to death right here, in the middle of the sea, and then kill Susannah. He pulls the rope tighter and I can feel my eyes bulge. I see purple spots in my vision, yellow stars, blue rain.

Suddenly, in between the colours and shapes and visions, there is Susannah, right behind Johno. She is holding a curved metal spar and she brings it down over his head.

He releases his hold on the rope and staggers forward. But Susannah is weak, and the only impact of the blow is surprise. He puts a hand on the back of his head, looks at a few specks of blood on his palm and laughs.

He strikes Susannah with the back of his hand, and the force spins her around and knocks her onto the deck. She coughs out blood and rain. I have loosened the rope from around my neck and am spluttering my way back towards normal vision, but he's upon me again, this time with his hands around my throat. Normally, I could take someone like him in a heartbeat – me, tall and strong; him, wiry and weak. But I'm winded, and when I try to pull in air, it feels as though I am doing so through a straw.

My vision narrows again, and I think: *This is it. This is how it ends.*

The words come out of my mouth, as though spoken by someone else.

'I'm your daughter.'

He hears me. His blue eyes bore into mine. And he sees something, something he cannot unsee. It's him. He sees himself in me, sees his eyes in mine. He knows I am not lying.

He staggers to his feet, clearly horrified that he just had his hands around his daughter's neck. Maybe he's thinking of his email – *a daughter for a daughter*. How does this end now?

Then, from behind, Susannah lurches forward, and pushes him once. He stumbles towards the edge of the boat but catches himself and turns around. Looking as though she is summoning energy from a place that she hardly recognizes, Susannah hurls herself forward and pushes him again. He takes another step, and I see a look cross his face, a look of horror. He has gone too far.

As Johno Fogarty goes over the side of his beloved boat, Susannah Brown's face is the last thing he sees.

Instead of the life he's lived flashing before his eyes, he sees a different one.

It is Monday, 4 April 1983, on the strand. The locals and tourists are so busy marvelling at the unseasonable heat that no one notices Susannah Brown is drowning. Except in this life, as he stands at the edge of the surf, Johno does not gaze at the trawler in the distance wishing his life away. He does not feel trapped. He is happy to work on the farm and have his children run wild and free.

And instead of his eyes dropping below a trawler and seeing a girl drowning, he looks down at his wife Maggie, and he wraps a loving arm around her waist. They turn to leave.

The girl in the water watches him walk away. She thought, for just a second, that he was looking at her. But it's too late, he's gone.

53

Blue lights flash and ambulances line up side by side, squeezed haphazardly into the roads leading up to the harbour. The rescue helicopter has been and gone, having tried and failed to rescue Johno from the waves. But he was no match for the sea. I watched his body being winched up into the air.

Tara and Susannah sit at the back of the ambulance to my right, covered in foil thermal blankets, arms around each other while they receive medical attention. What a sight it is to see them together. That, at least, is something good that has come from all this.

The wind has eased, and the hammering rain has turned to drizzle.

After I was seen to medically, and had my neck checked, I decided to ring Patrick, the man formerly known as Dad, to fill him in. It comes strangely easy for me to think of him as Patrick – I guess he was never much of a dad to me. While his reaction to hearing his eldest daughter almost died is predictably callous – *I always said that bollocks was a savage!* – I'm relieved that it doesn't upset me. Instead, perhaps for the first time ever, I talk to Patrick without looking for something I will never get – interest or compassion.

It turns out, he already knew about Olivia – who she was and why she was looking for him. Inevitably, the early coverage of Susannah's success mentioned her background, so Olivia knew her father was 'Patrick Brown'. Through some online sleuthing Olivia dug out an email address for Patrick from the British Irish Commerce Association web page. She must have tried a few other Patrick Browns from Dublin who seemed about the right age, but without ever knowing if she had hit the bullseye. Except Patrick chose to ignore her message.

'Yeah, I got an email – she was on a trawling expedition. Clever girl, in fairness. But I wasn't going to open that can of worms. Very sad what's happened to her. Look, Lucy, the past is in the past. I'm happy now. There's no point raking over the coals,' he said.

No time like the present, I decided.

'Do you know you're not my real father?'

He didn't answer the question. But he didn't ask any questions either. That told me all I needed to know. I didn't press him. I'd had enough, at least for now. I was – I am – spent.

It's weird how you can not know something for your entire life and then the truth of it dawns on you – at first slowly, and then with sudden blinding certainty. That's what's happened in the last two days. From when Susannah mentioned Mum's return visit to Dunmore East when she was revising for her Leaving – *April 1994* – to the moment Jack Fogarty said *I thought they would have told you*, my subconscious had been joining the dots. And in that conversation with Jack, everything clicked. What I had not seen I could no longer unsee. The links between Mum's general evasiveness *and* her bizarre hostility towards a place she owned a house in *and* her ban on any of us visiting it *and* the timing of her second visit to Dunmore East – suddenly these told a story.

Having been released from the garda station after making her statement, and being told what was happening on Johno's boat, Mum and Tara raced to Passage East. The look of anguish and relief on her face when she saw Susannah and me will stay with me forever. If my system hadn't already been pushed to its limits, feeling Mum's inner turmoil put me over the edge and I had to take refuge in an ambulance. Just breathing and trying to calm down.

I watch Mum now, pacing the length of the high harbour wall, pausing occasionally to look out to the sea, as if the Johno Fogarty she once loved might materialize before her. I know nothing yet about the story behind my conception, but I have seen enough to know that Johno was her great love. And how confusing must it be to love a man who saved one daughter's life and fathered another, and later tried to kill them both? I can't begin to wrap my head around that. I want to help heal her broken heart. I want to tell her that whatever happened in the past – in 1983 or in 1994 or even in the last few days or ever – that I love her regardless, and that everything is going to be OK.

I stand up to go and tell my mother these things but before I can hop off the back of the empty ambulance Inspector Menton appears before me. He hands me a mug. It's half-full of whiskey and I laugh, possibly for the first time since I arrived in Dunmore East.

'I don't know whether to go after you for impeding my investigation or shake your hand for making my life a whole lot easier,' he says, rolling back and forth on his shoes, his whole persona transformed.

'Not to mention me saving my sister's life.'

He chuckles.

'What has you in such a good mood anyway? I thought I was the bane of your life, with my "amateur-hour crap"?' I smile at him as I make air quotes.

'Sorry about that! But in answer to your question, and strictly off the record, we found the murder weapon on the boat.'

'Huh?'

'A rock, covered in blood. I'm willing to bet when the forensics come back it'll be her blood and his DNA will be all over it. We think he took it in a panic and was going to get rid of it once he'd got enough fuel to drive himself and your sister into never-never land.'

'Jesus!' I take a good long gulp of the whiskey. It burns beautifully. 'Has Susannah told you what happened yet? I didn't want to ask her, not until she has more energy.'

'She'll have to make a full statement but the gist of it is that she invited Olivia over for dinner to talk about her real parentage, and she wanted you in on the chat. She got a text from Olivia then, basically panicking and saying she couldn't face it, that she was turning around. Your sister texted her back straight away, asked her to come back to the cottage. Susannah tried to ring her, and although Olivia didn't answer at first, she did ring back almost immediately after. Susannah said that on that call, Olivia was freaking out. She said she had seen Jack Fogarty at the door shouting, and it panicked her. Then, Susannah says, Olivia just became more anxious, saying she was being followed by a man in the park, which she was cutting through on her way back from the cottage. Looks like Johno had been making his own way down towards the cottage and was now bearing in on Olivia, and she didn't know what to do. Susannah told her to get to the main road or duck into a cove, and she went down into Badger's Cove. Susannah told me that she ran there to find her . . . and instead she found old Johno there, rock in hand, Olivia at his feet, deed done.'

'But . . . why?'

'Have you seen a full-length picture of Olivia Philips?'

'No, I haven't.'

'Same height. Same colour hair. They look very similar, especially in the dark, especially when you're blinded with fury because you've just discovered who killed your daughter and she's in a cottage just down the road. From tracking Johno's phone, we reckon he saw Olivia fleeing the cottage, his son not far behind her down the hill, that he put two and two together and . . . well, got the wrong woman.'

'You're sure he was after Susannah?'

'Absolutely,' Menton says, 'Susannah said that he turned to her down at Badger's Cove, a mad look on his face, and said something to the effect of, "It was meant to be you." He kept saying it. He must have thought, though, that of all people to witness what happened, at least it was Susannah. The very person he had set out to hurt. Then he walloped your sister, I'm sorry to say, to shut her up.'

'What happened then?'

'Susannah was unconscious and so he risked leaving the two women on the beach to get his boat – just a stone's throw across the water from the cove. By the time Susannah came to, she was in the boat and tied up. She says he thought Olivia was still alive. It looks like he was trying to figure out what to do with Susannah, looking for a way out, but he seems to have cracked when he saw the news that Olivia was dead.'

Menton shivers and takes a slug of his whiskey.

'I have to say, Lucy, you got here just in time. How did you know his email was a ruse?'

'Any detective worth their salt would have had the boat checked,' I say with a smirk. He doesn't bite, but his lip curls up ever so slightly.

'Susannah will need a good few stitches for that head, too. Sure, you'd know all about that – stitches, wha?' he says, winking.

Menton is the first person in eleven years to slag me about my scars. And it's a revelation to discover that I don't mind. In fact, I like that he's not treating the scarring as something too horrific to be mentioned. Taboo. Maybe I could learn from him.

'How much whiskey have you had?' I say.

'Not enough, although I am glad that I don't have to fish any more bodies out of the deep.'

'You have a way with words, Inspector Menton.'

'You've a sharp tongue yourself. Look, I'm sorry to hear what happened to you—'

He clocks my puzzled look.

'You know, in Finglas. I've been told by a little bird, though, that you weren't fired. You resigned. And I've seen you in action. I think there's a path back for you, Lucy.'

I check to see if he is joking and he looks completely serious. How much I have longed to hear those words – what they would have meant to me only yesterday! Yet I feel my head shake and hear myself saying 'no'.

'You found out my detective was hiding something. You found out your sister's last known location. You found out the link between Susannah and Olivia. You tracked down the killer's house. You were the first to cotton on about the boat. You were the one who moved so fast that you saved your sister from taking up residence with the sharks. Ultimately, you found the baddie. I dunno – I'd say you've come very far from shitting your pants.'

We both burst out laughing, causing David, who had been holding Susannah's hand in the next ambulance, to give us a quizzical glance. Menton picks up on it.

'C'mere, don't go telling them I'm drinking on the job. I've had the fucking day of my nightmares. And it's nowhere near over. You really won't consider it, Lucy?'

I want to say yes. I want to go back to who I used to be. But I can't. When you've changed, you've changed. The clock does not roll backwards. I now know I need more control over my life than being in the force can offer me.

'I think I can find other ways to put my skills to good use,' I say.

'Ohhhh no, no, no. Don't tell me you're going to become one of those saddos, the private detectives chasing insurance fraudsters, missing pets and cheating husbands?'

'Maybe there's another side to it. Cold cases, missing people, the old stuff the gardaí don't have time for anymore. Things you don't see.'

He regards me with both disapproval and admiration.

'Well, I owe you one. If you ever need a favour, you come to me.'

He winks and saunters off and I watch him go, feeling like a woman reborn.

54

As I stroll back to the cottage on Wednesday evening, I'm startled to see Susannah and Tara sitting side by side at the picnic table, the glassy sea just beyond them. The two of them are bathed in pre-dusk evening pastels as they share a bottle of wine. They have the look of two long-lost pals having an epic gossip after not seeing each other for an age. Which is one way of describing their current relationship. The relief in the air is palpable.

After giving our statements we didn't get to bed till 2 a.m., all of us too shattered to say another word. It's been a day of napping and snacking and I needed to stretch my legs and get some time on my own. I have so much to think about and I'm still trying to fit all the pieces together in my mind. Coming back to this sight is both unexpected and heartwarming.

'There she is, our hero. Our detective,' says Susannah.

'Do you want a glass, Lucy?' Tara says, about to get up out of her seat.

'No, I'm grand. Sit down,' I say, sitting opposite them. 'But it would be good to have a chat.'

Susannah drinks deeply from her glass and eyes me up over the rim. 'You're right,' she says, 'shoot.'

'Well, to start with a simple question, what was the idea of bringing us all here Monday night? I want to hear it from you.'

'I really thought—' she starts, and her eyes fill with tears. She takes a deep breath and starts again. 'I really, really thought that if we could meet as sisters, the four of us, we could start the work of building a new family, an honest family. That if there were no more secrets, there'd be so much less suffering.

For instance, you could stop chasing something that would never come.'

'What do you mean?'

'Patrick's love.'

Though she's not telling me anything I haven't figured out, it's still upsetting to hear it stated so baldly. Tara reaches over and gently pats my arm.

'I was going to tell you the truth that was kept from you, set you free from being so tethered to Dad, so held back by waiting for something that was never going to arrive.'

'How did you find out, Susannah?'

'The usual way – Mum and Dad fighting. Most of the time I zoned out but one day I heard your name being mentioned and Mum saying "for the sake of the baby" and I perked up. Then I heard her asking him to treat you "as if she's your own". And he went on a rant about not bankrolling the daughter of "that fucker, Johno Fogarty".'

I flinch and Susannah gets teary again.

'I couldn't believe it, Lucy. That Dad could be so vicious, especially when you were the best thing that had happened in our family in the longest time.'

Now all three of us are in tears.

'I just put it to the back of my mind,' Susannah continues. 'It wasn't going to change how I felt about you. Years later, not long after I met David, Mum and I were having a few drinks one night and she was saying how lucky I was to have met the love of my life at a young age. When I saw the open goal, I ran towards it. I said, "Was Lucy's father the love of your life?" There was a split second when I could see she was tempted to lie, but then she just sighed, as if she was relieved that the secret was out. She asked how I knew and when I explained she said that yes, it was Johno Fogarty – that she'd got in touch with him again the time she ran away from home – and her only regret was that they'd had just the one night together. The next morning, he told Mum there was no future in it, because every time he'd look at her, he'd think of how he lost Katie. Her heart was broken but deep down she knew he was right. When she realized she was pregnant she thought it was the universe's way of rewarding her love. You know how woo-woo she is sometimes.'

We all laugh at that. Mum has aged in reverse, becoming more open-minded as the years have gone on. After Dad left, she trained as a yoga teacher and went into mindfulness and reiki and all kinds of new age stuff. She has made a good living out of it.

'Did you know, Tara?' I ask.

She moves her head slowly from side to side, and although I feel she's not being fully forthright, I leave it for the moment.

Susannah takes another sip of wine, cocks her head to one side and says, 'Next question?'

'What's the story with *Sea of Mirrors*? Why is there a garda called Lucy in it? And an Olivia Philips – that nearly gave me a heart attack when I saw it. Are you going to publish it?'

'Oh God, Lucy. I'm sorry you ever saw that. I was trying something with a young garda character and used your name as a placeholder, but as I worked, little details from real life crept in. I was never going to leave them in. I had the script with me to work on it, highlighting all the stuff that needed to change. I would start working on a story, based on real-life stuff, before ditching it to work on another storyline. So, Olivia's name was in there, before I came up with a replacement. The whole manuscript is a mess of ideas – I'm not even going to send it to Summer. I was just trying to find something real to get myself going again.'

'Don't say that, Sass – it can't be that bad.'

'Oh, it is, Lucy. I have to face facts – the last few books have been shite and I seem to have run out of ideas. When I go back to Dublin, I'm going to talk to David honestly about what I'm going to do. I think it's time to take a break – let him be the novelist in the family for a bit.'

She looks over at me, as if to check that we're done. She all but sighs when she sees that I'm far from done.

'What else, Lucy? Spit it out.'

She knows me too well. Her eyes are filled with trepidation. Tara just looks confused.

'David beat a fast track out of here?' I say, keeping my eyes locked on hers.

'He had to get back for a thing. I said it was fine, that we'll head back together once we get the all-clear from the gardaí.'

She's trying to come across as chilled, but there's a tightness to the set of her lips that I feel in my own.

'Hmmm. Maybe he knows something we don't?'

They glance at each other, and then expectantly at me.

'Like what, Lucy? Come on,' Susannah says, the curtness in her voice so familiar.

How should I say this?

From the moment I learned what Susannah did in 1983, there was something that just didn't sit right with me. *Yes, she's ballsy*, I thought, but I kept asking myself how she could be so relaxed, so at ease, in a place where she did something so terrible? How could she just sit around in the local hotel drinking rosé while carrying this horrific secret? How come, when Jack Fogarty came to the door to warn her to leave, she could just casually tell him where to go?

Then there was the puzzle of why David, when time was of the essence, needed to read a book that he had worked on closely – he'd have known *The Broken Bay* inside out.

And so, when everyone was finally in bed after we got back to the house, I went into Susannah's emails and found what he had been reading – the first draft of *The Broken Bay*. I've never been more disappointed to be right.

'I saw the first draft of the book you won an award for in New York,' I say without further explanation.

Susannah sucks in her cheeks and her shoulders rise as she takes a long intake of breath.

'How?'

I don't answer. That doesn't matter, and she knows it.

'What? What are you talking about?' Tara says, head swivelling between the two of us. Her reaction is genuine: she doesn't know what I'm getting at.

'Lucy, could you just drop this,' Susannah says, rising from the bench.

She is in a half-standing position when I turn to Tara and say, 'You two have never talked about it, have you?'

Susannah is suspended there in that position, sea breeze running through her hair. She sits back down slowly, reaches for the bottle of wine, and fills up her glass.

'What's she talking about, Susannah? What was in your first draft?'

Susannah says simply, 'The truth.'

A heavy and expectant pause lingers between us. I think I've said enough. I'll wait this one out.

'The truth?' Tara says.

Susannah looks at her. Tears spill down her face.

'I would never have published it, Tara. I just wanted to get the basic story written first, and I sent it to David in a rush of excitement when it was done. But I knew I would never let that version come out. I would never have done that to you.'

Tara has her face in her hands and her shoulders are lightly shuddering. She takes a breath and then looks directly up at me, wretched and desperate.

'What are you going to do, Lucy?'

It's not up to me, and it never has been. When I read that original draft, I saw what David must have seen over in the bar last night – the closest version to the truth. A story of a family visiting a small coastal village for a sunshine-filled holiday. And how one of the daughters pushes a local girl to her death. And how her older sister takes the blame. And how the weight of the secret is the kiss of death for their relationship – fostering fear and resentment in one sister, and an unbearable superiority in the other.

The version of *The Broken Bay* on the shelves is very far from that. There's an unflattering portrayal of a meek, cowardly sister, but nothing worse.

Just as I wondered how Susannah could be so relaxed in the place where she did something so terrible, I also wondered how she could ever have written a fictionalized confession. The answer, of course, was that she had nothing to confess to.

Once David heard Mum's story and made the connection with the plot of *The Broken Bay* – he was on to Tara. What he found in the first draft was his proof. He was still processing everything when I said I'd bring Tara with me when he was watching Jack Fogarty. That's why he reacted so strongly. Even when we were in Passage East, I noticed him avoiding Tara.

'Katie was just a little girl, and so were you. So why did you do it, Tara?'

Susannah's breath catches when I ask this. I'm confident this is a question she has never asked. How could she? It must have haunted her.

Tara pulls her cardigan around herself and looks off to the left, towards where the sea licks the sand as it edges closer.

'You're looking at it with an adult's eyes. Try to imagine yourself as a child. As a little girl, I idolized Susannah. She was my protector when things were bad at home, she was bold and brave and strong, but I knew already that I was shy and scared. I know I clung to you, Susannah.'

Susannah reaches a hand under the table and squeezes Tara's knee.

'That holiday was strange. We only met the Fogartys early on, after Johno rescued Susannah. But suddenly everything was about them. And every time Katie was around, I didn't exist. I didn't like Jack, I thought he was weird, but I was left with him all the time. Even at that young age, I was more jealous than you can even imagine. It made me furious. Nobody noticed though.

'That day, out on the cliffs. God, it was the simplest thing. The most stupid thing. Susannah hugged Katie and they looked like sisters. I was just invisible. It is blurry, I swear. But a few minutes later, Katie had moved a few metres further away, towards the grassy area, and I followed her.'

Tara gulps. I wonder if this is the first time she has described what happened out loud.

'She told me to get lost, go away, stop following her – something like that. Then she called Susannah over instead. I don't know what you were doing, Susannah, but I just . . . I just felt so enraged. And I pushed her. She stumbled backwards and suddenly one of her feet had gone from behind her. I didn't even see the gap. I can't remember if we even knew the cliff edge was close or anyone warned us about it. She sort of fell sideways, and then she was gone. I must have shouted, or made some kind of noise, because Jack looked up at me then. He was crouched over picking up rocks. He ran over, and then he shouted for his mum. That's the last full memory I have.

'I didn't mean to do it. I never meant for that to happen. I can't tell you the nightmares I've had. I don't think I can ever forgive myself for what I did, and for letting my own sister take the blame. It sounds lame, but it's true. It has ruined my life.'

She lets out a sob and clamps a hand over her mouth. Susannah stands up and wraps her arms around her.

'But why did *you* take the blame? Why didn't you tell the truth?' I say to Susannah.

She looks at me over Tara's head.

'You don't know, Lucy, what it was like for us when we were kids. The arguments, the tension in the house, how hard some of those days were. From the day she was born, I protected her. I always will.'

Now the secret is out, and it lives between us, between us three sisters. As I watch them embrace, I think about the unknowable consequences of seemingly simple choices. How decisions made on an impulse can change it all. Mum and Patrick's decision to come here. Johno's decision to go to the beach that day. My mother's decision to befriend their family. Patrick's decision to sleep with Maggie.

I think of another tiny decision that changed all our lives, and I watch Tara struggle with it. I know what she's going to say. I can see it in her – when the truth starts to come out, it comes out as a torrent.

'Lucy, there's something else,' she says, before breaking down, unable to say it. I move around the table to her and join Susannah in wrapping her in a hug.

'Don't, Lucy, don't hug me; I have to tell you, I have to tell you both—'

'Stop,' I whisper in her ear.

'But—'

'Let me guess, you're to blame for Susannah having no cigarettes that morning in New York? So what? You weren't to know, were you? You're not the one who attacked me. The only person to blame is that person. Not you.'

She pushes me away, aghast, and I laugh. I can't help it. The look of shock is almost comic, her mouth hanging open.

'How did you—'

'Your reaction yesterday. When I let slip about being out to get cigarettes—'

Susannah winces, but I ignore her and continue.

'You said, "You went out because of *the smokes?*" You knew

exactly what I was talking about. I've never felt such guilt emanate from a person before. What did you do? Steal them? Throw them away?'

Tara looks at Susannah sheepishly, her chin tilted downwards.

'I threw your bag in the bin. You left it on a ledge when we were on the rooftop of that restaurant we were in the night before.'

'You wagon!' Susannah says, but she's laughing, and when I laugh, Tara does too.

'Like I said, you weren't to know, Tara. None of us were. Forgive yourself. Because I forgive you,' I say, and I mean it with all my heart.

Susannah straightens up and walks into the cottage, emerging with another bottle of wine and an extra glass for me. I accept it when she hands it to me, but she can see me hesitate, my gaze unsure.

'You're wondering what to do, aren't you? About Katie?'

She's spot on. I haven't a clue what to do next.

'It's up to you,' she says, and sits back down. She seems looser, easier in her own skin. I see now that this is the secret that weighed so heavily on her for all this time.

'In case you're wondering – David gets it. He's sorry for Tara. He's sorry for me. For the Fogartys, of course. He thinks it was a tragic accident. He just needs time to wrap his head around it all.'

David's probably right. Ultimately, is there any other way to look at it, other than a tragic accident? Weren't they just little kids?

Now the burden of the secret is spread out. And maybe we can carry the load together, as a family.

Epilogue

Inspector Menton didn't hold a press conference as might be expected at the conclusion of a high-profile murder investigation. At noon, he had issued a statement that Olivia Philips' killer was found at 10 p.m. last night attempting to flee the county by boat. He gave the mere basics and said that the gardaí were still looking into a motive. Of course, the Waterford journalists knew that a local garda, Jack Fogarty, had lost his father in these tragic circumstances. But they didn't know why. While they knew that the Fogarty family had been hit by a previous tragedy nearly four decades earlier, when a child fell to her death at the cliffs, that was all they knew. The bare bones of it.

Maybe it would all come out one day, maybe the Philips family would demand an inquiry. Right now the worst of the details remain under wraps. Some news outlets have put up reports with all kinds of speculation about Johno from 'sources' – that he was a sad loner driven crazy by the loss of his daughter so many years ago; that he was intending to strike another victim he had been 'stalking'; that he was a bad father who made his stand-up son look bad in front of his colleagues.

The truth seems destined to stay amongst a small circle – at least for now.

In the cottage, I pull Mum's bedroom door towards me gently, pausing just before I close it, when I can see just a sliver of her face on the pillow, eyes closed, hands clasped together under her chin.

Of all the hills I've had to climb since things came to a head on the *Dunmore Rogue*, this is the one that has completely undone me. Mum is so utterly heartbroken that just looking at her, I feel my own heart shatter. I know that even if I didn't have these synaesthetic traits, I would feel the same way. There has been a vulnerability in her hollow expression all day, the way she couldn't lift her eyes off the floor and seemed to exist in another dimension. It's guilt and it's loss and it has put years on her.

Seeing her as she was today has made me aware of her mortality like never before. She has lived a life before me and I will live a life after her, when she's gone. These two worlds, two worlds in which we exist without each other – well, I almost don't want to know about either.

While I'm not sure what kind of relationship I'll now have with Patrick, if any – and I know I'll have to be OK with whatever happens – Mum, on the other hand, is a rock. It was no joke being a single parent, effectively, to two warring teenagers and a demanding baby while setting up a business. And she fought for me every step of the way, often when no one would listen to her. The more I think about it, the more I love her.

I go into the bedroom where I slept for a short time in the small hours after we got back from Passage East last night. I close the door, curl up on the bed and bury my face in the pillow, and I sob. It's been building up for a long time – maybe not just in the last few days – and now that I've let it out, I don't try to stop it. There are so many questions and so many emotions. It feels like there is almost too much to handle.

Because of how she's been, I haven't talked to Mum about the past and everything that happened. She's not ready, and in any event, I think I understand, and because I understand, I forgive her – not for having an affair – how could I judge her for a love affair that led to my existence? But I'm still getting my head around her keeping such a big secret from me about my own identity. All of my family keeping all these secrets.

How I untangle the strands of the secret, and figure out the Fogarty part of my identity, it's too much for me to imagine. As he left Johno's house, Jack looked back at me and said, 'You're quite tall. Same as my granny. I bet you have her intuition, too. I bet you feel things differently, just like she did.' That's been ringing around my head all day – like it might be the key to unlocking who I am. Like it's an invitation. But I'll think about that another day.

When I reach further down inside, as deep as I can go, there is something beyond all this confusion about family and secrets and figuring out who I am, something that lifts me out of the morass.

Pride.

I have achieved something I was convinced I could never do – focusing on the job at hand and taking control of my condition when it mattered most rather than letting it take control of me. Having failed so badly before this feels miraculous. Though I take nothing for granted, it seems like a turning point. I am taking control of my own life again. I am capable of this. And it starts now.

I get out of bed and hunker by the window, gazing out onto the strand, at the lighthouse across the water, at the trawler passing in the distance. I can let sorrow and shame about the past live in my heart, let it eat away at my soul. Or I can trust that the universe has a plan for me. I cast my eyes to the cliffs and the coves. What will be will be, as sure as the sand meets the sea.

Acknowledgements

Like most writers, my road to publication has been long and littered with rejection. I tried to write my first book when I was twenty-one and, unsurprisingly, it was a hot mess. It would take another fifteen years of trial and error to find a way through.

Although there were many times when I felt like packing it all in, Alan, my husband, never gave up on me. Thank you, Alan, for always having my back, for your love and enduring patience, and for sharing this journey with me.

We may never forget having one holiday semi-ruined by a rejection landing on the first day, but we'll also never forget that trip to Galway when this book officially went to auction. Thank you for bringing me to Dunmore East, the place that inspired it all.

I have to single out Brian Sherry, my father-in-law, and Patricia Sherry, my mother-in-law, too. There wasn't a Sunday lunch in the Sherry household when Brian didn't gently prod me to get back writing, always urging me not to give up even when I said I was done. This book wouldn't exist without you, Brian.

I also want to thank Paul and Ethna Sherry, who saw some excruciating early drafts of this novel and laughed with me rather than at me. That's the last time I try to write fiction after a few glasses of wine.

My life changed on 31 January 2024, when I received an email from Florence Rees, agent supremo at A. M. Heath, asking to set up a call after reading my novel submission. I couldn't believe it. She loved the book and wanted to represent me; I was so excited I nearly passed out. The last two years have been a rollercoaster in the best possible way. Thank you, Florence, for your patience, knowledge and talent, and for being the best cheerleader an author could ever want.

A million thanks to Alexandra McNicoll, Lucy Joyce and Jack Sargeant in the A. M. Heath foreign-rights department. It's hard to describe the excitement of seeing a foreign-rights deal land in your inbox on a random Monday.

Securing an agent is often a huge part of the process. But finding the right publisher is the big, scary mountain just beyond it. The multi-talented Patricia Deevy of Penguin Sandycove lit a fire under me when she heard me mention on a podcast that I was finishing a mystery novel. She saw some potential when, after I hastily put my skates on, she read an early version. It is down to Patricia and Joyce Dignam that the novel is in such good nick and I'm beyond grateful for their careful editing and for their vision and experience.

The work that goes into making it all happen is awe-inspiring. Thank you, too, to Michael McLoughlin, Cliona Lewis, Carrie Anderson and all the team at Penguin Sandycove, for everything you've done to make this book a success.

Thank you to Kasia Lipnicka-Koltuniak at Muza in Poland and Martina Pfitzner at Penguin Verlag in Germany for bringing this book to your two beautiful countries.

I am blessed with so many wonderful brothers and sisters who have always been so supportive, and who have my heart. Thank you, Stephen, Johnny, Joey, Rachel, Liz, Harry and Hazel.

If there was anyone who got more excited about book news than me, it was probably my sister Jessica, who is the biggest champion of us Bray siblings, and my brother-in-law James too.

This book is also dedicated to our brother Michael whom

we all miss terribly, and whom we think of every single day. I hope I made you proud, Michael.

Thank you, too, to my parents Sharon and Joe who ensured I got to study English in college, a hugely formative experience.

Every writer needs sustenance, and I found it through cuddles with my beautiful, adorable nieces Ellie, Rose, Síomha and Sibéal.

I am also so lucky to be blessed with amazing friends who inspire me with their own fantastic writing. To Ellen Coyne and our tiny book club of two: we did it! No words on this page can ever do justice to how grateful I am for your existence. Thank you to Rosita Boland for your incredible guidance and friendship, and to Ali Bracken, Elizabeth Lavin, Sarah Furlong, Leah McDonald, Elaine Loughlin and Mark Brady for being there since the very start of this process. My deepest gratitude, too, to Niamh, Aoife and Aideen, three of the smartest, most talented women I know who give the best advice. Early readers can make or break a writer's confidence, but I struck gold with Jacquelyn and Philip who supported this book from a fleeting idea on a train in France, to the final product in your hands.

Thank you to my colleagues in the *Sunday Times* and to former colleagues in the *Irish Times* for such incredible support throughout this long process.

The ultimate thank you goes to you, the reader. My ambition is to give you another world in which to escape, just when you need it the most. If I succeed in that, everything else is just a bonus.